KU-536-300

Seen to Be Believed

Louisa Scarr studied Psychology at the University of Southampton and has lived in and around the city ever since. She works as a freelance copywriter and editor, and when she's not writing, she can be found pounding the streets in running shoes or swimming in muddy lakes.

Also by Louisa Scarr

Butler & West

Last Place You Look
Under a Dark Cloud
Blink of an Eye
Seen to Be Believed

LOUISA SCARR

SEEN
TO BE
BELIEVED

C CANELOCRIME

First published in the United Kingdom in 2022 by

Canelo
Unit 9, 5th Floor
Cargo Works, 1-2 Hatfields
London SE1 9PG
United Kingdom

A CIP catalogue record for this book is available from the British Library.

Print ISBN 978 1 80032 352 0
Ebook ISBN 978 1 80032 351 3

Cover design by Dan Mogford

Cover images © Shutterstock

Look for more great books at www.canelo.co

Printed and bound in Great Britain by Clays Ltd, Elcograf S.p.A.

I

For Susan and Jon.

Prologue

Her body instinctively recognises the danger. A prickle of adrenaline down her spine; a tensing of her shoulders; hair rising on her arms. Amber stops and listens: a shout, then the slam of their front door. She pauses, the music blaring through her headphones. Nothing else comes. She goes back to her picture, adding sparkly stars, a moon to the sky.

But then she hears it again. An angry bark. A man – there's no mistaking it this time. Her heart races. She takes her headphones off. She waits. Frozen.

Another crash, something breaking. Her mother screaming, rising to a howl of pain. Her brother now. Frantic sobs. Unlike anything she's ever heard before.

She jumps off the bed, and creeps towards her bedroom door. Hands shaking, she slowly presses the handle down, opening it a crack. What's going on? What should she do?

She opens it wider and peers out. She can just see through the banisters to the hallway below. The front door is closed, the light on. There is a brown cardboard box on its side next to the door.

And then— Her hand flies to her mouth in horror. There's a man there – a big man. Dressed in black, wide shoulders, shaved head. She darts back into her bedroom, heart racing as she closes the door as quietly as she can, wincing at the slight click. She racks her brain, but she hasn't seen him before. Nobody like *that* comes to their house.

She stops and listens. She tries to still her frantic breathing. There's more shouting – the man, then her brother's answering cry. She can barely understand the stranger – his voice has an odd accent – but he's angry. Heavy footsteps thunder through the house below.

What should she do? She starts to cry. Her mother is silent now. Her dad is at work, he won't be back for hours. She came up here to get away from her annoying younger brother but now she wishes he were here. Panic clouds her brain until she remembers the phone in her hoodie pocket. The phone she relentlessly pestered her parents for. The phone she got years before her friends. The phone that could save her now.

She dials 999.

The operator comes on the line.

'Police,' she whispers frantically. 'Please. Quickly. There's a man in our house. He's… he's…' She can barely speak through her sobs.

'Police are on their way,' the operator confirms once she gives her address. 'How old are you? Is your mother around?'

'I'm nine. My mummy… She's downstairs… she…'

'Okay. That's okay, honey. Stay on the line. Are you in danger?'

'Yes. No. I don't know. I'm upstairs. He doesn't know I'm here.'

'Find somewhere to hide,' the woman tells her, her voice stern but calming. 'Lock the door if you can.'

'I… I can't.'

She looks around for a hiding place, her eyes darting towards the bed, then the wardrobe. She hears her brother screaming again, more crashing and then quiet. The silence is worse; Amber can't bear to imagine what's going on downstairs. What's happened to her mother? Is she dead? Is Tim okay?

She gets up on wobbling legs, stumbling to her wardrobe and opening the door. She pushes her clothes out of the way and awkwardly sandwiches herself into a corner. Among the shoes and rejected toys. But before she pulls the door shut, she hears a sound that makes her breath stop in her chest. Slow footsteps on the stairs. Closer.

'Please,' she squeaks down the phone. 'He's coming.'

Smashing in the bedroom next door. The furniture in her brother's room being turned over. What is he doing? What does he want? What's going to happen to her? She just wants her mummy.

Tears blur her vision. She still has the phone clamped to her ear; the operator is talking but terror obliterates any coherent thought.

The pacing stops outside her bedroom. She watches through a gap in the wardrobe door as the handle moves, downwards. A pause, then slowly, it opens.

She closes the wardrobe door. She is in darkness now. Alone.

Her hand reaches down and grasps at a soft teddy, one long discarded. She picks it up and pulls it tight to her chest.

'Please,' she repeats, her voice no more than a whisper. 'He's here.'

Part 1

FRIDAY

1

The lighting is low, the mood romantic. Next to him, a beautiful woman is holding his hand, ushering him forward to where one of his closest friends waits. He can smell delicious aromas wafting from the kitchen; he should be looking forward to tonight.

But Robin has never felt more uncomfortable.

He sees an enthusiastic wave from the back of the restaurant. Freya stands up with a big grin and he can't help but smile in response. She looks nice. Better than nice – stunning. He's so used to seeing her in the drab world of policing that here, in a smart dress, her long blonde hair loose and shiny over her shoulders, Robin's momentarily taken aback.

'Isn't this place great?' Freya says cheerfully as they arrive at their table. The waiter pauses while they say their hellos.

'Jo, this is Josh. Josh – Jo.'

Robin's girlfriend receives a kiss on the cheek from the annoyingly handsome man stood next to Freya.

'I've heard so much about you,' Jo gushes. 'All good,' she adds quickly, and Robin frowns. Not from him it wasn't, but he shakes Josh's hand agreeably.

'Sarge,' Josh offers as a greeting.

'Robin's fine tonight,' Robin replies, and Josh nods.

They all sit down; the waiter presents his napkin with a flourish. Robin murmurs a thank you as he's handed the menu.

This dinner out – it's Freya's idea. Detective constable to Robin's detective sergeant, they've been partners for just over eighteen months, and while Robin sees Freya every day, Freya felt it was time for a double date.

'You only see Josh at the nick,' Freya had argued. 'You never have a chance to get to know him.'

'Maybe that's enough,' Robin replied, little love lost between the charming DC Josh Smith and the more unrefined DS Robin Butler.

'And I want to get to know Jo,' Freya finished, ignoring his quip.

Robin grumbled and agreed, but now he's here, it's exactly as he imagined. The restaurant is posh. Too posh for Robin's liking – and it was Josh's choice, of course. Josh now pores happily over the wine list, eventually selecting a bottle of unpronounceable red as they order their food.

They've made initial small talk, and the women are chatting happily, Freya telling Jo about a film she saw recently, a description that's going on far too long. But it's a conversation, of sorts. The gaping silences between Josh and Robin are worse. Josh gives a tense smile across the table; no more than a thin line, his lips pressed together. Robin tries – fails – to return it.

Their starters arrive. Tiny pieces of salmon on a massive square plate with artful blobs evenly spaced around. But it tastes good, albeit lasting three forkfuls.

'But you said it was crap, didn't you, Rob?' Jo asks, turning her attention to him.

He has a mouthful, he can't answer, and in the space Josh laughs.

'But the cinematography was incredible! The director is a genius!'

Robin swallows. 'I got bored. Things blowing up. People getting shot. It's unrealistic.' He holds his hand over his glass as the waiter comes round with the bottle. 'Not for me, thank you.'

'It's a superhero movie,' Josh replies. Next to him, Freya also turns down the wine. 'You have to suspend your disbelief.'

'For two and a half hours? Jo can go with you next time.'

'I might do that,' Jo laughs, a little too loudly. She takes a sip of wine.

Robin glances across at her. They've been together for four months now. He has a girlfriend, a concept he still finds slightly odd.

'So how did you two meet?' Josh asks. 'Freya told me, I forget.' He shrugs, like the information was too trivial for him to retain.

'Crime scene,' Robin says, bluntly.

'A little more than that,' Jo laughs. 'I was the SIO on a suspicious death in Reading. Robin was there for Finn.'

'Oh, yes,' Josh interjects. 'Your best mate. Accused of murder.'

Robin glares. He's right, but he doesn't appreciate Josh's barely suppressed glee. Jo – or DI Craig, as he'd known her then – had been the senior investigating officer when Finn had been found confused and disorientated in a van with a dead body. It wasn't an auspicious start, Robin challenging her authority until the final – and correct – outcome was discovered.

'He was a right surly twat,' Jo finishes. 'A good job we bumped into each other again on New Year's Eve. Things went from there.'

She looks across at him and squeezes his hand affectionately. He returns the smile, feeling awkward – public displays of affection have never been his thing.

'So here we are,' Freya says. 'Four detectives from Major Crimes. All of us investigating violent murders for a living.'

'You'd have thought we could find something better to talk about than Marvel movies,' Robin comments. It subdues the conversation for a moment.

'See?' Jo retorts with a forced laugh. 'Still a surly twat.'

Despite himself, Robin makes a quick chuckle. That's one thing he finds attractive about Jo: she doesn't play games. She likes him and doesn't shy away from telling him that. And he likes her. He does. He's just not sure how much.

Their mains arrive, and any awkwardness fades. A perfectly cooked steak is placed in front of Robin; he tucks into it with zeal.

Despite his remark, Jo and Josh are still waxing lyrical about some director from New Zealand – a guy with too many t's in his name. Robin turns his attention to Freya.

He meets her eyes across the table. She widens them a little, as if to say *behave*, then gives him a small smile. She can't be enjoying herself, he thinks. Surely?

'I'm not saying it's not there,' Josh is saying to Jo. 'I've just never witnessed it first-hand.' Robin catches the gist of the new topic – misogyny in the police force.

'Nor have I,' Jo replies.

Freya's interest diverts away from Robin. 'You've never been asked to make the tea?' she counters. 'Take notes in a meeting even though you're one of the most experienced DCs there?'

'Nope.'

'Called love or doll or darling?'

Jo shakes her head. 'Maybe I make it clear I won't take any shit.'

'You're saying it's my fault the men take the piss?'

'I'm sure Jo's not saying that—'

'Josh, don't speak for her.'

'That wasn't what I was getting at,' Jo says with an attempt at a placatory smile. 'I've just never seen it as a problem at work. I don't know what it's like at Hants, but at TVP—'

'Hants is fine,' Freya interjects.

Josh tries to chip in again. 'And you're a DI, so it's clearly never held you back.'

'I worked hard for those promotions, Josh,' Jo replies.

'I didn't say you hadn't. I meant—'

Next to Robin's plate, his phone bursts into life. The discussion stops and all eyes shift to it, vibrating on the table. Robin recognises the number and feels a sudden flood of relief.

'I… Sorry.' He gets up and answers it.

'DS Robin Butler?' the voice from Control asks. 'You're needed.'

They relay the information: a vicious home invasion, two in hospital. Any more than that is unknown. Robin confirms he's on his way and hangs up.

He looks back to the table; the disturbance has luckily moved the conversation on. Jo has her head thrown back in laughter as Josh is telling a story. Her cheeks are flushed. Freya is watching her boyfriend, her chin cupped in her hand. Her expression is inscrutable as she turns her attention to Robin. She tilts her head to one side: *And?*

He walks back over.

'Sorry,' he says, pushing regret into his voice. He looks at Freya. 'We need to go.'

She nods and takes a last sip of her Coke. Jo looks at the half-full wine glass in her hand.

'You stay,' he adds. 'No reason work should ruin everyone's night.'

Jo looks at Josh, questioning.

'Why not?' Josh replies and reaches for the wine bottle. 'We'll get a taxi back later. Maybe have a few more heated debates,' he throws Jo's way with a wink.

Robin gives Jo a quick kiss and follows Freya, who's already walking towards the bar.

'I'll get it,' she says, passing a card across to the barman.

'You shouldn't—'

'I should.'

Their coats are retrieved. As they wait, Robin glances to the table. They're laughing again, and Robin feels a twinge of irritation. Why does Josh have to be so bloody charming to everyone? he thinks, before pushing it away.

He feels a nudge on his arm: Freya passing him his coat. Freya gives one final look back. Regret, or a different feeling? He can't tell.

'Come on,' she says. 'Let's go.'

–

It's a quick walk to where Robin's old Volvo is parked. The two of them get in and drive quickly to the address, Freya uncharacteristically quiet next to him.

'Are you okay?' he asks. She grunts in reply. 'You knew getting called out was a possibility tonight.'

'Yeah, of course.' She looks his way and smiles, but to Robin it looks unnatural.

He wonders if she's angry with him, but lets it go. If she is, he knows from experience she'll tell him soon enough.

Roads get wider as they drive. Bunched terraced houses give way to large empty driveways, entrances signposted with tall metal gates. In the distance they see the unmistakeable fluorescent yellow of a police car. Robin pulls up alongside. The uniform standing guard bends down to Robin's now open window.

'DS Robin Butler, DC Freya West.' The policeman peers at their IDs. 'Major Crimes.'

'Drive through,' he says. 'They're in there.'

Robin puts the car back into gear and cruises slowly through the open gates onto the driveway. It's a long, tarmacked path, spots strategically lighting their way. In front of them, the huge modern house is bright, every one of the many windows illuminated from inside.

Freya whistles softly under her breath. 'Must be, what? Five, six bedrooms?'

'Maybe more,' Robin replies. 'Lots to nick.'

Freya strains in her seat, looking back to the gates. 'But it's tricky. How would you get in?'

Robin pulls up next to a large white Audi Q7, his crappy Volvo estate looking out of place next to the brand-new four-by-four. The front door is open, two uniforms waiting inside.

Robin and Freya walk up three steps to the grand entrance, passing between two tall white pillars. As they go through, Freya taps Robin's arm, pointing to a small white box in the corner.

He nods in acknowledgement.

The hallway is double height, a large oak staircase winding its way up the left-hand side to a first-floor walkway, bordered by a carved wooden balustrade. Robin looks up, mouth slightly open. There are doors off the walkway, a few of them ajar. On the ground floor Robin can see through a set of double doors into a sleek black kitchen, a large formal dining room on the far side. But before he can gawp anymore, a man comes charging towards them.

'Are you the detectives?'

Robin nods and introduces himself and Freya. The man's wearing a smart navy suit, pinstriped shirt open at the neck. He's tall, bulk round his middle balancing out his impressive height. A young girl stands next to him, hanging off his arm. She winds a strand of her long brown hair round her finger. 'Come through, please,' he says.

He escorts them to a large sitting room, a huge television on the wall to their left, sofas all around. For the first time, Robin's glad of the tie Jo forced him to wear earlier this evening.

'Andrew Grace,' he says, holding out his hand. Robin shakes it. 'And this is my daughter, Amber.'

'How are you, Amber?' Robin asks. She looks like she's been crying.

'Okay—'

'She's badly shaken up,' her father interrupts. 'She was the one who called the police. She's only nine.'

Amber pulls her sleeves down over her hands and shuffles up closer to her father. She posts a thumb into her mouth; her demeanour makes her seem much younger.

'You've been extremely brave tonight,' Robin says gently. 'Could you tell us what happened?'

The girl nods. Her father smiles reassuringly, then puts his arm around her. 'Do you want me to start?' he asks. 'Then you can take over?'

The girl agrees, and the four of them sit down on the sofas.

'Amber called me, just after eight tonight. She was...' He glances at her. 'Upset. She said that some man broke in. That her mum was unconscious.'

Andrew Grace tries to lean back on the sofa, but stands up again, restless. He paces the floor, then walks across to a small pine cabinet, opening it and taking out a large bottle of whisky. 'Do you want one?' Robin and Freya shake their heads quickly. 'No, I guess not.' He pours a large measure in a wide crystal glass, then brings it back to the sofa, putting an arm round his daughter.

'How is your wife?' Robin asks.

'Laura's at the hospital now, along with my son.' He takes a sip; Robin notices his hand is unsteady. 'Her mother, their grandmother, is there. We should be with them. I want my daughter checked out.'

'Dad, I'm fine—'

'I know. But still, let's have the doctors take a look, shall we?' He turns his attention back to Robin and Freya. 'Will this take long?'

'No. We just want to get an initial statement, then you can go. And you called the police, Amber?'

'Yes,' Andrew Grace cuts in again. 'They got here quickly, thank goodness. Before he could... before he went into her bedroom. I think he heard the sirens and ran.'

Robin tries again. 'Can you tell us what you saw, Amber?'

This time Grace lets his daughter speak. 'Not much. I heard a crash and some banging. I looked out of my door and I saw him. Downstairs. I saw him... hit Mummy.'

Her chin wobbles and tears spill again. Robin knows the mother was knocked out by the intruder. The son pushed around. Who would do that to a seven-year-old boy, Robin thinks angrily. And for what?

Robin leans forward, resting his arms on his knees. 'You're doing very well, Amber. Did you hear him say anything?'

'Yes. But I couldn't make it out. He had some sort of accent.' She frowns. 'I don't know. I can't say what.'

'That's fine. Thank you, Amber.' Robin turns back to Grace. 'Do you know what was stolen?'

'Not much, as far as I can tell. He didn't touch the safe, and I noticed Laura still had her engagement ring when they took her away in the ambulance.'

'Any other jewellery? Electronics?'

'I'd have to get Laura to check her valuables. And she's... she's...' He bends his head to his hands for a moment, screwing his eyes tightly shut. 'I was at work. I should have been here.'

'Do you always work late on a Friday night?'

'Yes. Most nights I'm not back until past nine.'

'So he might have known you wouldn't be there?'

'Maybe. That's why we have the... Oh, shit.' Grace stands up quickly. 'Have you got the video? The CCTV?'

'Not yet. We noticed the camera at the front door. It records whoever rings the bell?'

'Yes. I'll get it for you.'

He stands up quickly, leaving the room. Robin and Freya follow, the girl trailing in their wake.

'This should be quick,' Freya says to Robin, sotto voce. 'If they have this guy on film.'

'Let's hope.'

Andrew Grace comes back in, his eyes wide. 'Laura's laptop, all the tablets. They've gone.'

Robin's optimism fades. 'All of them?'

The girl takes a quick gasp in. They all turn to face her. 'That's what he was shouting. Laptop. Laptop.'

'But the footage will be on my work computer too,' Grace adds. 'And that was with me.'

He leaves the three of them in the hallway, going out to the driveway. They hear the peep of the car, then the opening and shutting of the car door.

He returns with a large black bag, and places it down on the hallway table. He takes out his laptop. For the first time Robin notices two of Grace's fingers on his left hand are splinted and bandaged together.

'What happened to your hand?' he asks.

Grace glances at it for a second. 'Oh, that. Fell over. Wasn't looking where I was going. It's nothing.'

He dismisses Robin's question and goes back to the laptop, all of them waiting while it loads.

'Yes, look, here.' Grace pulls back so they can see the open web page. A list of videos and locations appear. 'We have cameras in every room,' he explains. 'Three round the outside, one on the gate, plus the one out the front. We have it set up so they record once motion is detected, and the footage is kept for a week. Here, this is the one from the door.'

Robin leans in closer as the video plays. A hand draws back from pressing the bell, revealing a man waiting. He's white, potato-faced, with a shaved head. Wearing all black, with a brown box in his hand. He's not the sort of person you'd want to meet in broad daylight on the street, let alone breaking into your house.

The girl starts crying again. 'That's him,' she says. 'That's the guy who hurt Mummy and Tim.'

Robin nods. 'And this gives us one hell of a head start to catch him.'

2

Freya's stunned. The clarity of this footage, the fact the man didn't even try to cover his face – it's madness. He must have known there would be cameras, how could he not?

'Have you seen him before?' Robin asks. Both Andrew Grace and Amber shake their heads. 'Not hanging around outside the house or following you?'

'No. Never,' Amber replies, and her father shakes his head again in agreement.

Freya waits while Grace downloads the videos to the police network via the secure link. She then takes charge, quickly contacting the duty sergeant, ensuring the image is sent out to the cops on Response and Patrol.

'What exactly do you do, Mr Grace?' Robin is asking as she taps away on her phone.

'I'm the CEO of my own company. A software engineering start-up.' He laughs awkwardly. 'Or rather, we used to be a start-up. We're considerably bigger than that now. Hamilton Grace Software – have you heard of us?'

'No, sorry. What do you do?'

Freya waits for confirmation that the video has been received, then turns her attention back to the conversation.

'We make virtual reality software.'

'For video games?'

'Yes. But it's so much more than that. It can be configured to any real-life location, so it's transferrable to a huge number of industries. The emergency services use it to practise evacuations – the same for oil rig workers and other high-risk professions.

Power stations. Exposure therapy for phobias. Shopping. And those are just a few examples. We're in the middle of trying to get a deal with Peloton, for their cycling and running routes.'

'We?'

'Me and my CTO. Tiller Hamilton. He's the genius behind the code. I'm the suit who runs the business.'

His mobile phone buzzes, and he looks at it. 'I'm sorry,' he continues. 'That's my mother-in-law. We need to get to the hospital. She says Laura's woken up.'

'That's great news. Yes, please go,' Robin confirms. 'We'll be in touch shortly. And I'm sorry, but you might want to find somewhere else to sleep tonight. If it's okay with you, I'd like to get the forensics team in to look for prints and footwear marks – anything that might help us find this guy.'

'Of course,' he replies. 'Whatever you need. Can I pack a bag for us all?'

'Yes. But someone will need to go with you.'

Robin gestures to one of the uniforms and passes on the instruction.

'We'll try and be as quick as possible,' Freya confirms.

'We'll need a statement from you, Amber,' Robin adds. 'And your wife and son when they're well enough.'

'Anything we can do.' And with a final shake of the hand to them both, Andrew Grace and his daughter head upstairs, followed by the officer. Freya watches them go.

'That makes things easier,' she says to Robin, his gaze fixed to where they've just gone. 'That he's actually being helpful.'

'Hmm,' he replies. Then he shakes his head quickly, turning his attention back to her. 'So, what's your theory?' he asks. 'Excessive violence, no provocation as far as we know. That's unusual. And why target the electronics?'

'Looking for files? For extortion or blackmail? Access to online banking?'

'Maybe,' Robin concedes. 'But he doesn't seem the type for anything complicated. This guy breaks in to a multimillion-pound house, doesn't try to hide his identity and nicks nothing but laptops? A thug, looking for a quick buck? How much is an iPad worth nowadays? A couple of hundred quid?'

'Transportable and easy to shift?'

'Yes, but compared to the engagement ring of the woman he knocked unconscious? Probably worth a tidy few grand.'

'If not more,' Freya agrees.

'Right. So what does that say to you?'

Freya frowns. He's got a point. For once Robin's cynicism seems warranted. She stares up the stairs where they can hear the opening and closing of drawers as Andrew Grace and his daughter pack.

'That nothing is as it seems,' she replies, deep in thought.

3

The next few hours are spent overseeing the crime scene. Andrew and Amber Grace leave with a growl of V8 engine; scene guards swap out as shifts change; SOCOs arrive in their Scientific Services van, quickly covering everything in a fine layer of grey dust.

For Freya and Robin, the priority has to be the CCTV.

They leave the house and sit in the front of Robin's Volvo. Even in April, it's cold and dark and damp, but they need space away from the bustle. Freya notices the clock as Robin turns the engine on, attempting to get some warmth into the car – it's fast approaching midnight. But she knows why they're there. This guy is nasty and violent – and there's a good chance they can catch him fast.

Robin reaches backwards and grabs his laptop, pushing his seat back and resting it on his knees. It's a common occurrence for police officers, working in their cars. Laptops whirring as the radio crackles and the windscreen steams up with condensation.

'Why would someone have CCTV in every room?' Freya wonders aloud as Robin boots it up, loading the videos from the police network.

'To check up on cleaners, housekeepers. Staff.' Robin shrugs. 'You know. The people that look after your house when you're rich.'

Freya mulls over that thought until the screen jumps into life. The first camera angle comes into view, capturing the hallway and the front door. Robin scrolls forward to an estimated time, then rewinds quickly as the man appears. He presses play.

The video shows a woman approaching the entrance. She opens the door without hesitation, but jumps backwards as it's forced hard into her face. There's no sound but Freya can see her mouth open, her hands in front of her in surprise. The man barrels into the house, discarding the cardboard box in his hands and charging at the woman. He hits her – once, twice – and Freya gasps. There's no hesitation – no chance for the woman to comply to his request before he goes for her. She falls to the floor but he doesn't stop there. The man stands over her, and Freya watches as he grabs her by the hair and hits her again. It's unflinching. Brutal.

Then the son comes in. Freya tenses, readying herself for what's to come. Sure enough, the man turns, then grabs his arm, shaking him and pushing him to the ground. The man stands over him, fist raised. Shouting something loudly, his mouth wide open. A seven-year-old boy, poor kid. He just lies there, his hands over his face, as the man leaves, running out of the room.

She glances quickly to Robin; his eyes are narrowed, his hand covering his mouth. It's clear he's feeling the same way as she is, her stomach churning with disgust and anger.

The man goes out of shot to the left, and Robin changes views, looking for the study. For the few minutes while Robin looks for the correct time, Freya sits in silence, reeling. Then it's up and running again. The man is moving fast, searching through the desk and cupboards. He finds an iPad and takes the black rucksack off his back, putting it inside, before turning his attention to the chest of drawers by the desk.

'There,' Robin says, pointing at the screen. Freya can see what he's referring to – he places his hand flat on the top of the wood. 'We'll get a print from that.'

'Why's he not wearing gloves?' Freya asks.

'No mask either. Same as with the doorbell. He doesn't give a shit.'

Robin presses play again and the man continues his search. A new room, a new recording. The lounge. He ignores the television, the expensive speakers and the surround sound. He opens a few more cupboards, finds another laptop.

The hallway again now, and the man runs up the stairs two at a time.

'To the boy's room?' Freya says. Robin checks.

'No camera in there,' he replies. But the man comes back into view within minutes, a tablet clutched in his hand.

They watch as he pauses outside what Freya assumes is the daughter's bedroom. He tries the handle; he pushes the door open, then he pauses. Freya imagines the sound of sirens as he turns and leaves, the rucksack slung on his back.

'She was lucky the first responders were so quick,' Robin notes.

'Very.' But she worries about the after-effects – what an incident like that will do to the girl going forward.

Freya's phone buzzes and she gets it out. It's Josh.

> Home now. Tell Butler Jo in taxi. Excellent company. Went for a few more drinks. Don't know what she sees in him. How's it going? x

She turns the screen away from Robin so he can't see Josh's rude comment, then replies:

> Going to be a late one. Don't wait up. x

'Captain America?' Robin asks.

'Josh, yes. And you agreed not to take the piss anymore. No more nicknames.'

'Sorry. Hard habit to break.'

She notices Robin roll his eyes but ignores him. 'He says Jo is in a taxi home,' she adds instead.

'Good.' Freya notices him glance at his own phone, then puts it down again quickly.

'Has she messaged you?'

'Yes,' he replies, but he doesn't elaborate, shoving the phone in his pocket.

Freya thinks back to the dinner. When she suggested it, she thought it was a good idea. Josh and Robin are her two favourite men, the people she spends the most time with, but they exist in a constant state of passive-aggression, sniping at each other whenever they get an opportunity. All she wants is for them to get along. Freya knows that Josh doesn't like how close she and Robin are – but he's with Jo now. He has a girlfriend.

Robin rarely talks about her, except if Freya asks what he did at the weekend.

'Jo came down,' he'll say, but that'll be it. Freya doesn't push for more. Robin seems happy with the arrangement. With Jo.

She was surprised Robin agreed to dinner. But maybe he just didn't know how to refuse without seeming churlish. And Jo is lovely. She *is*. So why doesn't Freya like her? She can't put her finger on it. Maybe it's that Jo is so much more successful than she is. A detective inspector, more senior than both Freya and Robin. And had she been flirting with Josh?

Freya sighs, then catches Robin looking at her.

'I'll pay you back,' he says. 'For dinner. You shouldn't have had to pick up the tab.'

'It's fine. You're always buying me lunch. And I didn't pay for all of it. I'm sure Josh and Jo ordered a few more bottles of wine after we left.'

'They seemed to get on, didn't they?' Robin comments.

'Everyone gets on with Josh,' Freya says, sounding more bitter than she intended.

Robin scoffs in reply. She turns to him and he smiles.

'Robin?'

'Yes?'

'Let's not do that again.'

'No,' he replies sternly. 'Let's not.'

4

They head back inside, donning the usual white suits as they go through the door. They've seen the whole house now through the lens of the CCTV, but Robin is curious: how do these people live? If you have a few million, what house do you choose?

To him, the place seems completely devoid of personality; a showroom example of a home. There are posed school photos on the white marble mantelpiece, next to one of the whole family. Robin picks it up. Two kids, a girl and a boy. He can see the similarity in their faces, and the boy has inherited Andrew Grace's propensity towards a rounder build. The wife is delicate and blonde. Pretty, like her daughter.

'What have you got there?' Freya asks, coming into the room behind him. He holds the photo out to her. 'Ah,' she says. 'Perfect happy family.'

'Apparently so.' He looks around again. 'But where's the mess? The dust? The discarded newspapers and books and kid-related crap?'

'Tidied away by the cleaner? All in their rightful place?'

'Hmm,' Robin replies. 'Shall we head up?'

They leave the living room and ascend the grand wooden staircase to the first floor. All the bedrooms lead off the main walkway; instantly Robin can see the open door leading into Amber's room.

'Poor girl must have been petrified,' Freya says. Robin follows her inside.

To Robin, it looks like a normal nine-year-old's bedroom. Not that he's had much experience of that. A poster of Harry Styles is on the wall. Clothes are messily discarded over a chair, a bookshelf is full of Harry Potter and Roald Dahl. Soft toys with weirdly big eyes line up on a shelf. Robin goes to the bed and picks up the gaudy picture lying on the bright pink duvet cover. He imagines her drawing, hearing the commotion going on below.

There's a shout, and they leave the room, looking over the banister to the SOCO standing in the hallway.

'DS Butler?' she calls up. 'We have a number of prints. Good strong ones. Some you need to see.'

He recognises the voice and the posture: Crime Scene Manager Jess Derby. Quick, efficient. He likes working with her. She's flexible when it comes to letting him follow a hunch, but never where the integrity of exhibits is concerned. He owes her more than a few favours.

Robin yells his agreement, then takes a quick step back, the height making him queasy.

Freya has already started heading down the stairs, but Robin pauses in the son's doorway. The room has been completely turned over. All the drawers have been pulled out; the bedclothes discarded on the floor. No regard for personal property or the well-being of the people whose house he so callously broke into. This was one determined offender.

When he gets downstairs, Jess and Freya are waiting for him in the hallway. The CSM starts talking the moment he joins them. No time for niceties or hellos.

'We've not bothered with the obvious places the family would go – such as bedrooms and door handles – but we have found a few where you directed.' She gestures with a wave of her hand and they follow her to the study. 'Andrew Grace mentioned the laptop his wife uses is usually kept here.' She points to a small chest of drawers under the desk. It's coated with dust, and they strain forward to look at it. Sure enough, there's the handprint, clear against the dark walnut.

She points with a gloved finger. 'Excellent detail, strong characteristics. Look at the size—' She places her own gloved hand alongside and it's huge in comparison. 'Would bet my life that's a man. We took a comparison card of Andrew Grace before he left, to rule him out, and in my quick assessment it's not him. See here?' She points to a ridge on the tip of the middle finger. 'This is what's known as a double bifurcation, and Grace doesn't have it.'

Robin cranes forward, squinting at the print. He can't see a thing. 'I'll take your word for it,' he says.

Eyes crinkle about the mask. 'We'll run a search on that, Butler. Good chance that's your man.'

Robin and Freya eventually depart at two a.m., leaving Jess at the crime scene.

'You'll call me?' he asks, and Jess gives him a look. 'When the prints come back?'

'Yes, Butler,' she confirms, patronisingly.

He drops Freya off at her house and waits while she trudges inside.

When he gets to his own home the whole place is in darkness. It's a compact terrace in a small row, bought ten years ago when he first got promoted to sergeant. His sister had just got married and he'd fancied a shot at responsible adulthood himself, buying one of the first places he saw and could afford. But he likes living here. His own space, his own bit of calm.

He lets himself in quietly, closing his front door with barely a click. He kicks his shoes off; leaves his coat where it falls. His tie has been long since discarded, and he undoes the buttons to his shirt as he plods up the stairs to the bathroom. The light makes him blink; he puts toothpaste on his brush still half blind.

He scrubs for a moment, his eyes partly closed. Then he looks up, catching a glimpse of himself in the mirror. He pauses, his toothbrush in his hand, his mouth white with foam.

It's not an attractive sight. He's tired, body weary for bed, stomach grumbling from lack of food, the steak feeling like days ago rather than mere hours. He leans forward and peers at his reflection. In this light, his hair seems more grey than brown; the lines round his eyes and across his forehead now deep furrows.

The start of a new case. His ambition to catch this guy is burned in him, as much as it always is, but the tiredness, the constant bloody ache in his bones – is this it, now? he wonders.

He leans forward and spits. Rinses his toothbrush and drops it into the glass. There's a blue one there, too, nowadays. It's a nice addition; the slow encroachment of Jo's belongings is a necessity given she lives in Reading, nearly fifty miles and over an hour from his house in Winchester. And he likes it. The feeling that someone likes him. The promise of a future.

And the rest? That's what he signed up for. A life on the force. A case to solve. A man who brutally beat up a woman and terrorised a child without hesitation. The sort of man who deserves to be put away – and fast. Who knows what else he is capable of? The next person he encounters could end up in the mortuary rather than the ICU.

Robin switches the light off in the bathroom, then creeps into the bedroom, discarding his clothes in the dark and crawling under his duvet in just his boxers. In the dim light he can see a lump – Jo, sleeping on her side, facing away from him.

He lays his head on the pillow, then – not able to resist – he shuffles up next to her, his legs behind hers. She shifts; her hand reaches for his and pulls it around her in a hug.

'You're cold,' she moans.

'I'm sorry,' he whispers. 'How was dinner?'

'So good.' She pauses. Her voice is slurred. 'I drank too much.'

He laughs quietly. 'You can sleep it off in the morning.'

'You're going in?'

'Yeah. Burglary. Definitely ABH, maybe GBH. And we have him on CCTV.'

But she's asleep. Jo's fingers are limp, her breathing steady and slow. He keeps his hand in hers, taking comfort in the sensation of someone in bed next to him. Maybe this is it, he thinks, as he slowly drops off to sleep.

SATURDAY

5

Robin wakes to the sound of vomiting. He opens his eyes, blearily lifts his head and squints into the early dawn. He hears retching this time. From the bathroom. The bed is empty next to him.

He smiles ruefully and replaces his head on the pillow, waiting for Jo to return.

He must have dropped off to sleep again because he is woken by a kiss on the cheek and a scalding hot mug of coffee placed down on his bedside table. Jo climbs back into bed and entwines her legs round his.

'Feeling better?' he says.

'You heard that?' She groans quietly. 'I blame Josh. Leading me astray. I don't know why you give him such a hard time. He's fun.'

'He annoys me,' Robin mutters. He slowly pulls himself to a sitting position. 'He's always so...' He places his hand directly in front of his face, almost touching his nose. 'Right there.' Jo laughs, and Robin smiles in return. 'You can spend all day in bed if you like,' he says to her. 'Recover.'

'Without you? No, I'll head back.'

'You don't have to—'

'What's the point of staying here? Hanging around, waiting for you to come home.'

'Cooking me dinner?' he tries, half serious.

'You won't be back for dinner. You'll get some awful takeaway with Freya.' She leans up, giving him a quick kiss on the lips, then pokes him in the tummy. 'Something you need to watch out for.'

'Yeah, yeah.' He pulls the duvet up over his chest, self-consciously, as she climbs out of bed. 'You give up the wine, I'll give up the takeaways.'

She laughs and carries her coffee with her to the shower.

He sits in bed for a moment, enjoying the warmth and listening to the water running in the bathroom. He glances at the clock: 8.15 a.m. Early, in his opinion, for a Saturday, but late given the state of the case.

He picks up his phone and calls Jess. She answers straight away.

'It's not back yet, Butler,' she says, anticipating his question about the handprint.

'How long?'

'As long as it takes.' He waits, then he hears a sigh. 'I'll chase,' Jess says, then hangs up.

Freya next. She answers on the fifth ring, her voice heavy.

'Are you awake?' he asks, carefully picking up his coffee and blowing on it.

'What do you think?' she grumbles.

'I'll pick you up in half an hour. Bright and early.'

'It's definitely early. I may be bright. But don't count on it.'

–

Andrew Grace isn't answering his mobile, and when they call the number he gave as a contact, the woman tells them he's at work.

'Hamilton Grace,' she says gruffly, her voice dripping with disapproval. The mother-in-law, he presumes. 'Do you know where that is?' she asks.

'We'll find it,' Robin replies.

30

But it's proving a challenge: Hamilton Grace Software is located in the middle of nowhere. Robin follows the satnav down single-lane potholed tracks as Freya reads out instructions from the company website on her phone.

'Follow the country road until large gates appear on your left-hand side,' she repeats.

'I am!' he exclaims, annoyed, debating turning round in a farmer's field and trying again, until a massive iron entranceway looms up in front of them.

He indicates and turns in, driving carefully through.

Off the bumpy country road, the driveway of Hamilton Grace is smooth black tarmac, lined either side with long grass and wild flowers in a riot of yellow, white and red. They cruise in silence as a slick glass building emerges. Sunshine sparkles off the glass. It's two floors, and they can see a spiral staircase running up to a balcony. A bright blue sign announces they have arrived at HGS. Hamilton Grace Software.

To the left of the glass cube is an older brick house. It's clearly a big place, but dwarfed by the modern building next door. It's pretty. Green wisteria covers the front sash windows between the bright purple blooms. Two tiny dormers poke out of the roof. It's surrounded by a low white wall; a narrow gate leads to a gravel driveway.

Robin follows the signs to visitors' parking and pulls up neatly between two vivid parallel lines. The car park behind is nearly empty, but a white Audi waits to their left, close to the entrance.

'He's here then,' Freya says.

'Apparently so.'

'Strange place to go when your wife's in hospital and your young kids are traumatised.'

Freya had called the hospital first thing, filling Robin in on Laura Grace's prognosis the moment she'd got in the car.

'She's awake but barely. Fractures to her left eye socket and cheekbone. Drugged up to the eyeballs. Doctor said to give it a few more days before we speak to her. We'll not get much sense at the moment.'

'We can wait,' Robin agreed. 'We have the CCTV and the handprint. They're our best bet in finding him.'

But Response and Patrol are coming up blank. And Jess is quiet, so here they are. Maybe Andrew Grace can offer more insight in the cold light of day.

They get out of the car and make their way to the main entrance. But before they do Robin glances up – and two figures catch his eye. Caught perfectly in the glass of the exterior he can see two men facing each other in an expansive office on the first floor. One has the pot-bellied silhouette of Andrew Grace, while the other is shorter, with a narrow build. Grace is gesticulating wildly while the slimmer man faces him, hands on hips.

Robin pauses and watches them. Freya follows his gaze. They're clearly arguing, then they stop and the unknown guy storms away.

'Wonder what that was about,' Freya muses.

Sleek glass automatic doors open smoothly, welcoming them into a cool, bright interior, a white reception desk taking centre stage. Given it's a Saturday, they're surprised to see a smart blonde-haired woman as sentry, unperturbed by the presentation of an official police badge.

'DS Robin Butler and DC Freya West to see Andrew Grace.'

'Is he expecting you?'

'No.'

The woman stares for a second. 'He's working. He doesn't like to be disturbed.'

Robin smiles tightly. 'Disturb him, please.'

She frowns, then picks up the phone, making a call. She talks quietly, waits, then replaces the receiver. 'His PA will be down to get you shortly, please take a seat.' She gestures to the area by the door, a row of soft expensive brown leather sofas, artificially aged for an 'authentic' look. 'Help yourself to a tea or coffee,' she adds, insincerely.

Robin moves away, leaving Freya at the reception desk.

'Do you often work on a Saturday?' he hears Freya ask.

'Not usually.'

'Sucks, doesn't it?' Freya says in a soft voice. 'I could be in bed with a croissant and a Bloody Mary, and instead he—' Robin imagines the glare in his direction '—makes me come in.'

Robin hears laughter from the woman and glances back to Freya with a small smile. Her blue eyes and blonde hair give her an air of innocence, meaning people let their guard down around her. Sure enough, the receptionist checks around, then leans forward conspiratorially.

'He's expecting visitors. Some people he doesn't want the other staff to meet.'

'Who?' Freya asks in a theatrical whisper, although Robin can hear them clearly in the silent reception area. He turns his attention to the line of newspaper clippings displayed in frames on the wall.

'Don't know. Wouldn't say,' she replies, looking visibly disgruntled. 'But he insisted on me being here this morning. Also,' she laughs, 'that man wouldn't know the way to the kitchen if we gave him a map. God knows he needs his caffeine. Grumpy as hell.'

Freya chortles in reply, then comes to join Robin at the ego wall. He points to the first clipping, looking at the picture, then reading the text below.

Set up in 2006, he reads, *Hamilton Grace Software is the brainchild of Teàrlach Hamilton, a software engineering graduate of UCL. Hamilton first came up with the VR Tourist as his final year project, the first program of its kind to combine virtual reality with the exploration of real places, initially designed to help autistic children feel comfortable in unfamiliar environments.*

Andrew Grace, a business graduate living with Hamilton, saw the commercial potential in Hamilton's ideas, and Hamilton Grace Software was born.

Today, Hamilton's revolutionary algorithms mean that the interactions between VR and a user's movement feel instantaneous and natural, avoiding the sickness-inducing lag present in many modern-day applications. Combined with Grace's commercial nous and natural charm, the company continues to move from strength to strength, attracting outside investors.

'Well, good for them,' Robin mutters, his gaze drifting back to the photo. It shows what looks like a pale, thin teenager, grinning broadly, his arm thrown round Andrew Grace. Younger, but unmistakably him. He checks the date – it was published ten years ago in *Computer Weekly*, the headline declaring them 'The Talent of Tomorrow'. He's about to read the next article when he's distracted by a small birdlike lady scuttling into view. She twitches in front of them, hopping from one leg to the other.

'I'm Diane, I'm Mr Grace's PA. This is most inconvenient. He's busy today.'

'So your colleague said,' Robin says, drily. 'But you told him Detective Sergeant Butler would like to speak to him?'

She hesitates, nibbling on her fingernails. 'Yes. Come up with me.' She scurries away to the staircase behind reception, Robin and Freya rushing to catch up with her.

'Thank you,' Freya says to the receptionist as they pass, the woman nodding in return.

Diane continues at pace through the double doors at the top of the stairs, round a corner and through another set, leading to a grand suite of rooms overlooking lush green countryside through three full-height windows.

'Impressive, isn't it?'

A voice speaks from behind them and they turn. Andrew Grace is standing there, looking much more relaxed than he had a few minutes ago.

'Wonderful view,' Robin agrees. 'How long have you had these premises?'

'About five years now. We bought the old manor house first – you must have seen it when you drove in.' Robin nods. 'We worked out of there for a few years, then the draughts and old electrics weren't fit for purpose so we built this place here.'

'It's very modern,' Freya says.

Grace smiles. 'There was no point in trying to match the architecture of the old place. And I think the contrast emphasises the beauty of both. Shall we go through to my office?'

They follow him past a large boardroom into an equally spacious office. Again, the full-height windows look out to rolling fields, a few sheep scattered in one, hedges bordering them into picture-perfect squares. Grace gestures to the two chairs in front of the desk and they sit down.

'How is your wife, Mr Grace?' Robin begins. 'And your son?'

'Andrew, please. And she's on the mend, thank you. My son and daughter are both at home with their grandmother. Tim's fine. The hospital checked him over. Just a few bruises.'

And the mental trauma, Robin thinks, but doesn't say.

'And you're at work today?' Freya asks.

'I have a company to run,' Grace replies with a tight smile. 'How can I help you? I'm sorry to be short, but I have work to do.'

'Of course. We have a few follow-up questions about your break-in, if you don't mind.' Grace looks hesitant. 'And an update on the case.'

Another forced smile. 'Fire away.'

'As you know, we got a good image of the man who broke into your house and attacked your wife. Here.' Robin pulls a printout from his bag and sets it on the table. 'Has anything jogged your memory overnight?'

'No. Sorry.'

'You've never seen him before? Not even hanging around your neighbourhood?'

'My wife is home more than me, she'd have a better idea. And as I said last night, I don't recognise him. Don't you have better ways than this to identify him?'

'We do, yes. The image has been circulated round the drug and fraud teams, and every PC on Response and Patrol will be

35

on the lookout for him today. We also got a good handprint from your study, which we're running through the database now.' Robin pauses. 'In the meantime, we were hoping you could shed some light on what he was looking for.'

'Looking for? What makes you think he was searching for something specific?'

Freya passes Robin the open laptop and Robin puts it in front of Grace. He presses play on the video.

'In all this footage, he's only after laptops and tablets. He ignores the more valuable items, including your wife's engagement ring, and only goes after the electronics.'

'Maybe he was interrupted?'

'No. Even in your main bedroom, he doesn't touch your wife's jewellery box. Fingerprinting confirmed it. Why might that be?'

Grace stares at the video for a moment then pushes the laptop back to Robin. 'I don't know, Detective. Does that mean your forensic teams have finished with my house?'

'Yes, it does. You're free to return when it's convenient. And it would be helpful if you could take another look around. In case there was something additional stolen.'

'I will.'

'What sort of data do you keep on your laptops, Mr Grace?' Freya asks.

He turns to her. 'Amber has the usual stuff. Homework, downloads from Netflix, photos. Tim only has an iPad. My wife, I don't know. You'd have to ask her.'

'What does your wife do?'

'She's a housewife. She goes to the gym. She sees her friends. She looks after the kids. She doesn't *do* anything.'

Robin's sure his wife wouldn't appreciate that description, but he lets it go.

'What about you? What's on your laptop?'

'Work stuff. Spreadsheets, presentations. All boring. But that was with me. Anyone breaking in would have known that, as soon as they realised I wasn't there.'

'Anything commercially sensitive?'

'Yes, all of it. But it's encrypted. Even if they had stolen it they wouldn't have been able to access the hard drive.'

'Could any of your competitors have benefited from the information?'

Grace laughs. 'We don't have any competitors, that's the beauty of it. We're bleeding edge. Our software model is unique – no other company has anything even close to being as quick and realistic as us. They're at least five years behind.'

'So your code is worth a lot of money?'

'Our *code*, as you put it so simplistically, is buried in IP and copyright and patents. Even if someone did steal it, they couldn't do anything with it without having to pay us a shit tonne of money. Besides, it's locked down. Never released. There's no way it could be stolen.'

They all hear a noise outside the office, then a knock on the door. The PA stands on the other side.

'Your visitors are here, Andrew,' she says.

He turns to Robin and Freya. 'I'm sorry, I have to go. Diane will show you out.'

Robin and Freya stand, but Robin pauses.

'Who were you arguing with earlier?'

'Pardon?'

Robin points at the glass window. 'We saw you from the car park. You, with another man. Who was that?'

Grace glances out of the full-height window, down to Robin's car. 'That was probably Tiller. Tiller Hamilton. We own the company together. Now—'

'What were you arguing about?'

'Just the usual disputes that arise from running a company. Now, if you'll excuse me.'

He says it with more certainty this time and Robin takes the cue to leave. 'Thank you for your help, Mr Grace. And if you see your wife before we do, could you let her know we'll be by the hospital to interview her as soon as we can.'

'I will.' He stands up and the thin-lipped grimace is back. 'Thank you.'

Twitchy Diane resurfaces and leads the way out of the office. They follow, Robin looking around as they go. He can't see any sign of an office with Hamilton's name on the door.

'Where does Tiller work?' Robin asks Diane as they walk.

She peers backwards. 'Not up here. Down on the lower floors. With the engineers.'

'Still? Even though he owns the company?'

'You'd have to ask Mr Hamilton about that,' she replies.

'We would love to,' Robin says. 'Can you show us the way?'

Diane pauses, her mouth opening and closing. 'But he's... he's...'

'Now,' Robin says with a big smile. 'Thank you.'

6

Tiller Hamilton's working environment couldn't be more different to the sleek, modern glass of Andrew Grace's office. Diane escorts them down a metallic-trimmed staircase towards the depths of the building, Freya following, Robin behind Freya. Tube fluorescents flick on; there is little natural daylight here, the sun blocked by the rows of tall trees at the back of the premises. Freya peers into the rooms as they pass. Offices, lit only by desk lamps. Darkened cupboards with racks of metal shelving. Computers attached to multiple massive screens.

'How long have you worked for the company?' Freya asks Diane, her voice little more than a whisper. Talking any louder seems intrusive to Freya, like it would in a church or a cathedral.

'Since the beginning. So… coming up to sixteen years. Gosh,' she says, turning to Freya with a smile. 'Doesn't time pass quickly.'

Freya laughs in return. 'Do you enjoy it?'

'The boys are like family to me.' She stops at the doorway to a small room. 'Even though they're hardly boys anymore. Tiller?' she calls out.

Freya peers past her into the office. Piles of paper rest on every surface. There are crowded messy bookshelves on one wall and a filing cabinet, half open, paper peeking out of the stuffed drawers, against the other. A head pokes out from a cupboard.

'Hello?'

In contrast to the doughy features of his business partner, the man is sharp and pointed, with deep-set, slightly hooded

39

eyes. He reminds Freya of a wolf, albeit a friendly one. Lean build, white teeth and a long thin nose. He's wearing a baggy T-shirt with a Space Invaders graphic on the front, black jeans and Dunlop Green Flash trainers. All look worn and faded.

'Mr Hamilton, we're the detectives investigating the break-in at Mr Grace's home last night and the attack on his family,' she begins. 'DC Freya West…'

'DS Robin Butler,' Robin finishes.

Hamilton reaches out and shakes each of their hands in turn, but Freya notices he doesn't meet their eyes. 'Teàrlach Hamilton.' He has a strong Scottish accent and pronounces his first name something like *char-loch*. 'An awful thing to happen. I hear they're okay?'

'Yes, on the mend.'

'That's good to hear. Thanks, Diane,' he addresses to the PA, and she leaves them. 'Come in.'

He gestures into the cramped office; Freya and Robin shuffle inside.

'We won't keep you for long,' Freya says. 'Diane said you have visitors.'

'Oh, they're Andrew's visitors, not mine. How can I help?'

He sits down behind a rickety wooden desk. Freya stares at the chair, then moves a pile of paper off it.

'Dump it on the floor. There.' He points. 'No, there. There,' he snaps. 'Intricate filing system,' he adds. 'I know where everything is.'

'Do you know this man?' Robin clears the chair next to her according to Tiller's precise instructions and sits down. He takes the photo out again, and places it on the desk. Tiller looks at it for a moment, then shakes his head.

'No. I'm sorry. Is he the guy?'

'We believe so, yes. Do you have any idea why he would target your business partner's house?'

'Not a clue, I'm sorry.'

'And where were you on Friday night, Mr Hamilton?'

'You're not suggesting I did it?' he asks bluntly.

'Just helps to get the full picture.'

'I was here. Until about ten. My security pass can confirm it. Then I went home.'

While Robin's been talking to Tiller, Freya has been looking out to the darkened corridor. 'Who works down here, Mr Hamilton? It seems a strange place to have an office.'

Tiller looks over to her and grins. 'The techies. Most prefer it. Down here, in the peace and quiet, nothing to disturb them. It takes a certain type to be a software engineer. You think in a specific way.'

'Introverts?' Freya asks.

'And the rest. You'd classify a few of the guys working here as autistic, formally diagnosed or otherwise. I think you have to be, a bit at least, to do what we do.'

He talks quickly, in sudden bursts, big gaps in between his sentences. Freya has to concentrate hard to keep up.

'And what's your role in this? Andrew explained a bit about what your company does, but it would be good hearing it from you.'

'Have you heard of virtual reality?' he begins. Freya nods. 'Well, forget everything you know. It's the easiest way to describe our technology, but it's so much more than that. We're looking at world modelling, in the same way that traditional VR does, but we take it one step better. Augmented, virtual and mixed-reality technology, totally immersive. You engage fully with the world around you – but better than that. We're talking machine learning, AI—'

'Artificial intelligence?' Robin asks.

'Aye. The prediction of behaviour before even you know what you're going to do based on micro-expressions and move-ment. Temperature, heart rate. Biometric parameters. Combine that with other sensors like RF and acoustic and you have a self-learning computer system.' He grins. 'It's no OASIS, but we're years ahead of Facebook's Meta or whatever the hell it's called now. D'ye ken?'

'Not really,' Freya admits.

He runs his hand through his shock of grey-brown hair, clearly in frustration. 'Have you heard of the Turing test?'

'Where you have to guess if the player you're interacting with is a human or a robot?'

'Exactly. Our AI is almost indistinguishable from a human. We've been training it up for years. Combine this with VR and the applications are endless. A lot of people want it. And that makes Hamilton Grace valuable as a company.'

'And you designed it.'

He smiles, proudly. 'Originally, aye. But we have a team of clever people working on it now.'

'So what does Andrew do? If you're the brains behind the company?'

'He's the personality. Someone like me, I could never sell the damn thing. Stand in front of investors and ask for money. Andy's the driving force. We met at uni. I was lucky. He saw the potential in what I was developing and took it out to market.'

'And the split? It's fifty-fifty?'

'Absolutely. You're surprised by that?'

'He couldn't do it without you.'

'And I wouldn't be here without him. Without Andy I would have probably gone on to work at some tech giant like Google or Twitter. Sold my soul, God forbid. But here we're actually doing some good. And I'm making money for myself, rather than the devil.'

'Pardon me for commenting, but you don't seem to be the sort of person who's bothered by material goods.'

Tiller laughs. He smooths down a crease on the front of his T-shirt. 'And you'd be right. But I do value my freedom. I work the hours I choose, in the company I've helped build.' He gestures out of the open door to the deserted corridor. 'With like-minded people who are happy here. What more could I want?'

His computer makes an odd noise, the sound of a Pac-Man dying, and Freya sees an error message appear on the screen.

Hamilton frowns at it, then begins typing, seemingly no longer noticing they're in the room.

'We'll let you get on, Mr Hamilton,' Freya says.

'Tiller,' he says without looking up.

Freya's confused for a moment. 'I'm sorry,' Freya says. 'But what is your real name? You called yourself something else earlier.'

His fingers pause on the keys. 'Nobody's actually called Tiller. Teàrlach. It's Gaelic. But nobody could pronounce it at uni so this is what they settled on.' He shrugs. 'I kind of like it now.' He picks up the desk phone and dials a few numbers. 'I'll get Diane to take you back.'

'We can find our own way.'

'No, Diane should take you,' he replies, curtly. Then he catches himself. 'Diane likes to do things properly. She'll flap if I let you wander, and the one rule of business is you don't mess with PAs. The eyes and ears of a company.'

'And you're Scottish?'

'Aye,' he says proudly. 'Fife born and bred.'

'So how did you end up down south?'

'UCL is one of the best places to study software engineering, but I couldn't stand London. Andy's from here. It seemed like the best place to go after uni.' He turns his attention back to his screen.

'Tiller, one last question?' Freya tries. He grunts but doesn't look up. 'Do you have any idea why someone would break into Andrew's house and steal his laptops?'

'That's what they were after? His tech?' Freya nods. He frowns. 'Nobody with any sense, that's who.'

'What do you mean?'

'Stealing laptops is pointless. Especially anything Andrew owns. In the old days everything would have been stored on servers, but nowadays it's all in the cloud.'

'So even if they could get into the laptops, they couldn't access your systems?'

'Not at all.'

'Who does have access?'

'The techies – our programmers. It's all built through collaborative development.' He pauses. 'But it's distributed in small parts, so no one person has access to the whole.' Then he smiles. A brief grin, little more than a smirk. 'Except me, that is,' he concludes.

7

Diane arrives and shows them back through the building, up the stairs until they emerge, squinting, into the sunlight of the bright reception.

The blonde receptionist gestures to Freya as they pass.

'You need to sign out,' she says, and Freya picks up the pen. Robin waits while she scribbles a time in the relevant box. 'Did you get everything you need?'

Freya glances around then bends towards her. 'Did you catch the name of Mr Grace's visitors?'

'Couldn't possibly say,' she says, with a small incline of her head towards the visitors' book. Freya notes the top name quickly.

'Thank you,' she says, and follows Robin out of the building.

They walk out into the car park; there is now an extra vehicle in the visitors' area. A black BMW; Robin looks at it with interest.

'Parapet Holdings Ltd,' Freya says. 'And the name written in the book was G. Kepner.'

'Doesn't tell us much,' Robin says, sneakily taking a photo of the number plate of the BMW.

'No. Or if it's even relevant.'

She waits for Robin, who's making no move to climb into his Volvo. He's lifted his head to the sun, closing his eyes. It's a perfectly dry, crisp day. Freya can only hear the sound of birdsong, the rustle of the wind gently moving the trees.

He opens his eyes again and glances down at the practical boots on her feet. 'Do you fancy a walk?' he asks with a smile.

'Have we got time?' Freya asks as she follows Robin to the far side of the car park. In the distance she can see a gap in the hedge, and a green field beyond.

'I've got my phone. If anything happens someone will call. Besides,' he says, turning back for a second. 'My doctor says I should get more exercise. Do me good.'

Freya jogs to catch up, joining him at his side as they step off the tarmac away from Hamilton Grace. He's the man in charge, she thinks. Who is she to argue?

They walk in silence for a few paces, the ground turning to grass and mud. A well-worn path is evident through the field and they follow it, Freya falling into step behind Robin when it gets too narrow.

From this view, she can't help notice the mark on the back of his head, a patch where his hair has grown back unevenly, unable to cover the scar that lies beneath. It's been four months since he was attacked in the line of duty. Striking out alone, Robin had eventually been found unconscious, attempting to apprehend a murder suspect.

Four weeks in hospital as a result, another six with him recovering on his sofa. Freya has since forced him to share the location of his iPhone with hers in case he goes off-piste in the future.

She had initially been worried sick. And then, when it was clear he was going to be okay, she enjoyed their time together. Visiting him after work, bringing the gossip from the station. Josh grumbled, and was ignored. She rarely saw Jo, although she knew from the food in the fridge and the cleanliness of the kitchen that she visited.

It felt like the old days again. Just the two of them, watching terrible police dramas, Robin dropping off to sleep without notice, leaving her talking to no one.

And she missed him while he wasn't at the nick. Seeing his face every day, bossing her around, his omnipresent frown as she divulged her latest theory. She had worried at the time – what if things weren't the same when he came back? But on that first day, five weeks ago now, she'd received a call.

'Pick you up?' he'd said, without introduction. And she hadn't been able to help grinning like an idiot when his Volvo had pulled up outside.

'What did you think of him?' Robin calls back now. He turns a little as he walks.

'Who? Andrew Grace?'

'Both. What did you make of them?'

'Grace is trying hard to come across as helpful, but in reality he'd like us as far away from him as possible.'

'Do you think he's lying about something?' His voice carries easily in the quiet of the countryside; it feels a long way from the hubbub of their office.

'I wouldn't go that far. But there's definitely something he's not telling us. All is not well in the world of Hamilton Grace.'

'Agreed,' Robin replies. Now they're at a wider point in the path, Robin slows so she can catch up. 'But could it just be the strain of working with someone like Hamilton? I did a bit of googling this morning. Definitely the child prodigy. He was programming at the same time he was learning to read and write.'

'He's clever, that's for sure,' Freya says. She grabs at a bit of tall grass next to her and breaks it off at the stem, running it through her fingers. 'And a little bit awkward.'

'A little bit?'

Freya smiles. 'Okay, more than a little. But it's worked in his favour. He clearly loves his job and what he's achieved with his company. He's odd, but no more than some people we've met.'

'True. And some of those we work with.'

Robin's phone rings, interrupting them. He answers it and listens for a moment. 'Okay, Mina,' he replies. 'We're on our way back.'

He hangs up, then turns. 'She's just arrived at the office. She's wondering where we are.'

47

'In a field,' Freya says, with a smile. She looks at Robin. He seems more like his usual self today. When he first came out of hospital he was pale, shrunken in, quiet. But he has colour back in his cheeks, and a little bit more padding round his middle.

'I'm glad you're back, Sarge,' she says, feeling a tug of affection.

He squints at her in the sunshine, a slight smile on his face. 'What's brought this on?' he asks.

She shrugs and turns back. 'Just… you know. Being around nature. Out in the sunshine. It makes you think.'

'It does, Frey,' he replies. They head back to the car, Robin following her this time down the narrow path. And after a moment, she hears him.

'It's good to be back,' he says.

8

'Are you coming?' Andrew stands in the doorway of Tiller's office, glaring. 'Well?'

'Andy, I've told you. No.'

'You should at least meet with them.'

'No.'

Andrew pauses for a moment. He's silhouetted, his large bulk almost fully blocking out the light from the corridor.

'Don't you realise how much this could change our lives?' Andrew says, quieter now. 'For the better?'

Tiller looks up from his computer screen, at the man he's known for nearly twenty years. So much has changed. When they started the company it was all about the excitement. The potential of what they could achieve. The first time someone invested they celebrated with a bottle of cheap Asda sparkling wine and two plastic glasses, sat in Andy's rusty Ford Fiesta. Tiller had felt blessed by his own fairy godmother. First, because he had met Andrew – someone who could actually sell this bunch of incomprehensible code – and secondly, because Grace believed in him enough to put his own money on the line and join forces.

But now? Now it was all about becoming bigger, making more money and making it faster. No matter what the consequences.

'Why are you even here, Andy?' Tiller asks. 'Shouldn't you be with your family? With Laura, in the hospital?'

'Typical that she's the only thing you're concerned about, Tiller,' Andrew says snippily. 'And this was arranged weeks ago. As you know. These aren't the sort of people you cancel on.'

'Not the sort of people you say no to, either.'

Andrew narrows his eyes. 'They had nothing to do with what happened last night.'

'This is just coincidence, is it? The very week we need to decide, some thug breaks into your house, terrifies your son. Puts your wife in hospital—'

'I know what happened, thank you.'

'And you don't think the two are related?'

'They're not that stupid. They don't need to resort to such tactics. Not when we're going to sign the papers.'

'I'm not. I've told you that.'

'But you have to! We need both signatures on the contract.'

Tiller stops. Andrew's voice has taken a different tone. Where before he'd met Tiller's refusal with anger, now he seems desperate.

'Why, Andy?' he asks, slowly. 'Why are you so keen for this deal to go ahead?'

'We're not going to get a better offer.'

'How do you know? We've had others, we'll get more. We're waiting to hear back from Peloton. And Zwift.'

'But not…' Andrew runs his hands down his face. 'Not soon enough.'

'Why? Why does that matter?'

But he just shakes his head. 'Meet with them? Please.'

'I'm not selling to these people.'

'They're not going to use it to—'

'How do you know?' Tiller interrupts. 'Because they say so? Because they've given their word?' he mocks. 'I don't trust them. And you shouldn't either.'

'Please, Teàrlach.'

He's using his proper name. Always a bad sign.

'You can't always get what you want, Andy,' he says quietly. 'This is my company too.' And Tiller turns away, looking back to his computer screen.

He hears Andrew sigh. There's a flash of light as he moves out of the doorway, then it darkens again as he turns back. 'I'm going to meet with them today,' he says. 'And then we have until Friday to make our decision. One week and all that money can be ours.'

'I don't want it,' Tiller says. He looks up into his best friend's eyes, knowing that this could be the decision that breaks them, for good. Andrew turns and walks away, his heavy footsteps getting quieter as he retreats back down the corridor.

Tiller stops, thinking for a moment. One week. A lot can happen in a week. Slowly he places his fingers on the keyboard, opening a new terminal window and creating a batch script over the package of data. After last night, something niggles. Something that tells him he needs to protect the company; protect what they've built. Something he wonders if he'll regret.

'They cannae have it,' he repeats to himself. 'Not them.'

9

DC Mina Desai greets them happily, black curls bouncing, as Robin and Freya arrive back at the police station.

'Thank you for coming in on the weekend, Mina,' Robin says. He hands her a coffee, which she takes gratefully. Like them, she's a long-standing member of the Major Crimes team, and had been dispatched to the grandmother's house to formally interview both children.

'Happy to. Any scumbag who scares the shit out of kids deserves to be thrown in jail.'

'How is he?'

'Shaken up, poor boy. With a nasty bruise on his arm where that bastard grabbed him.'

The three of them sit down at their desks, Robin and Freya eager to find out what she's discovered.

'I interviewed them separately, both with the grandmother present. Nothing either of them told me differed from what we saw on the CCTV, although Tim could offer a bit more detail. The offender pretended to be an Amazon delivery driver. That's why Laura Grace opened the door.'

'And why there was a discarded cardboard box there.'

'Absolutely. Tim was in the living room, got up as soon as he heard his mother cry out, then got shoved around for his efforts.' Mina frowns. Mina's own children are still tiny, but Robin knows her mothering instincts must be kicking in. 'And this guy was definitely after the electronics.' She picks up the written statement from her desk and reads from it. 'He was shouting, "Where are your computers? Where are your laptops?" And he described the bloke with an accent. I pushed, and his best guess was Spanish or Italian. Not Irish. Not American. Nothing closer than that. Did you get any thoughts from Andrew Grace about why he would want them?'

'Nothing helpful,' Robin replies. 'Did the son have any idea why the laptops were targeted?' Mina shakes her head. 'So what do we think?'

'Something on there they wanted?' Freya suggests. 'For blackmail? Photographs, video?'

'Sex tape?' Mina adds with a grin.

Robin returns her smile. 'Maybe. But look at the house. It's obvious they have money.'

'Do you think it was random?'

'It can't have been. If it was a random break-in they would have gone for the other valuables, surely? And the man certainly knew what he was looking for.'

'Is it related to the company?'

'Even knowing Grace's work laptop was in the back of his car, with him?'

'Would they have known that? He was working late, on a Friday night. Most people, even the most devoted CEOs, are home by eight when that guy broke in.'

This is the part of a case that Robin enjoys the most. This sparring, throwing ideas to and fro. Especially with Freya. They work in the same way but she doesn't think like him – her point of view always offers something new.

'But Hamilton said there was nothing to gain from stealing Andrew's laptop,' Robin counters. 'And if it was related to the company, wouldn't you go after Tiller? He's the man with the brains.' He pauses. 'What could Laura or the kids have?'

Robin gets up, grabbing a marker pen and standing next to the spare whiteboard. 'So, let's assume it's an outside job.' He starts to write, until Freya gives him a look and holds out her hand. She takes the pen and they swap places, Robin acknowledging his scrawl will be incomprehensible. 'We know he was after laptops. Why?'

Freya writes *Why Laptops?* Then adds *Blackmail? Sex Tape?* next to it.

'Money? Access to banking apps and stored passwords?' Mina contributes. 'Identity theft. Or something as dull as they were pirating films?'

'Why would a family like that be pirating films?'

Mina shrugs. 'Access to high-value items then. Easy to sell.'

'That's what you thought,' Robin says with a gesture towards Freya. 'But a hard house to break in to.' He shakes his head, changing tack. 'I don't buy it. Let's work on the theory it's linked to the company. That they didn't know Grace's laptop wouldn't be there and were hoping to get something to defraud Hamilton Grace. Insider trading? There's a lot of money tied up in that code.'

Freya writes it all up. 'None of which helps us actually catch the guy,' she finishes.

As if listening in on their conversation, Robin's phone starts to ring. He sees the name on the screen and sits up straight in anticipation.

'Jess,' he says. 'Have you got something?'

'Sorry for the delay,' she replies. 'We had a few matches on the database initially, so we needed someone from the finger-print bureau to manually check. And she didn't like working on a Saturday.'

'But you have a match?'

'We do,' she replies. Robin can hear the satisfaction in her voice. 'We have your man.'

10

They have an ID. They know who this guy is.

Thierry Durand, French national. They pull up his record on the Police National Computer and his mugshot appears. Glaring into the screen, shaved head, fat face, piss-hole eyes. They compare it to the still from the CCTV: this is their guy, all right.

He's known to the police. Multiple arrests for assault, ABH, robbery – including a few stints inside. Quite a record.

Robin calls their superior officer; DCI Baker confirms he's on his way in. They mobilise Intel, the armed response team – everyone they need to get this guy behind bars.

'Look, here,' Freya says, pointing over Robin's shoulder. 'The last arresting officer.'

It was Detective Inspector Matthew Ratcliffe. Affectionately known around the station as Mouse.

Robin picks up his phone and calls him. He answers on the first ring and as Robin explains what they're dealing with, Mouse takes a long intake of breath.

'Yeah, I know him. A real thug. I tried to get him on a rape charge but the woman miraculously changed her mind about what happened. What did you say he was after in the break-in?'

'Laptops and iPads. Any insight into why he'd want them?'

Mouse scoffs. 'He knows bugger all about electronics. Thick as shit. His speciality is quick in and out and carnage for anyone who gets in his way. All fists, no brains. Either he thought he could sell them quick, or someone told him to do it.'

'A hired thug?'

'Exactly that. Listen, I can't come in this weekend, I'm out of town, but phone me if you need anything. I'll be back on Monday. Call the drug squad and the gangs unit. And the NCA. We don't want any blue on blue. He used to work as a muscle man for the Dahmer boys.'

'The OCG that hang out round Southwood way?'

Organised Crime Groups. Gangs, primarily overseen by the National Crime Agency. And the Dahmer boys are a particularly nasty bunch. So-called due to their well-known habit of drilling through people's skulls (or kneecaps, or other convenient body part) to get them to talk.

'That's the one,' Mouse confirms.

Robin puts in a call to the other teams – eventually someone gets back in touch. Yes, they've heard of him. But no, go ahead, arrest the fucker.

Everything is moving. Robin feels the charge of excitement. Soon, they'll have this guy in custody. And they'll find out exactly what has been going on.

–

Hours later, Robin's neck and brain and eyes are aching, but the plans are all in place. The risk assessment is done, the armed response team are ready to go bright and early the next morning. Sunday is a perfect time to pounce. Hopefully their shitbag will be in bed, hung-over and unsuspecting when the AROs arrive with the battering ram. In the meantime, he can't get up to anything nasty – surveillance are watching.

He drops Freya home, and can't wait to get through his own door. But when he arrives there's a familiar car in the street. He hurriedly parks up and heads inside.

'Jo?' he calls as he takes his coat and shoes off.

'In here,' is the answering shout back.

He's confused. She must have got in using the hidden key – something they've resorted to before – but back so soon? Hasn't she got better things to do on a Saturday night than drive hours to see him?

He goes through to the living room, slumping down on the sofa next to her.

'What are you doing here?' he asks. He smiles then reaches over and gives her a kiss. 'Not that I'm not glad to see you, of course.'

'How's the case going?' she asks. He notices she's avoided the question.

'We have him. CCTV, clear handprint, the lot. We'll do the raid tomorrow morning at six.' He grimaces. 'So I need an early night.'

'No, no, I get it, don't worry. But…' She pauses, then looks bashful. 'It's just… There was something I wanted to talk to you about. And I wanted to do it face to face.'

Oh, here it comes. Robin's been ready for this moment; he knew it was all too good to be true.

'Go on then,' he says, steeling himself for the inevitable dumping conversation.

'I was doing some work, because what else is there to do on a Saturday?' She grins.

'Right…' This isn't going where Robin expected, but he keeps quiet.

'And out of interest I was scooting around to see what jobs are out there.' She glances his way to confirm he's still listening, and Robin nods. 'There was one for a DCI position. In D and C.'

Devon and Cornwall. 'But that's a transfer. Would they let you…?'

'See, that's just it. I know the super down there and I called her and she said they were desperate and they'd love to have me. I just need to apply, and go through the usual bollocks, and…'

'So, you're moving to Devon?'

'Yes, but…' She turns excitedly on the sofa to face him. 'You could come too. I mentioned to Detective Superintendent

57

Holton that you were a DS in Major Crimes, and she said they're always looking for people with experience. You could transfer, wait a bit, then apply for promotion to DI. Wouldn't it be good? Move back and be closer to Finn and Josie? You're always saying how you'd like something new.'

'I never say that,' Robin says slowly, still processing.

'Okay, maybe not. But I think it would be good for you. What's keeping you here?'

'I have a house…' He gestures vaguely around his tiny living room.

'You could rent it out. We could get somewhere together. What do you think?'

'I… Er…'

'I know, it's a lot. Sorry, I shouldn't have sprung it on you like that. But what do you think? First thoughts?'

First thoughts? Robin doesn't think she'll like his first thoughts. He doesn't want to go. He likes his job. He likes his team. And he likes… Freya. But Jo's right, it does make sense.

Ever since everything that happened back last May, Robin's wanted to see more of his best friend, Finn, and Finn's mum, Josie. They are the closest thing to family he has, growing up next door in the tiny village of Kingskerswell in Devon. The fact he hasn't got down there lately to visit constantly plays on his mind.

And he's been a DS for years. Baker is always encouraging him to make a move towards promotion. It does annoy him that he now takes orders from people like DI Ratcliffe, someone who made sergeant after him.

But move? Pack up his life and go? Could he do it?

He forces a smile and takes Jo's hand in his.

'It's a good idea,' he says, and she beams back. 'But I'm tired. I have a lot on my mind. This raid tomorrow. Catching this guy. Let me think about it.'

'Yes. Yes, of course.' Jo sits back on the sofa, happy. 'Now, do you want to talk about work, or would you rather watch some TV?'

'TV, please. Something mind-numbingly awful,' he replies, and she grabs the remote, loading up Netflix.

She chooses a film; he doesn't care what. He's not watching it. Inside his head, everything whirs. The arrest for tomorrow. Whether the guy will be there, whether he'll go down without a fight. The ever-present worry that some of his colleagues will be hurt. And now this.

He's only been with Jo four months; he has ketchup in his fridge he's known longer. But he does like her. He enjoys her company. He fancies her. They have so much in common, they're good together. But to leave? To transfer to another constabulary, and live with her?

He has no idea.

SUNDAY

11

It's five in the morning, and Freya and Robin stand at the back of the briefing room. In front of them, a group of large men listen to their inspector as he goes through the plans for the raid. Behind them, DCI Baker observes carefully.

'Intel puts Thierry Durand living with his girlfriend, at a terraced house at 67 Beechmast Road in Southwood. The place is known to us, a regular haunt for druggies and pimps. This is not going to be easy – visibility is restricted, multiple entry and exit points, but we'll make sure we cover all possibilities. We've had eyes on him all night, he's definitely there.'

He clicks a button and the man's face appears on the screen. Freya remembers him from the CCTV of the burglary and she involuntarily shudders.

'Thierry Durand. Hired thug. Not afraid to use force, so we'll go in hard. We don't believe there'll be anyone else there but let's not take chances. Entry will be dynamic and forced. Clear the other rooms in the house fast, restrain and arrest anyone you come across.'

'Including the girlfriend?'

'Yes. Conspiracy, until we know more. Any other questions?'

The men in the room shake their heads. The inspector looks to Robin. 'Detective Sergeant Butler, do you have anything to add?'

Robin pushes himself up from the wall, standing straight. All eyes turn his way. 'This man has put a woman and her son in hospital, beaten up in their own homes, so make no mistake, he's a nasty piece of work. He's used to being arrested, but he's not the brightest spark so he may resist. Don't hold back.' Robin smiles. 'I know that'll be tricky for you guys to do.' A smatter of laughter echoes around the room. 'And thank you,' Robin concludes. 'You're doing the world a service, getting this shit off the street.'

Faces turn back to their inspector. They're fidgeting, eager to go.

'Get kitted up,' the inspector says. 'Be ready in ten.'

The room bursts into life. A rush of testosterone and muscled guys keen to get a result.

The inspector makes his way over to Robin and Freya.

'Are you joining us?' he asks.

'From a distance,' Robin replies, and the inspector nods in approval. He doesn't want anyone unarmed getting in the way. 'Suit up anyway,' he finishes and leaves them to it.

Wordlessly, Freya follows Robin out. They put on their black stab vests, police-issue coats. They hang back as the armed officers load into the van, clutching LMT Carbine semi-automatics, Glock handguns in easy reach. Freya hears the bark of a large German Shepherd and turns to see the dog unit ready to deploy.

The sun is slowly coming up – a globe of dazzling yellow, bright against the hazy blue and grey – as the procession of vehicles makes its way to their target. Freya enjoys the natural beauty of it for a moment, even in such insalubrious surroundings.

Freya knows how the tactics work: minimising risk to officers in the position of threat, minimising any risk to the public. Going in first thing in the morning means their offender's defences will be low – hopefully he'll still be sleeping as the enforcer is bashed through the door.

The teams move decisively towards their target. Bent low, dressed all in black with stab vests and helmets, the only thing visible are their eyes behind safety glasses. Scopes train on the house. They crouch behind open car doors, hustle round the back, surprisingly quiet for such large men. The dogs wait, ears pricked, held tight by their handlers, poised to release at the slightest encouragement.

Freya and Robin watch from a distance, a radio clutched in Robin's hand. She feels butterflies in her chest, a jolt of anticipation. Authorisation is given, and the scene becomes a flurry of activity.

Shouting, the thud of footsteps. The bang as the front door is burst open. They hear the lead officer call out.

'Armed police. Anyone at this address, make yourself known. Come to the front door, your hands where we can see them. Armed police.'

There is no movement, and the officers barrel in. The sound of screaming – a woman – then she comes into view, escorted out of the house in a dressing gown, her hands behind her back.

'Where is he?' Freya whispers. 'Is he there?'

Robin doesn't reply, just holds his head closer to the radio. More shouts as the house is methodically cleared. And then a cacophony of noise. A bang of a door being forcibly opened, shouts from the officers, their loud voices blurring into an aggressive blare of confusion.

Then the confirmation.

'State nine, one in custody. AIO.'

All in order. They're clear.

They've got him.

12

The search begins. While Durand is taken to the police station – cuffed and scowling in his dressing gown in the back of the cold van – teams swoop in, Freya and Robin among them.

They suit up and enter the house. The front door stands wonky on its hinges, frame splintered, lock broken. Muddy footsteps litter the hallway.

The dog has gone first. An enthusiastic black and white spaniel, tail wagging, tongue lolling, the handler pulled along in its wake. Freya can hear them upstairs as they move from room to room.

The house is dark, and Freya clicks switches on as they go. Some of the lights are out, others are just bare bulbs, swinging from the ceiling. The carpet is dirty; the dated woodchip wallpaper scuffed and peeling.

And there is a smell. Even behind her mask, she can detect it. Old sweat. Spilled beer. Tobacco and joints – getting stronger as she goes into the living room.

The evidence is here. Overflowing ashtrays, butts bursting out onto the carpet. Empty beer bottles. A sofa that has definitely seen better days coated in stains of worrying provenance.

'What a shithole,' Robin says from behind her. She nods, and opens a cupboard next to her, rifling through the detritus within. Paper and old receipts and any amount of crap. Nothing incriminating, to her disappointment.

'Here's something,' Robin comments, holding up a battered tin – baggies of weed, next to crumpled five- and ten-pound notes.

'Small-scale,' Freya replies.

'Intent to supply. It's a start. Oh, hello...'

Robin shows her what he's found: a roll of twenty-pound notes. He carefully undoes the elastic band and counts it. 'Three grand,' he concludes.

'You don't get that from dealing a bit of green.'

'No.'

Robin places it all in an evidence bag and labels it, then continues the search. But there's not much. What belongings Durand does have are old and battered. Freya leaves Robin to finish the room and goes into the tiny kitchen.

The mess is worse here. The sink is full of dirty plates and pans, food dried on. The surfaces are filthy, the cupboards nearly bare. The fridge is much the same – empty barring beer and half-finished takeaway containers. But there are a few things that make her pause. Weighing scales, small bags, clingfilm. She bundles them up quickly.

A shout from upstairs diverts Freya's attention. She leaves the kitchen and heads up, Robin following.

The voice calls again from the main bedroom and she goes inside. This is clearly where they sleep: almost-grey sheets, indescribable stains. Even with gloves on, Freya doesn't want to touch it.

The dog is sitting obediently in front of the wardrobe, the doors open, his handler behind him. But otherwise it hasn't been touched.

'Here,' the officer says, pointing towards the bottom. 'Pepper went straight towards it.'

Freya scans the open wardrobe. It seems innocuous enough – a few clothes hanging up, shoes scattered in the bottom. She crouches down and pushes them out of the way, then taps on the base. It's hollow.

She glances back to Robin, then pulls at the board. It comes away easily, and what's revealed makes her gasp.

Packed into the small space are large white cuboid parcels, wrapped with clingfilm. Gently, she takes one out with a gloved hand – there's another layer below.

She hears a low whistle from behind her.

'Fucking hell,' Robin mutters.

He crouches next to her, then starts taking photos as she carefully removes the drugs from the hole. Seven perfect white blocks.

'What do you think?' Freya says. 'Coke?'

'If it's uncut, this lot would be worth hundreds of thousands on the street. Easily.'

Freya digs further. And her hand comes into contact with something else. Not plastic this time, but paper.

She pulls it out. It's a bundle of fifty-pound notes. Smaller lots wrapped with colourful elastic bands then looped together in one large sheaf. Freya counts up the smaller bundles.

'Ten grand,' she says.

She looks back into the hole and slowly pulls out another, and another. She passes them to Robin, his eyes widening above the mask.

She looks at it all, shaking her head in disbelief.

'Thierry is going to be in big trouble,' Freya notes. 'And not just from us. All this, seized by police. Someone is going to be seriously out of pocket.'

Robin sits next to her, idly thumbing the money with his gloved hand. He looks up, his eyes crinkling as he smiles.

'What do you say, Frey? You and me? Tuck this in our pockets and who would know?'

She looks at the money in front of her. 'Fifty grand, Butler?' she replies with a grin. 'Wouldn't even begin to support my lavish lifestyle.'

'No? We could go somewhere hot and inexpensive. Thailand? Nice little wooden hut on the beach. Our own tropical paradise.'

'I'd drive you mad within a fortnight. Either that, or bore you shitless.'

'You, Freya? Never.'

She glances to him, and for a second makes eye contact. And she feels that feeling again – those butterflies in her stomach. The electricity of connection. She swallows hard, glad that most of her face is hidden behind the mask, then hurriedly sticks her head back into the wardrobe, emptying it of the last of the haul.

She senses Robin move away from her side, and when she looks up again he has evidence bags in his hand, slowly putting the money away. The moment has gone, as quickly as it arrived.

–

The money and the drugs are catalogued and carefully removed; few people remain in the house. Freya and Robin stand outside, trying to avoid the glare of the nosy neighbours and the lens from the local press.

The search of the house is ongoing. Before she left, Freya had poked her head round the doorway of the spare bedroom. It was full of stuff. Just stuff. An old exercise bike had clothes draped over it, some of them still with labels. Freya opened the cardboard box closest to her – it was full of old iPhones and tangled cables. Stolen goods waiting to be fenced. Nothing of great value, but a pain in the arse to catalogue and match to potential burglaries from the area.

But it's one for later. For now, they have Durand to consider.

Next to her, Robin yawns.

'Do you want to get a coffee?' he asks.

She stifles a yawn of her own and nods.

A patrol car drops them at the Costa closest to the nick, and, cardboard cups in hand, they walk slowly back to the station.

'Was Jo okay the other night?' Freya asks. 'Being left with Josh?'

'Yeah, she didn't mind. She knows what the job's like.'

'Good to be with someone who understands,' Freya says.

66

'Hmm.'

They walk a few more steps in silence. Freya senses Robin's holding back; there's something he's not sharing.

'And everything's going well with Jo?' she prompts. She glances his way. His brow is lowered, head tilted down. A sure sign something is bothering him.

'Yeah, really well. I think.' Another pause. Freya waits. 'She's looking at a transfer. Down to D and C. There might be a promotion in it for her.'

'That's amazing. But what about you two? I guess you could always try long-distance,' she rambles. 'Backwards and forwards. Not much different to what you do now.'

'She's asked me to go with her.'

Freya stops dead on the pavement. Robin takes a few more paces then looks back, noticing she's gone.

'But that... that's unexpected,' she manages.

'It was.'

'And what did you say?'

'That I would need to think about it.'

They start walking again, and Freya gathers herself together. She's shocked. The thought that Robin would leave Southampton. That he would leave her.

'It makes sense,' Robin continues. 'I'd be closer to Finn, and apparently they're short on DIs, so I might even get promoted.'

'That's good,' she murmurs.

'And you could apply for DS.' He turns to her with a slight smile. 'Without me holding you back you'd be a sure thing. Baker would promote you in a second.'

'But... But...' They're at the nick now, and Robin holds the door open for her. 'But we wouldn't work together,' she blurts out.

Robin pauses, the door in his hand. He nods slowly.

'I know,' he says quietly.

And the door slams shut behind them.

13

Durand is talking to his lawyer. They've had to wait a few hours for the translator – a pinched-looking man with a sensible short back and sides and thin glasses. It's not hard to see that there is little love lost between the two professionals and their client.

Freya peers through the window into the interview room, then joins Robin where he's waiting to the side of the corridor.

'Ugly fucker, isn't he?' Freya observes with a smile.

Robin snorts. He really is. Usually a mugshot is unflattering, painting an offender in the worst possible light, but in this man's case it seems to have done him a favour. He's sweaty and pale, shaved head misshapen. His nose is flat to his face, like it's been broken too many times. Durand is out of his robe and pants and into the standard grey tracksuit with minimal improvement – the cheap material is stretched against his arms and across his chest. He's big – and not just with muscle. Rolls of fat billow around his non-existent neck and seem to render his arms unwieldy. But not so cumbersome he couldn't punch the living daylights out of an innocent woman, Robin reminds himself.

He appreciates the moment of levity with Freya. Ever since Robin shared his news about Jo's proposal, she's been quiet. He hasn't wanted to ask why. Maybe she's thinking about the possibilities with him out of the way. Promotion. An easier working environment, that's certain, without the antagonism between him and Josh.

There's a shout from the corridor. Robin and Freya look up as the door opens and the solicitor stands waiting.

'We're ready,' he says.

He looks sweaty and harassed, even before the interview has begun. They've shared limited information in the preliminary discovery conversation – no lawyer likes to go in blind.

Robin and Freya file in. They sit opposite Thierry Durand and his translator, placing the bulky file of evidence in front of them. The solicitor sits at the end of the table, next to Durand.

Robin clears his throat. He begins the interview slowly, reciting the date, the time and the people present. The solicitor and translator include their introductions. Durand grunts in agreement to his name. The caution comes next; Durand doesn't flinch.

Robin looks across the table at the man. The stench is palpable inside the close quarters of the interview room. Body odour, fried food and something biting and bitter, like rotten meat. Durand stares back, his piggy eyes blank.

'We would like to begin by asking you about the evening of Friday the twenty-second of April, beginning at nineteen hundred hours. Seven p.m.' Robin waits while the translator relays the message. The man's gaze doesn't shift from Robin's face. 'Where were you?'

'J'ai rien à dire,' he replies.

'My client has nothing to say,' the translator repeats. 'No comment.'

'Do you know a man called Andrew Grace?'

A pause while it's translated.

'J'ai rien à dire.'

'No comment.'

'Have you ever been to his house? Twenty-seven Honeysuckle Drive?'

The same.

'Did you assault the occupants of that house? A woman and her young son?'

'J'ai rien à dire.'

'No comment.'

69

'Yeah, I got that,' Robin snaps with a frown to the translator. He turns his attention back to Durand. 'Let me share something with you. Some video footage from that night.' He pulls two stills from the file and pushes them over the table. The man doesn't even look at them.

'No comment,' he says in heavily accented English.

Robin shows him another photo from the CCTV.

'This is the moment you punched Laura Grace unconscious,' Robin says. The solicitor looks at the photo, then away again quickly. 'Would you like to see the video? It doesn't make great viewing. Not for you, at least.'

He pauses, watching the man's face while the translator talks. His expression doesn't change.

'Non,' Durand replies. This time he adds the flicker of a smile. 'Merci.'

'There were five cameras in that house, Thierry,' Robin continues. 'One in practically every room. Three round the outside. Plus this one on the doorbell.'

He pushes the original shot towards him. There is no mistaking the punchbag features of their suspect. The solicitor winces.

'Plus, here—' Another picture is passed across, a grey apparition of fingerprinting dust. 'A handprint taken from the house. One that matches exactly to yours. We can prove you were there. As if the video showing what you did to Laura Grace and her son isn't enough.'

Durand doesn't move, his eyes fixed on Robin.

'Okay,' Robin says, admitting defeat. 'Let's move on to something new. What we found when we searched your house.'

Durand frowns, then barks a sharp torrent of French to his solicitor. His translator passes on the message, and Robin catches the tail end of the question: *Are they allowed to do that?* Robin tries hard to withhold a smirk.

'You've been arrested,' his solicitor replies, his tone jaded. 'Under section 32 of the Police and Criminal Evidence Act, they're allowed to search your house.'

Durand turns back with an expression that tells Robin he'd like to punch a pudgy fist into his face. Robin smiles, slightly sarcastically.

'Now we've established that, let me tell you what we found.'

He opens his file again and takes out two photos. He places them in front of Durand and his solicitor leans forward. The lawyer studies them closely, then looks to Robin, his mouth open.

'This here,' Robin begins, 'is just over fifty thousand pounds in cash. And this is seven kilograms of high-purity cocaine. We found it at the bottom of your wardrobe.'

'You put it there,' Durand says, clearly, ignoring his translator.

'We have more than enough witnesses to say we didn't.'

'It's my girlfriend's.'

'Really, Thierry?' Another photo – this time a close-up of one of the packets of coke, a clear row of swirls in the grey dust. 'Make up your mind which defence you're going with, bearing in mind these are your fingerprints, and next door your girlfriend is talking to my colleagues. You're not going to come out well in this, I imagine.'

'C'est une salope doublée d'une pute,' he spits in French. 'She lies.'

'And you're the paragon of virtue, are you, Thierry?'

Robin's aware he's being less than professional but his confidence in their case against this man is making him smug.

'But I don't think you're the brains behind any of this,' Robin says. The translator gabbles next to him, but from the hatred on his face Robin's sure Durand's having no problem understanding Robin's English. 'From what I hear you're no more than a hired goon. A man the important people send in to do their dirty work. The crappy iPhones and the knock-off electronics. The small-scale distribution of weed – that's more your style. I don't think you deal in cocaine. I think you were holding onto it – for some people who are going to be very angry when they find out where their merchandise has gone.'

Durand looks to his solicitor. He speaks quickly in French.

'My client has no more to add at this time,' the lawyer says, dejectedly. He has sunk so far down in his seat he is almost horizontal.

'Then perhaps you would like to relay this. We're going to charge you for the GBH and the burglary.' The translator interprets as Robin talks. 'And because of the violent nature of these attacks it's unlikely you'll get bail. You will be remanded in custody until your trial, and the evidence we already have means you'll be staying in prison for a very long time. And that's even before we talk about the drugs charges.' Robin pauses, waiting for the translator to catch up. He doesn't want any misunderstanding on this. 'But,' he continues. 'If your client helps us,' he turns his attention to the man, 'if you tell us why you robbed this house, what you were looking for, who paid you, then maybe life will be a little bit easier for you from now on.'

The translator finishes. The solicitor looks hopefully at his client.

'Va te faire foutre,' Durand says.

The translator looks embarrassed. 'Go fuck yourself,' he repeats, quietly.

14

Robin and Freya file out into the corridor; Durand is taken back to his cell. The solicitor pauses, watching his client leave.

Robin waits until the man is out of sight, then turns to the solicitor.

'Listen, there is no way he was acting alone. His previous offences indicate he works for anyone who will pay him, and you know we'll get a warrant for his mobile phone data.'

The solicitor nods wearily. 'I can't comment, you know that, Detective.'

'I know. But you're here to act in the best interests of your client. And if he tells us who was behind this attack, who owns the drugs and the money, then surely that works in his favour.'

'My client may disagree. But yes, I take your point.'

And with that he trudges away, head tilted to the floor.

Mina comes to join them, a beige file in her hand.

'How did you get on?' Freya asks her.

'Well, she's a charmer,' Mina begins. 'Every other word a profanity. Has nothing good to say about your boy there.'

'Let me guess, she knows nothing about the drugs?' Robin says.

'Nothing,' Mina confirms. 'But actually, I believe her. She was all "no comment" until I showed her the picture of the coke and the cash and then she became quite chatty. Her eyes opened so wide I thought her eyeballs would drop right out of her head onto the table.'

'You have such a way with words, Mina,' Robin laughs.

'I try. Did you find any of her prints on the wrappings?'

'No, none,' Robin confesses. 'Did she say who the drugs belonged to?'

'No, just that it was all down to Terry. She pronounced it like that – Terry. Like he was some English bloke down the boozer.' She grins. 'She didn't know anything about the burglary Friday evening, either. She just said that Terry was out all night. Didn't come home until ten Saturday morning and passed out on the bed.'

As they're talking, Robin notices the large six-foot-plus figure of his boss appear at the other end of the corridor. Robin raises a hand and DCI Baker heads towards them.

'Did he have any laptops with him when he came home?' Freya asks.

'No. Not that she knew.'

'And we haven't found them at the house, either,' Robin says. 'So where are they?'

'Passed on to whoever wanted them nicked,' Freya suggests. 'In exchange for an additional roll of cash?'

'I guess so,' Robin replies. 'But it's going to take ages to get all that money from the house fingerprinted. That's assuming he brought it home and didn't spend it at the pub. Afternoon, guv.'

Baker greets the three detectives warmly. He's dressed in smart trousers, a smart shirt and matching jumper: the off-duty uniform of a man supposed to be at Sunday lunch somewhere posh. But contrary to appearances, Baker is a beat cop through and through, doing the majority of his training in the Met. There's no way he'd want to miss following up on a juicy raid like the one that went down that morning.

'Have you got anything?' Baker asks in his rough east London accent.

Robin fills him in on their interviews.

'It's not surprising he's keeping shtum about where the drugs came from,' Baker replies. 'Opens his mouth and next thing he knows his tongue will be cut off and shoved where the sun don't shine, all his blood disappearing through the nearest prison drain. No, keeping quiet is the only way he'll survive from here.' He turns to Robin. 'Are you happy with this as a conclusion, or do you want to keep pushing?'

Both Freya and Mina look to Robin. He thinks for a moment.

'Honestly, guv? I'd rather keep looking. From the testimony from the son, Tim Grace, we know Durand was targeting the laptops, and I can't for a second believe that house was chosen at random. Someone paid him to be there, and I'd like to know who.'

Robin glances to Freya; she smiles in agreement.

Baker nods approvingly. 'Fine. Do it. And tomorrow I'll get some other poor sod to work through that pile of stolen goods you dug up at the Durand house. Maybe something will come of that. Now, if you'll excuse me, there's a beef roast in a cosy New Forest pub with my name on it.'

The three of them watch him go and once he's out of sight, Mina jokingly pulls on Robin's arm. 'Please let me work with you,' she begs. 'I don't want to trace dodgy iPhones.'

Robin laughs. 'Since you gave up your weekend, anything. Although I can't guarantee this is going to be more interesting. Until forensics return, let's go back to Andrew Grace, find out a bit more about the company. Let's see what we can dig up.'

–

Hours later, the five a.m. start is making itself known. Robin's eyes droop, his head dips at his desk. Laura Grace is still too ill to be interviewed, so he's been looking into the company. He hasn't got far. The website talks about state-of-the-art algorithms, real-time software, data fusion – an array of technological terms he doesn't have the energy to decipher.

He scowls and flicks away from the website, then opens a new screen. He looks at the name jotted down from their visit to Hamilton Grace yesterday. Parapet Holdings Ltd.

He pulls up a Google search and types it in. The top result is a dissolved company on the Isle of Man. He frowns, reading the information. Nothing useful; this can't be it. He moves on.

He spends the next half an hour exploring options to no avail. Real estate in Illinois; finance and insurance in Lancashire. Parapet investments, properties, enterprises – a whole load of names that don't seem to have significance. It's a needle in a noun-ridden haystack. He tries another direction, pulling up the PNC and typing in the number plate from the BMW.

Registered owner: Giles Kepner. *G. Kepner.* The name written on the sign-in sheet. No surprises there.

He tries Google again – including the name – and this time the record for Companies House appears on his screen. He clicks through – incorporated on 30 June 2021. So, what? It's less than a year old? The next tab: no accounts filed. The next, and only one appointment registered: Giles Kepner. Role: Director. Occupation: Director. With a correspondence address here in Southampton.

He frowns. It tells him nothing. Nothing that will help, anyway.

'Defence activities?'

Freya appears behind him, a mug of coffee in each hand. She passes one to him as she sits down.

'What are you looking at?' she asks. 'Why don't you leave this to Intel?'

'Because they're backed up and I don't want to wait two weeks.' He points to the screen. 'Parapet Holdings. The company that was visiting Grace on Saturday. What do you mean, "defence activities"?'

'Here,' Freya leans forward, pointing at the screen. Under *Nature of Business* the website is showing a list of codes.

71122 Engineering related scientific and technical consulting activities

84220 Defence activities

'What does that tell us?' Robin asks.

'Not much,' Freya smiles. 'What does it say about Hamilton Grace?'

Robin scrolls back up and types the name in the search box. A list appears and Robin selects the correct one.

Freya looks over his shoulder at the screen, then flaps a hand at him, as if to say, get out of the way. He does as he's told and she takes over the mouse, scrolling down the page.

Nature of business: 62020 Information technology consultancy activities

'So far, so boring,' Robin says.

Freya clicks on the *Filing History* tab.

'So, Hamilton Grace Software Ltd were incorporated in 2006, which we already knew, and here—' She scrolls down. 'Here are all their financial statements.'

Robin sits up straight, suddenly interested. 'So can you tell me how much money the company makes?'

'Of course.' She opens a document and quickly flicks through the pages of incomprehensible numbers. 'My dad was the managing director of a manufacturing company – I didn't grow up talking profit and loss at the dinner table for nothing. Look, here.' She points to the screen. 'This is their balance sheet. And they are doing well. Really well. Last year, the company made eight hundred grand profit.'

'So who would get that? Grace and Hamilton?'

'Some of it goes to the taxman. I'd guess some of it is invested. And the rest, to the shareholders.' Freya clicks the *People* tab. At the top: Grace, Andrew. Role: Director. Occupation: CEO. Below him: Hamilton, Teàrlach. Role: Director. Occupation: CTO.

But the next row makes Robin frown.

'There, stop,' he says, but Freya already has. The mouse hovers above the name. Somerset, Chloe. Role: Director (Resigned). Occupation: Finance Director.

Freya turns, frowning at Robin. 'Nobody's mentioned her before, have they?'

'No.'

Robin watches as Freya flips away from Companies House and loads up LinkedIn. She types the name into the search box and a few options come up. The first one is an attractive brunette wearing a smart dark grey suit.

'Here. Chloe Somerset. Finance director at Hamilton Grace Software. Joined in October 2015, left... Oh, interesting.'

Robin leans forward. 'Left November 2021.' He looks at Freya. 'Six months ago.'

15

Tiller pauses in the entrance of the hospital, feeling the small twitch of anxiety bloom. He's never been here before, he doesn't know where he's going, and that alone makes the discontent breed. He should have brought something – chocolates or flowers. Do they even allow flowers in hospitals nowadays?

He doubts himself. He thinks about turning back but makes himself push through the double doors. Inside the heat is stifling and he pulls at the neck of his T-shirt. He pauses and takes a long deep breath. You need to do this, he repeats on loop in his head.

Laura's his friend. He owes it to her to make the effort. He met her on a train – Tiller on the way back from Scotland, Laura getting on at York. The company was only six years old by that point, their future still uncertain, and Tiller had managed to snatch a quick trip home to clear his head before investors were due to visit. The only empty seat in the carriage was beside his, and he'd reluctantly moved his bag for the petite blonde. Being close to people in confined spaces – aeroplanes, trains, cars – is one of Tiller's pet hates, but his curiosity had been caught by the book she had in her hand. *Ready Player One.*

'What do you think of it?' he'd asked.

She smiled. 'I expected it to be all complicated and nerdy, but actually I'm enjoying it. It's a lot of fun.'

He laughed. 'I love it. It's an unapologetically nostalgic nose-dive into the best and worst of eighties pop culture and the spiritual dawn of the new tech era. Some of the concepts are outdated or just plain wrong, but in terms of what a first-person immersive graphics engine could be, it's spot on. I played so many of those games as a kid. It's wonderfully geeky.'

She'd looked at him, her mouth half open in confusion. 'Laura,' she'd said, and they'd talked the whole rest of the journey until Laura got off at London.

Of course, any budding romance had been over the moment Tiller introduced her to Andrew. They hit it off immediately, and Tiller had long learned to get out of the way when he saw the signs. But over the last few years Tiller's felt closer to Laura again. Bonded out of necessity. Because of Andrew, and in spite of him.

Tiller follows signs to the ward, one step at a time, and arrives in the doorway, looking down at the small bay of beds. And then he sees her. She looks tiny. A withered shell of her former self. He takes a slow step towards her. He can see the extent of her injuries now. Her face is puffed into a mass of red and purple. Her left eye is almost completely swollen shut, a large cut stitched above, a swoop of black bruise below. Her lip is split, her face double the size it should be. Her eyes are closed and he takes a moment to compose himself, to force back the anger and the disgust towards whoever did this to her.

'Hi Tiller,' she says. She's half-opened her good eye and is looking at him.

'Hi Laura. How are you feeling? I'm sorry, I didn't bring anything. I should have…' He shrugs apologetically.

'Don't worry.' Her speech is laboured and slurred. She slowly lifts an arm, tubes connected, holding her hand out to him.

He touches it awkwardly, then quickly pulls back. 'Don't talk if it hurts…' He pauses. 'Does it hurt?'

She manages a small nod. Of course it does, he thinks, internally cursing himself for his stupidity.

He sits down on the chair next to her bed. 'Have the police spoken to you?' he asks quietly.

She shakes her head. 'I can't remember much,' she mumbles. 'But Andy said...' She pauses, her hand going up to her face with a wince. 'Andy said they've caught him?'

'Aye. Some thug from Southwood way. Listen, Laura. The police said the man was after your laptop. Do you know why?'

Another shake of the head, and a small frown. 'Where is it?' she whispers. 'Does Andy know?'

'Does Andy know what?'

The voice comes from behind them and Tiller jumps. Andrew stands there, tall and dominating in his suit and tie.

'Hello,' Laura says with an attempt at a smile.

'Does Andy know what?' Andrew repeats.

'What was on the laptops,' Tiller replies quickly.

Andy glares at him. 'Tiller. Can I have a word?'

He follows the angry point of Andy's finger into the hospital corridor.

'What the fuck are you doing here?' Andy barks when they're in a quiet corner.

'Calm down. I'm just visiting Laura. I thought she might want the company. While you were at *work*,' he says, with more venom than he intended.

'Someone has to keep everything moving.'

'On a Sunday?'

'This is business, Tiller. Not a hobby.'

'Look, I know you're stressed but you don't need to be like this—'

'Why are you visiting my wife?' Andy snaps again.

'She's my friend. Why shouldn't I?'

Andy just glares.

'Oh, you're kidding me. Not this again.' Tiller pauses, taking in Andrew's defensive stance, his anger and his scowl. 'How many times? I am not sleeping with your wife!'

'You were. Why not now?'

'That was ten years ago. Once! Before you and Laura were properly together. We're just friends.'

'And you expect me to believe that?'

'Yes! There's nothing going on. What proof do you have, Andy? What evidence?'

'I know what I see.'

'Nothing. You don't see anything. We're two friends, talking. For Christ's sake, Andy. Get over it.' Tiller shakes his head with exasperation. 'I can't take this. Get a grip. Tell Laura I'm sorry, but I had to leave.'

Tiller turns on his heel and walks away. Behind him he hears the squeak of Andrew's shoes as he turns.

'That's right! Walk away, you fucking coward,' Andy shouts after him. 'When the tough decisions need to be made, when someone confronts you, you can't take it, can you, Tiller?'

But he doesn't stop. He carries on walking. With the sure certainty that whatever their company was, whatever their friendship was, it isn't anymore.

16

When Freya makes it home it's nearly six. She's tired, a headache starting, a quiet evening on the sofa the only thing on her agenda. But when she pulls up in her driveaway she can already hear music, all the lights on her ground floor on.

She wearily pushes her key in the lock. She can feel the tension grow. There was a reason she'd lived alone. Despite the cost of it all, taking the weight of household domestics by herself, she liked the peace and quiet. The knowledge that at the end of a long day she could do exactly as she wanted. And this – this noise, this onslaught – it's too much.

She pushes the door open to the kitchen. She's met by a pleasant aroma of garlic and tomato; it makes her stomach rumble. Josh is standing at the stove, spatula in hand. He turns when he sees her and instantly turns the music down.

'Spag bol okay?' he says with a grin. The table has been laid, a glass of red waiting for her. There are even candles. She goes over to him, wrapping her arms round his waist.

'Yes, perfect.' She smiles and lifts her face towards his. He bends down, planting a soft kiss on her lips.

'Long day,' he says. 'Did you make progress?'

'That thug isn't getting out any time soon. But he didn't give us anything we can work with.'

'He didn't tell you where the drugs or the cash came from?'

'Not a word.'

'So you've got your man.' Josh takes the pan off the heat and adds two large dollops of sauce into pasta steaming in a bowl. 'What more can you do? Case closed.'

'Is it, though?' Freya counters. 'Somebody paid this guy to break into the house. Robin thinks it's related to the company. The one the husband runs.'

'But no evidence?'

'He's got a sense for these things.'

'But no evidence,' Josh repeats. He places a bowl of delicious-smelling pasta in front of her. Freya doesn't want to argue about this now. The difference of opinion between her boyfriend and her boss is long-running, and she hasn't got the energy to rehash the same debates. She takes a mouthful.

'This is amazing,' she says. 'I could get used to this.'

'You can,' Josh grins. 'I'm nearly unpacked.'

'You live here now,' she says with a smile.

'I do.' And he reaches over for another kiss.

–

Food eaten, Josh diligently tidies up and loads the dishwasher. Freya feels restored as she slumps on the sofa, the empty wine glass resting between two fingers. Josh comes over, bottle in hand, and she holds it up to him. He refills it, then does the same for his own before collapsing next to her.

'You're the talk of the station,' Josh says, as Freya swings her legs up and rests them on his lap. 'That raid. Was it really seven kilos?'

'Yeah. And fifty grand.' Josh raises his eyebrows. 'The NCA says that he'd probably taken our burglary job as quick cash, but any OCG's going to be pissed if that's what brought us to his door. A smash and grab, and suddenly they're seven kilos lighter.'

'Can't you offer him protection?'

'I'm sure that's what the NCA are doing. It's with them now. You know what they're like – the sniff of a bit of kudos and off they go.' She takes a sip from her wine, then quickly follows up with another. 'It doesn't help us much. I don't think our little burglary is high on their list of priorities.' She glances at Josh.

His gaze is off in the middle distance and the wine glass is loose in his hand.

'We're going to interview the ex-finance director tomorrow.' She nudges Josh's leg. 'Hey!' she says, and he looks up and blinks. 'At least try to pretend you're listening.'

'Sorry, sorry, I am.' He pulls himself up a little bit on the sofa and smiles. 'Did you get anything from his mobile?'

'It's with Greg,' Freya tries, referring to one of the analysts in the Digital team, but her heart's not in it. She's too tired to talk about the case now that Josh's lack of enthusiasm has broken her train of thought. 'Are you all unpacked?'

He nods, with a smile. 'I just need another drawer or two. Could you clear one for me?'

Another? Freya thinks. For a man who's lived out of one small bedroom in a shared house for the past eighteen months, he certainly has a lot of clothes.

But, 'Yes, absolutely,' she agrees.

She finishes the last dregs of wine in her glass and puts it down on the coffee table. She wriggles up next to him, resting her head on the soft cotton of his sweatshirt.

It's worth it. To have Josh here, on her sofa – *their* sofa, she mentally corrects herself. Cooking her dinner, when normally she would have ordered a takeaway or cooked pesto pasta, *again*. So what if he's a bit noisy? If he always leaves the lights on and never puts the toilet seat down?

This is right. Living together, moving forward into the next phase of their relationship. This is what they're supposed to be doing.

She's growing up, and it's about bloody time.

MONDAY

17

Freya finds Chloe Somerset suspicious from the word go. She refuses to let them near her house, instead agreeing to come to the police station. Who willingly *asks* to come to the nick? Most people do their utmost to get out of a trip here.

She arrives on time, and Robin shows her through to the consultation room. It's a crappy place, usually used by lawyers and offenders, but all the nicer visitor rooms are taken. Monday morning – everyone has something to say.

They offer her tea or coffee but she declines, taking small sips from a plastic water bottle. Freya and Robin sit with steaming hot mugs in front of them.

'I just don't like it,' she explains. 'Would rather drink water.'

Who gets through a Monday morning without caffeine? Freya thinks, the one glass of red wine too many making itself known. She takes a gulp from her mug; the headache threatens again, a thump just behind her forehead.

'I'm not sure why you need to speak to me,' Chloe says. 'You mentioned it's to do with an attack on Andrew's wife, but that was at his house, wasn't it?'

'Yes. But we believe it's connected to the company—'

'I don't work there anymore,' she says quickly, interrupting him.

'And why is that?' Freya interjects.

Chloe turns her attention to Freya. Her eyes are light blue, almost grey. She has long brown hair, with a severe fringe she peers out from under.

'Politics,' she says briefly.

'You left six months ago?'

'Yes.'

'What do you do now?'

'I'm looking for a new opportunity.'

'You left without a job to go to?' Freya responds.

Chloe turns to Robin. 'Why do I feel like I'm the suspect here?' she says. 'I've come in, of my own accord. Why does it matter why I left Hamilton Grace?'

Robin flashes a quick warning look to Freya. She can tell what he's thinking: what's got into you? Normally, she's the charming one; the good cop to his scowl. She's tired, Josh waking her early, singing loudly in the shower. But that can't be it. Why is she in such a mood? She sits back in her seat and crosses her arms, trying to concentrate on Chloe Somerset and the job at hand.

'We believe that the attack on Laura Grace has something to do with the company,' Robin explains with a smile. 'And you were the only other person in senior management. We're hoping you can shed some light on what it's like to work there. The culture, and so on.'

'Fine.' Chloe smiles tightly at Robin. She ignores Freya. 'When I first joined, it was a small company. Agile. Fun. We could make decisions fast, ensure the company was always on track.'

'And was it?'

'Yes. It made money. Quickly. And it grew. But then I noticed the disagreements between Tiller and Andrew. Small differences of opinion at first, like how much bonus to pay the employees, or introducing regular hours. Tiller was all about profit-share, and letting the engineers do what they wanted. Andrew was stricter, wanted the shiny and new.' She pauses.

'Andy even wanted to knock down the old manor house, build a larger place on top. But Tiller said no. Turned out it was Grade Two listed, so there wasn't much Andy could do in the end. The old house is lovely, have you been inside?' Robin shakes his head. 'Original fireplaces, sash windows, rickety old staircase. I mean, it's freezing cold and it was hell to work out of but Tiller fell in love. He'll do it up properly, eventually. It's just Tiller's style. Rattling around by himself with only the ghosts for company.'

'Sorry, what do you mean?' Freya asks, confused.

'He lives there. Didn't he say?'

'He didn't mention it.' Freya glances to Robin, who looks just as baffled as she is.

'Well, that's Tiller for you. Bloody nightmare of a man. No wonder Andrew loses his shit sometimes.' Chloe pauses, lost in thought for a moment. Then she shakes her head, pulling herself out of it. 'But generally, I kept out of the arguments. Both of them were right to some extent. The company was growing. They needed rules and regulations, otherwise people would take the piss. But Tiller understands engineers. He's one of them. He knows how to keep them happy. And it was certainly working. I liked it there. Being a part of something big.'

'What changed? Why did you leave?'

'Andrew.' She reaches for her water bottle again. Takes another sip. 'He was getting more secretive. And there were aspects to our financials I couldn't substantiate. As an FD, there are rules I have to stick to. Accounting regulations and legal requirements. We need to account for every penny going in and out, otherwise it raises questions.' She stops again. Sip sip sip. It irritates Freya. 'Andrew was treating Hamilton Grace like his own personal bank account. Money – large amounts, thousands – would go out, then come back in a week later. Postings in our accounts I knew nothing about. Auditors don't like that sort of thing. I told him to stop.'

'And did he?'

'Not at first. So I had no choice but to tell Tiller. They had a massive row, and after that it stopped. But Andrew wouldn't talk to me. Like a little child. If I was in the room, he'd walk out. You can't run a company like that. So I confronted him.'

'Then what?'

'He wrote me a cheque. I left.'

Freya's surprised. 'Just like that? No arguments?'

'They made me sign a settlement agreement. So I couldn't take them to court. But yeah.' She meets Freya's gaze again. 'If someone offered you a year's salary to leave your job, would you?'

Freya raises her eyebrows. 'And have they replaced you?'

'Not as far as I know. Which is a dangerous position for the company to be in. I've told Tiller to keep an eye on Andrew.'

'You're still in touch with Tiller?'

The water bottle again. Another sip. 'We've stayed in touch, yes.'

Freya notices her face colour.

'What do you think Andrew was doing?' Robin asks.

Chloe holds the water bottle in her hand, thinking. 'I don't know,' she says slowly. 'I wondered if it was something dodgy. Brown envelopes, a few backhanders to grease the wheels. But when I mentioned it to Tiller, he laughed. Said it was just Andrew being shit with money. He's been like that since he was at uni. Tiller said he was always lending him cash.'

'Are you close?' Freya pushes. 'You and Tiller?'

'Just colleagues,' she replies, her eyes firmly focused on her bottle.

'Ex-colleagues,' Freya adds. She feels a nudge on her leg under the table. Robin telling her to back off.

Chloe glares. 'Yes. Now, if that's all? I have to be going. I need to get back for my dog.'

Robin stands up as Chloe does. 'Thank you for coming in, Ms Somerset. We appreciate your time.'

Chloe nods in their direction, then leaves, her now empty water bottle clutched in her hand.

Freya makes an annoyed grunt. 'She's shagging him, you know,' she states as they walk out of the consultation room back to the office.

'She probably is, but how is that relevant? What's got into you this morning?'

Mina comes over as he's asking and looks between the two of them, detecting trouble.

'Nothing, I'm fine. Just didn't warm to her.'

'That's unlike you,' Robin says.

'Yeah, well. You don't have the monopoly on being a grumpy bastard.'

Robin raises his eyebrows but says nothing. He turns to Mina. 'Have you got anything interesting?'

'Phone records for Durand,' Mina replies. 'Plus cell sites. Greg's waiting at your desk.'

They look over; Greg turns and waves gleefully. Robin mutters a quick thank you and heads across.

Mina turns to Freya. 'Why are you being so pissy?' she hisses. 'And it's nothing to do with that woman.'

Freya glances Robin's way, then, seeing him talking to Greg, hustles Mina towards the kitchen.

They cram into the tiny space. Freya fills up the kettle and switches it on. 'Jo's asked Robin to move to Devon with her.'

'What? Why?'

'Something to do with a promotion for her. And she says there are opportunities for him.'

'That's good, isn't it? He has friends down there. And he seems happy?'

'He's only been with her four months! And for two and a half of those he was ill. They've never lived together. She wants him to uproot his whole life and move?'

'It's hardly—'

'And what about me!?'

90

Mina's forehead creases in a sympathetic look. She hands Freya three clean mugs. 'You'll be fine, honey. With or without Robin Butler. Baker will reassign you. You'll probably end up working with me again, reporting to Mouse.'

'I don't want to work for someone else,' Freya says, sulkily.

While Robin was recovering at home, she'd been temporarily moved to work for DI Ratcliffe, but it wasn't the same. She missed Robin. Their easy banter. Their partnership – always equal, despite the fact that on paper Robin is her superior.

But it isn't only that. Freya knows their partnership goes further than just friendship. She remembers the feelings she had following those desperate few days at the hospital just after his attack. The worry that he would die, that she would lose him. That they'd never— What? She hasn't yet managed to reconcile it all in her head. It's a line they've never talked about. Would never cross.

And the thought that he might move – might leave her – has taken her by surprise. She wants to grab hold of him. Tell him not to go. But who is she, to Robin?

She miserably spoons instant coffee into the mugs. She feels Mina's arm round her shoulders.

'Perhaps it's what you need. A fresh start,' Mina says gently. 'Things are good with Josh, right? You haven't got buyer's remorse? With the moving in?'

'No, not at all. He's wonderful. You know that. Everyone knows that.'

Mina stirs the coffee. 'I'm not the one living with him, hon.'

'No, no, Josh is great, it's just…'

They both jump as Robin appears in the doorway of the kitchen.

'What are you doing?' he asks.

'Making coffee.' Freya hands him his mug, but she can't help the hot flush spreading from her neck.

'Well, come on,' he says, grinning. 'I think Greg has something.'

18

With the boom of shows like *CSI* and real-life documentaries on the BBC, the police have found that offenders are more forensically aware now than ever before. They wear gloves; they're careful not to leave traces of where they've been or who they are.

But not Thierry Durand.

Greg's talking through what he's found on Durand's mobile, and Robin stares at the information on the screen in disbelief.

'You can see here, cell site data puts Thierry Durand's mobile right next to the Grace's house just before the time of the break-in. He even made a phone call – to this number.'

'The person behind the burglary?' Freya says, from her seat behind them.

Greg smiles back at Freya, a little too enthusiastically for Robin's liking. Greg's long-standing crush on Freya is well known, but it has a tendency to veer from sweet to creepy in a matter of seconds. 'Could be,' Greg continues. Today he's wearing a faded grey sweatshirt with a Star Wars logo and a liberal application of something that looks like ketchup down the front. 'Calls between them start about a month ago, with a flurry just after the attack.'

'So not only does he go into a house with full CCTV without a mask or gloves,' Freya says, almost unable to contain her mirth. 'He leaves his personal phone on, and makes calls from it?'

'The man's got the intelligence of a lobotomised gerbil,' Robin mutters. 'Can we get the data for this other number?'

'Already requested it,' Greg confirms. 'Although it's going to take a while. We're up to our ears with all those stolen iPhones you seized from his house.'

Freya leans forward. 'But Greg,' she begins with a swoosh of shiny blonde hair, 'I know how good you are at your job. You'll get through it all in no time.'

Robin contains a snort at Freya's blatant flirting. Greg turns bright red.

'I'll come back to you as soon as I can,' he says, pushing his glasses back up his nose. He bustles out of the office, paper flying in his wake.

Robin gives her a look.

'What?' she says innocently.

He shakes his head. 'Don't encourage him. And what do you make of Andrew Grace siphoning money out of the company accounts?'

'But he wasn't siphoning, he was putting it back again after. Money laundering?'

'Some sort of fraud? Or backhanders and bribes, as Chloe thought?'

'His PNC is clean.'

'Doesn't mean he's not up to anything. Just means he's never been caught. Frey, could you give the fraud team a call – see if they have anything on their radar we're not aware of?'

'Will do,' she says, and turns away, picking up the phone next to her.

Robin turns back to his computer, listening to Freya talk on the phone, the hubbub of the office a salve to his brain. He quietly sips his coffee, running his eyes down the rest of the phone data presented to them. He glances to Freya. She's still talking, so he shifts screens, searching for the internal jobs board for Devon and Cornwall. Selecting the right page, he selects Transferees, then clicks *Express an Interest*.

An extra line has been added on the page, stressing an additional request for DCs and DSs, but he hesitates before clicking

Apply. He knows this won't be the final part of the application, that he'll have to fill in forms, go for interviews – but this is the start. Is this what he wants?

He hears Freya shift next to him, and turns, guiltily. She's watching him, frowning.

'You're going then?' she says.

'No, I...' He turns back to the screen and closes down the website. 'I was just looking.'

'But you're considering it.'

'I don't know.' He sighs and sits back in his seat, cupping his hands round the remainder of his coffee. 'It's a lot. To move. I'm happy here. And I haven't been able to say that for a while. What if, by moving, I somehow end up where I started?'

He doesn't say any more. Freya will know what he's referring to. When they first met he was depressed, even suicidal. Every aspect of his life was going wrong and he was only just making it through the day. Not sleeping, not eating, barely talking. It was only when he started working with Freya, and everything that happened during those first few months, that he pulled himself out of the hole.

'Are you happy with Jo?' Freya asks.

'Yes. She's great. You've met her.'

Freya nods. 'She's great,' she echoes. 'But?'

'But.' He laughs. Freya's always been able to read his mind. 'But I feel like I've been swept up in this relationship. Ever since... the accident...' His hand goes up to the back of his head, where he can feel the bump under his hair. 'I've been focused on getting better. Going back to work. And Jo was a huge part of that. I just wonder whether... Is this what I want?'

He meets Freya's eyes for the first time, then shakes his head.

'I'm being daft. It's my usual pessimism, ignore me. I can't have anything nice in my life without assuming it's all going to come crashing round my ears.'

'That's understandable, Robin,' Freya says. 'Given what happened to your sister and the boys.'

Robin nods, mute. Robin's sister, Georgia, and her twin boys were killed in a hit-and-run, nearly seven years ago now. Out of nowhere, Robin lost his entire family.

Freya leans over to him and gently rests her head on his shoulder. She's done it before, but never in the middle of the office – where he's not her friend, he's her sergeant. Suddenly she realises what she's doing and sits up quickly. She pats his arm awkwardly.

'You'll figure it out,' she says. And she turns back to her own screen.

Robin stares for a moment, then frowns. She seems to be taking the news well, but then, what was he expecting? Hysterics? Tantrums? That she would hang off his ankle begging *please don't go*?

Freya was a frequent visitor when he was in the hospital. Jo – with work and her longer commute – had been by less. And it was Freya's visits he looked forward to. When he was still out of it, sometimes he wouldn't even know she'd been by, except for the note left next to his bedside. Or a book, or a magazine she knew he'd enjoy. When Jo was there he'd always felt he had to maintain some sort of image. She was ostensibly his new girlfriend, he had to at least try to stay awake. But with Freya there was no such pretence.

Later, she'd visit him at home. They made their whole way through three seasons of *Succession*, Freya explaining what he'd missed when he'd fall asleep in the middle ('Not much. Logan was a dick'). Life with Freya was comfortable. It was easy. But maybe that isn't what Freya needs now.

Maybe she is desperate for a promotion and doesn't know how to tell him. Maybe this is a way out for her.

'Freya?' he says. 'You should apply for DS.' But she's not listening.

Instead, she says, 'Here, look at this.'

She moves out of the way and he scoots next to her, looking at the article she has up on her screen.

It's the light pink website of the *Financial Times*, the heading Mergers & Acquisitions clear at the top. And the headline: 'Private equity firms consider approach for successful UK start-up Hamilton Grace Software'.

Freya glances back to Robin. 'They're looking to sell. We didn't know that, did we? Why are they being so secretive?'

'No, we bloody didn't,' Robin mutters. 'And what else might they be hiding?'

19

Tiller lies on his sofa, staring at the ceiling. He glares at the patch of brown damp, wondering if it's spread. This old house always needs something doing. A pipe that's leaking, a floorboard coming loose. He's done some work to the place, but lately he hasn't had the energy. The electrics are good now; he has super-fast fibre broadband straight to the door, a mesh Wi-Fi network in the house. What else does he need?

He hadn't wanted to go in to work today. He hadn't wanted to see Andrew, and besides, his mind is a mess. He can't focus, can't think. Instead, he has his laptop. He can work from here.

He's done a bit, idly tapping the keys, but he can't lose himself in the code as he always has before. There's too much going on. It churns in his head, an endless loop of worry and intrusive thoughts.

His phone rings and he picks it up warily. He answers with a sigh of relief.

'I need to talk to you,' the voice says.

'I'm at home. Come round.'

Twenty minutes later, here she is.

He lets her in, and she rushes inside, shaking rain out of her hair. She seems upset. She has a small black spaniel with her who does the same, droplets of water flying round the hallway. It immediately greets Tiller by jumping up and planting wet fluffy feet on his jeans.

'What's up, Chloe?' he asks, bending down and ruffling the dog's ears.

'The police wanted to talk to me.'

Tiller recoils. 'What about?'

Chloe quickly walks through to his makeshift kitchen, the dog following. 'About you, and Hamilton Grace, and the reason I left.'

'What did you tell them?'

'Nothing!' But she pauses.

'Chloe…?'

'I told them about Andrew. That he'd been messing around in the company accounts.'

'Shit, Chloe.'

'They seemed happy with that. They didn't push for more.'

They sit down on his dusty sofa, side by side.

'What's going on, Tiller?' she asks. 'I'm worried. I couldn't sleep at all last night. Laura's been attacked? And the police said they were looking for laptops. Could it be—?'

'No, that's ridiculous. How would a random thug know?' He's trying to be reassuring, but she's articulating the exact worry that's been going round in his head since he heard about Laura. 'But it's in a safe place? Right?'

'Of course. I promised you. But should we tell the police—'

'No.'

'Aren't you being a bit paranoid?'

He pauses. Maybe he is. But it's a risk he's not prepared to take.

'The fewer people that know, the better.'

She nods solemnly.

'Do you want a cup of tea?' he asks. 'Something stronger?'

'No. I just wanted to see you.'

Chloe leans forward and presses her body against his. Then she reaches up, grabs his face and snogs him. It's not subtle, but Chloe knows Tiller frequently misses less conspicuous social cues. He returns the kiss, pushing her coat from her shoulders, then pulling away and taking her hand. The kitchen is the wrong place for this.

He leads her towards the bedroom; she follows, pulling her boots off her feet as they go. Once there, he kicks the door shut, locking the dog outside, then kisses her again – his ardour a mixture of passion and relief. That she's okay. That she's kept quiet. Clothes are discarded; they make love quickly, urgently.

The ridiculous allegation from Andrew that Tiller's sleeping with his wife is misplaced. Andy suspected something was going on, but it was the relationship with Chloe he always missed.

Tiller hadn't wanted to tell him. He and Andy had grown apart over the years, and Tiller knew that Andy wouldn't like the fact he was sleeping with their FD. Two board members against one, Andy would see it as a loss of power. That the pillow talk between Chloe and Tiller could be detrimental to him in some way.

And Chloe agreed. In reality, there has never been anything serious between the two of them; Tiller's foibles are too much for the pragmatic Chloe. She wants a future, marriage, children. A normal relationship. There is no such thing as normal with Tiller.

He needs his life the way he designs it. Everything left exactly where it should be – from his shoes in the hallway to his stacks of paper in the office. There is no place for a child in this rigid routine. No place for a girlfriend. Not that Tiller would ever define Chloe as that.

Some would call it OCD. Others cite autism. But he's never seen a doctor; never been formally diagnosed. He just calls it wanting his life the way he has it. Structure helps him think. It helps him code. But it doesn't help his relationships.

Previous girlfriends have tried to change him. They've shouted in exasperation. Tidied his house, cleaned his car. But things went back to normal and soon they left. The only reason Chloe is still here is because she accepted him from the start.

'But I will date other people, Tils,' she'd said. And he'd nodded, knowing it was inevitable that one day she would find someone else to keep her company at night.

But maybe she would leave sooner if she knew. The risk he is taking – with her.

He comes with a gasp, his eagerness for her, and his stress and tiredness, preventing him from holding out too long. She rolls away almost instantly, and he looks across with mixed feelings for this woman that shares his life.

Tiller sometimes feels like Chloe sleeps with him out of boredom rather than any real affection, but still. He's not one to turn down the arrangement. He just wishes he wasn't such a convenience. That he was someone she actually cared about.

He stares at the ceiling, feeling a fresh surge of guilt.

She shouldn't have been pulled into this. But there had been nobody else he had trusted at the time.

What can he do? He can't tell the police. Not now.

He feels helpless; there's nothing he can do to stop the events he put into action. But he can, at least, try.

He waits until Chloe falls into a slow, soft sleep, the insomnia from the night before catching up with her. He picks up his phone, selects an app, then frowns at what he sees.

He won't be long, he thinks. He gets up, careful not to disturb Chloe; he'll be back before she even wakes up. He gets dressed quickly, steps over the dozing dog in the hallway and slips out into the cold, damp night.

20

Robin's late. He's always bloody late, but Liam is used to it by now. His brother-in-law waits patiently, book in hand, as Robin charges through the door of the bar.

'Sorry, mate,' Robin says breathlessly as he drops into the seat opposite him.

Liam looks up. 'Work?' he asks, resigned, peering over the top of his glasses.

'Always.'

'It's no wonder you cops end up with cops, no one else can stand you.'

'And no wonder most detectives end up divorced.'

Liam smiles, then points to the pint, waiting, tantalising on the wooden slats of the table. 'I got you a beer.'

'I love you.'

'I'm definitely not going out with you.'

Robin laughs and takes a long pull of the beer. They've both been here before – a craft ale house that also serves the best tacos in Winchester. Liam passes him the menu. He's bloody starving.

'Was it worth it then? Being late for me?'

'Not even.' Robin waits while the man comes over and takes their order. 'Procession of dead ends and shitty leads. How's your work?'

Robin drinks as Liam tells him about his day. It's been over ten years since Liam first met and married Robin's sister, but Robin still doesn't have a clue what Liam does. It seems to involve spreadsheets, and a series of increasingly incomprehensible meetings involving overhead digression, critical success factors and something called global utilisation. Robin doesn't mind. Food arrives and he eats happily, the chipotle chicken washed down nicely by the beer.

He had his first official date here, two months ago, with Jo.

He'd been out of hospital for four weeks, a bit wobbly on his feet but bored shitless of sitting on his sofa at home. He'd begged her to take him.

'No beer,' she'd told him sternly.

'One.'

'Low-alcohol.'

'Fine.'

But when they'd got there, he was nervous. Actually sitting opposite her, needing to make conversation. He'd smiled awkwardly in the silence.

'How do we do this then?' she asked with a grin. 'Do we talk politely about work?'

And they were off. Comfortable ground, police talk. Dead bodies, investigations, fingerprints, blood. The common language of detectives.

And Jo Craig is great company. That night, she told him about one of her latest cases, a man found dead in his house after six months, quietly decomposing under the window – the route her colleague happened to choose as an entry point.

Robin had winced at the image of his foot edging through, then coming into contact with the putrefying head.

'He'll never get the brain off those boots.'

'Sticking to the ground for weeks.'

He'd leaned back in his seat, pint glass in hand, getting his breath back from laughing so hard. It had been exactly what he'd needed. A boost of confidence; someone he fancied making him laugh. And this burgeoning relationship has been going well, trotting along nicely until this proposal out of nowhere.

He realises that Liam has stopped talking and is looking at him strangely.

'Everything okay, Rob?' he asks.

'How did you know?' Robin asks. 'With Georgia?'

Liam tilts his head at the question, coming apropos of nothing. 'I didn't. Not for sure. But I knew I was in love and couldn't imagine life without her, and that was it.' He gives Robin a supportive smile. 'Why?'

'Jo's asked me to move to Devon with her.'

Liam lifts his eyebrows so high his forehead furrows into deep ridges. 'That's quick.'

'Hmm.'

Liam nods slowly and takes a final bite of his taco. He stays silent for a moment longer, then wipes his mouth with a napkin. 'And?' he says at last.

'And I don't know.' Robin sighs quickly, then downs the last mouthful of beer and glances round to the bar. 'Do you want another?'

'No, I shouldn't,' Liam says apologetically. 'Early start. Five a.m. Lizzie wants to get twenty miles in on the bike before work.'

Robin recoils. 'Bloody hell.' Liam and his girlfriend Lizzie's cycling exploits always seem knackering to him. He raises his arm to the waiter and asks for the bill.

They pay and Liam grabs Robin in a tight bear hug as they say goodbye outside the bar. The rain has stopped, street lights reflecting in the puddles of dirty water on the pavement.

'I'm glad you're okay,' Liam says with a grin. 'You gave us all a scare back in January.'

'Yeah. All good now.'

He gives Liam a final manly clap round the back, then starts walking towards home.

'Robin?'

Robin turns; Liam's stopped a few metres away in the middle of the pavement.

'The fact you're not sure? About whether to go to Devon with Jo?' Liam pauses, as if uncertain whether to continue.

'Yes?' Robin prompts.

'Maybe that's telling you what you need to know.'

21

Another quiet night at home. Freya sits with her laptop on her knees, methodically working through the mobile data taken from Durand's phone. She's matching calls to the cell sites, but so far nothing new has come up.

Durand's life was fairly uneventful. He made the majority of calls from his house, with a few trips to the supermarket and the Ladbrokes on the corner. He didn't have a job – not a legal one anyway.

'He must have gone out sometimes?' Josh says from the sofa next to her. His own work has been done for the day, and he's watching a Newcastle game on Sky Sports – a new addition to the fast-accumulating streaming services Josh apparently can't live without.

'To the local Wetherspoons,' Freya replies. 'Every Friday and Saturday.'

'What a life,' Josh says, and goes back to the football.

Freya glowers at him, annoyed. He's a DC in Major Crimes, like her. How is it that he doesn't seem to work late as often as she does?

She looks down the phone list again. The more she studies the numbers, the more she's certain this number ending 897 is the brains behind the crime. She remembers the small roll of twenty-pound notes found in Durand's living room. Three thousand pounds was all it took to get this man to barge his way into someone's home and beat up Laura Grace and terrorise her seven-year-old son. And now, assuming justice is served,

Durand will spend most of the rest of his miserable life behind bars.

So who is 897?

Greg's initial information hasn't offered much to identify the suspect. An unregistered SIM, bought for ten quid from Tesco.

'This guy knows what he's doing,' she says to Josh.

'Huh?' Josh doesn't turn away from the football.

'The unregistered burner,' she says. 'That's crime 101. You buy a cheap burner to use for your dirty work. So how can we find out who's behind it?'

Josh pauses the football and turns her way.

'Have you got the cell sites or itemised calls yet?' Freya shakes her head. 'Then you're stuck, until then. Unless you can find out when and where it was bought and go through the footage from that particular shop?'

'Ugh,' Freya groans. Hours and hours of shitty shop CCTV.

'Unless the NCA get your man to talk. Which he won't.'

'They might offer him witsec?'

Witness protection. Josh gives her a look.

'You think he'd trust the cops? A man like that?'

Freya makes an exasperated noise. Josh, sensing the conversation is over, turns the football back on.

Freya knows he's right. You open your mouth to the police, and your days are numbered. Even now, his lips sealed shut, there's no way of stopping someone determined sticking a shank in this guy's gut.

It's just so bloody annoying.

She closes her laptop and picks up her phone, about to text Robin. But as if he's reading her mind, the phone starts to buzz, his name on the screen.

'It's Andrew Grace,' Robin says the moment she answers. 'He's been attacked. He's in a bad way.'

'I'll meet you at the hospital,' Freya replies, already on her feet.

Part 2

22

Robin has no wish to be back in a hospital so soon. His month-long stay lingers; a stain on his consciousness that no amount of scrubbing will get out. He doesn't remember his time in the ambulance or the Emergency Department, only the feeling of confusion and pain, waking up in the ICU, a tube down his throat.

Freya's waiting for him at the entrance to the ED, a doctor by her side. Introductions are made, and the doctor explains again, for Robin's benefit.

'He's lucky,' he says, his fingers toying with the stethoscope around his neck. 'The head wound is superficial, it didn't damage his skull. But he has broken ribs, a spiral fracture of his ulna, here—' He points to his lower right arm. 'A suspected torn rotator cuff and a comminuted fracture to the right femur.'

'What circumstances might lead to that pattern of injuries?' Robin asks.

'In my opinion, he was struck from behind on the legs, then his right arm was pushed up hard behind him.' He frowns. 'He told us he fell over, but he's lying. There's no way he got like this by accident.'

'Thank you for calling us,' Robin says. 'Can we interview him?'

'Yes, but not for long. He's going to be in a lot of pain. We'll admit him to the ward as soon as we can get a bed, and then he's straight to theatre to sort that leg. He's in for a long night.'

The doctor leaves them, and they look down towards the bay where Andrew Grace is lying.

'This case is going from bad to worse,' Freya notes, and Robin has to agree. They head towards Grace.

If this is lucky, Robin hates to think what the converse looks like. Andrew Grace is a mess. Clothed in a hospital gown, the head of the bed tilted up slightly, he lies still, his eyes closed. His arm rests on a pillow, tightly bandaged, only the tips of his fingers visible. His broken leg is secured to a board and elevated in front of him. A large graze of road rash runs down the left-hand side of his cheek.

He opens an eye, sees them, then closes it again.

'Andrew?' Robin begins softly. 'Do you remember us? DC West and DS Butler from Hampshire Police. Thank you for giving permission to the doctors to call us.'

'Of course I remember you,' he mumbles. But his eyes stay shut, his voice is slow.

They move closer to the bed, Robin taking a seat closest to his head.

'Can we ask you some questions about what happened?'

'I'm not feeling great.'

'No, I can see that. We'll only take a few minutes of your time.' Grace stays silent, so Robin continues.

'You were found in the car park at Leisure World, near West Quay. Can you tell us what you were doing there?'

He opens one eye. 'Going to the cinema.'

Robin frowns. 'To the Odeon?'

'That's the one.' Robin feels Freya's quick glance; he knows what she's thinking. 'What did you see?' Robin asks.

'Does that matter?'

'Did you keep the ticket? Can we check your belongings?'

Grace takes a long, painful breath in. 'Do what you want,' he says, apathetically. 'But I don't know where they are. They cut all my clothes off me.'

'What happened after the cinema?'

'I fell over. I smashed my face in.'

Robin looks to Freya. She raises an eyebrow.

'Andrew, I know you've had a bad night, but with the greatest respect, that's bullshit. Even I can tell that someone attacked you.'

Grace is still silent, but Robin can see the muscles in his jaw tensing.

'Anything you can tell us now will give us a head start on finding who did this to you. Don't you want that?'

He takes a long breath. 'I can't help you,' he says quietly. 'I don't know what happened. All I remember is getting to my car, then falling forward, my face against the concrete.'

'Did you see who did this?'

'No. Nothing. Did they take the car?'

'We'll find out. Do you think that's why you were attacked?'

'Why else?' He closes his eyes again. They're not going to get any more out of him today.

'We'll be back tomorrow, Andrew. In case you remember anything else.'

But Grace doesn't reply.

Robin follows Freya out of the bay and into the main part of the Emergency Department. The place is relatively quiet. A red board on the wall announces a wait time of two hours; people litter the waiting room in a variety of bloodied and battered states. A woman argues with her boyfriend, a large cut bleeding on his forehead. Next to her a toddler cries, his face puce with anger.

Freya returns with Grace's belongings – a plastic bag with a pair of jeans, trainers, shirt inside. She puts on plastic gloves and opens it, digging around in the pocket of the jeans.

Triumphantly, she pulls out his wallet, and starts looking through.

'Any tickets for the cinema?' Robin asks with a smile.

Freya gives him a sarcastic look. 'That place closed at the end of February. As you well know. If he's going to lie he needs to at least try to get the basics right.'

He laughs at her tone. 'First thing in the morning, let's get on to the CCTV for Leisure World, they must have something there. Plus we need to find his car.'

'You're thinking it's all linked?' Freya asks, placing everything into an evidence bag of her own.

'Must be,' Robin nods. 'Because if not, this guy is having one hell of a bad week.'

TUESDAY

23

One attack is now two. Three out of the four members of the Grace family are victims. And nobody is talking.

Robin and Freya stand in the car park of the Leisure World complex. It's nine a.m., the place is deserted. It's been this way for a while – the ASK restaurant long closed, the strip club vacant. The huge grey box of the Odeon and the Oceana club were the last to go, now shut up, awaiting redevelopment.

But there is ample CCTV, cameras on poles at every corner of the car park. Freya has gone inside to track down someone with access while Robin heads to Grace's white Audi.

It's here. Alone and abandoned on the right-hand side of the car park. Robin stands next to it, appraising the scene. It's parked up against a tall metal fence, relatively concealed. A prime target for a carjacking, if anyone fancied it. There is blood on the concrete – from Andrew's nose, no doubt – and scuff marks from the paramedics. Dark red spatters are visible on the white paintwork.

Robin puts gloves on and tries the door. It opens. He peers inside. A few coins rest in the centre cup holder but otherwise it's empty. He retreats, and in doing so, his foot catches on something under the car. It jangles. He reaches down and peeks under, pulling out a set of car keys and an iPhone. The screen is smashed; the phone is unresponsive when he presses the power button.

'They weren't trying to rob him then?' Freya says, appearing behind him.

Robin places the keys and the phone in separate evidence bags. 'Doesn't look like it. He still had his wallet on him. Phone and car here.'

'So why would someone jump him? Leisure World, of all places?'

Robin looks around the car park. 'Paramedics report a 999 call at just after ten. A security guard spotted him and administered first aid. Ambulance arrived to find Grace responsive but confused. Did you have any luck with the CCTV?'

'They're sending across the files for the car park, but I had a quick look at the footage while I was there. One camera captures him walking quickly across, here to here—' She points from the main road, then towards the docks, in the direction of the car. 'Just before ten. Then he disappears out of view.'

'So why was he here?'

Robin looks around. It's a bright sunny day; the rain has disappeared overnight, but a cold wind from the Solent tugs at his jacket. To his right, cruise ships wait in the docks, their massive hulls dominating the landscape. He can hear the rumble and beep of container ships loading, interspersed with the cry of seagulls. Behind and to his left is just car park and fences and hedges.

'Drugs?' Freya suggests.

'A quick buy?'

Freya nods. 'We know Durand was dealing weed and involved with cocaine. Perhaps they are more connected than we thought?'

'So where is it?'

'They mugged him, then took off?'

Robin frowns. It's a bizarre set of circumstances, one he can't get his head around. The burglary at the house, and now this? He doesn't believe in coincidences. Something's going on.

'Call Jess,' he directs to Freya. 'Get the Audi towed to the garage. See if they can find anything interesting.' She nods. 'And let's get back to the nick,' he says. 'Hopefully the CCTV will have arrived by then.'

It has, and Robin isn't thrilled. They divide the footage between them and sit, cross-eyed, staring at their screens. But there are blind spots, one directly next to Grace's car, although Freya catches him arriving, and points it out to Robin.

'Here,' she says, then indicates the timestamp. 'Twenty fifteen.'

'So he was there for nearly two hours. What was he doing?'

They watch as Grace walks away from his car towards the main buildings, then goes out of sight.

'Scroll forward to just before ten,' Robin directs.

She does, and here he is again. Head down, he walks quickly, his keys gripped in his hand. He stops at his car, into the blind spot, then, after a few minutes, they see him fall.

Robin scowls. 'But no sign of the offender,' he mutters, annoyed.

'Not on this camera. But there's no way they would have got in and out without being captured. So where did they go?'

'Keep looking. I want to make some progress on this at least.'

But before he can continue, he spots the bald head of his boss in the doorway. Robin looks up and DCI Neal Baker catches his eye. He beckons a finger in his direction.

'Back in a sec,' Robin directs to Freya. 'Guv?' he says to Baker, once he's in the corridor.

'Don't worry, Robin. I won't take up much of your time. I know you've got a weird one. Any leads?'

Robin smiles. The old detective in him couldn't help but ask.

'Not yet, but the place is smothered in cameras. We'll get something.'

'Good, good. Listen, I had a call last night. From Detective Superintendent Holton at Exeter HQ.'

Oh, shit, Robin thinks. What has Jo done? 'I'm sorry, boss. I was going to mention it, but I haven't decided myself yet.'

Baker holds his hands up. 'Not a problem, Robin. She just wanted the low-down on you. Says there might be some DI opportunities up for grabs in the near future. For the right person in the right place.' Baker smiles. 'I said you were shit, obviously.'

'Obviously.' Robin returns his grin. 'But honestly, I don't know yet. Jo only just started talking about it.'

'Yeah, she mentioned her too. Said she's a shoo-in for DCI.' He pauses, studying Robin's face carefully. 'It's a good opportunity for you.'

'So everyone keeps saying.'

'But?'

Robin can't help glancing back to their desks where Freya is working. Baker follows his gaze.

'You're worried about West?' he asks, confused.

'Not worried, just… I don't know.' Robin shrugs. Too many thoughts, none of which he wants to share with his boss, however close their working relationship. 'I'm still thinking.'

'Well, make your mind up soon. Apparently they have a few other candidates in the mix and they need to know about you and Jo. Things are moving fast, Robin. Don't miss out.'

With a reassuring squeeze of his shoulder, his boss turns and heads quickly down the corridor. For someone so large, he's surprisingly fleet of foot, the ex-boxer in him coming to the fore.

When Robin turns back, Freya is on her way towards him.

He waits, curious. She has a notepad in her hand, and a blank MG11 form.

'There's someone at the front desk,' she says when she's next to him. 'Says he witnessed an attack on a man last night. One in the car park of Leisure World.'

'Lead the way,' Robin replies. Anything to get out of watching CCTV.

24

Freya peers through the door into the interview room. The man sits on the edge of the chair, glancing nervously around.

Freya knocks quietly before pushing the door open. Robin wordlessly beckons for the paperwork – his way of telling her to take the lead – and follows. The man jumps up when he sees them.

'Please have a seat, Mr Cook.'

He does, but perches on the edge, back straight. 'Kurt,' he says. 'Will this take long?'

Freya smiles. 'I'm DC Freya West. This is DS Robin Butler. Would you like anything to eat? Drink?'

'No. Thank you.' His voice is rough, scoured by years of smoking, judging from the smell. He picks at his nails anxiously.

'We understand you saw an attack last night?'

'Yes. I think so. I don't know. It might not be important.'

'Tell us about it, Kurt. We never know what we'll find useful.'

He stares at the floor for a moment and Freya takes the opportunity to appraise him. Long straight hair, tucked behind his ears. Greasy face, a light port wine birthmark down the left-hand side of his cheek. Shirt and jeans, scruffy trainers. He looks late twenties. Maybe younger, but if so, he's had a hard life.

'I was walking back from work. Using Leisure World as a cut-through as I always do. And there was this man laying into this other bloke on the far side of the car park. It looked grim.'

'Where do you work?'

'At the cruise terminal. I finish at ten, so this must have been just after.'

'How far away were you?' Freya asks. Next to her, Robin is scribbling the details on the MG11 form as Kurt talks; Freya wonders if anyone will be able to read it after.

'I dunno. I'd just crossed the road, pushed through the gap in the hedge. They were across the other side. On the right, by the fence. But there was a street light,' he adds quickly. 'I saw them.'

Freya leans forward. 'And what did you see?'

'The bloke was lying on the ground, and the other guy was kicking the shit out of him. Proper going for it. Then he looked up, saw me and ran off.'

'And what did he look like?'

Kurt stops, thinking for a moment. 'Not big. Short. For a bloke.'

'How did you know from that distance?' Robin interjects.

Kurt stares at him. 'He just seemed... small. Skinny. Brown hair.' His face lights up, as if remembering something. 'And I saw him get into his car.'

'I thought you said he ran off?'

'Yeah, ran to his car. It was black. A Toyota Prius. And the plate began KL61.'

Freya glances to Robin. It's a strangely detailed account, but if it helps them get an ID she shouldn't complain.

'Do you remember anything else?' Freya asks.

'Nah.'

'And what did you do then?'

'I saw that a security guard had turned up, so I left.'

'You didn't call 999? Or see if you could help?'

'I'm here now, aren't I?' The man glares. 'Can I go now? I need to get to work.'

He shifts in his seat, picking at his fingers again.

'We'll just need you to check this statement.' Robin pushes the form across to Kurt and he stares at it.

'You want me to sign this?' He looks up again, his eyes darting around the room. 'You're not recording me today, are you?'

'No. Unless you want us to?'

'No,' he says quickly. He stares at the piece of paper. 'Why do you want me to sign this?'

'It's our standard witness statement. It means that if we arrest the man for the attack, we can use it as evidence against him.'

Kurt reads the first page. 'You can prosecute me?' he snaps.

'Only if what you're saying isn't true,' Freya says slowly. 'Are you telling the truth, Kurt?'

He stares at her for a moment. 'Yeah,' he says at last. He picks up the pen and signs the box. Under Occupation he writes *None*. He turns the page. 'And you want my address and stuff?'

'Yes, please,' Freya says sweetly.

'I'm not gonna court.'

'And why is that?'

'I've got a job. And stuff.'

'Well, let's worry about that when we get there, shall we?'

He stares at the form for a moment. 'All right,' he says eventually.

Kurt starts painfully making his way through the tick boxes on the MG11. Robin leans over to Freya. 'Can you finish up?' he whispers. 'I'll head back and crack on.'

She nods, keen for Robin to go back to the CCTV and start looking for the owner of the mysterious Toyota Prius.

Kurt tackles the form, cross-eyed in confusion at every question, slowly ticking the boxes. He runs his finger under the account that Robin has written, his lips moving along with the words.

Freya notices that as he's working his way down, he's getting more and more agitated. He's now sweating, his left knee jumping up and down under the table.

'Are you okay, Kurt?' Freya asks after five minutes of this.

He looks up, his finger resting on the page. 'Fine,' he says quickly.

He signs his name at the bottom. Finally.

'I'm done,' he says. 'You'll arrest this guy now?'

Freya smiles. 'I hope so. You've given us a lot to go on.' They both stand up, Kurt staring at the floor. 'Thank you for your help.'

'Yeah, well...'

His voice tails off and, his gaze firmly fixed on his shoes, Freya escorts him to the door. Seeing the exit, he picks up his pace, almost hitting a run once he's outside the double doors.

Freya watches him go, pondering his demeanour. He seemed anxious, desperate to get away – more than she'd normally expect from someone in these circumstances. Kurt disappears out of sight and Freya sighs.

No, he was nervous. He's probably not the most law-abiding of individuals, no doubt worried they'll dig up something from his past. Some low-level pot possession or something. It makes sense he'd be behaving strangely; not everyone loves being in a police station. With one last look, Freya dismisses her worries, then hurries off to Robin. To see what he's found out.

25

Back at their desks, she finds Robin staring at his screen. Chin resting on his hand, elbow propped up on the desk. He doesn't look over as she sits down next to him.

'There are more black Toyota Priuses with that plate than you'd think,' he says.

She loads up the CCTV again. A new perspective this time – footage taken from the road leading to the car park. Maybe she'll find the car that way.

It's a wide lens. On the left-hand side, Freya can see the entrance to the Hollywood Casino; a stark misnomer given its drab exterior and peeling paint. On the right, the sad boarded-up windows of the Quayside pub, long closed. And in the middle – the road. A few cars pass through, none of them the right colour or shape.

'There isn't a single Toyota Prius registered in this area with that number plate,' Robin says.

'Nothing?'

'Nothing. Which means it might be any one of these in the UK.' He sighs. 'I can't be arsed to go through every single black Prius ruling them out.'

'Try a variation? He could have remembered it wrong. You know how reliable eyewitnesses are.'

Robin harrumphs and goes back to his screen. As Freya stares at the CCTV, she hears him typing, and a quick grumble of 'Why can't Intel bloody well do this?'

She smiles indulgently. And then something on the footage catches her eye. Two figures have come into shot. One – tall, head tilted to the ground, almost completely blocking the view of the other. Freya tries to zoom in but to no avail – the image just pixelates into tiny blocks of colour.

Robin makes another disgruntled noise next to her. She shuffles across, looking over his shoulder; he's scrolling down the search results on the screen. Then he jumps, so quickly he bumps the back of his head against hers.

'Ow. Sorry.' He vigorously rubs his skull, then turns. 'Look.' He points to a line on the monitor with a grin. 'That can't be coincidence.'

She stares, then glances back to the CCTV.

'No, it bloody can't,' she replies.

26

Footsteps thunder down the corridor, Diane's chirping voice behind them. Tiller looks up from his computer screen. Down here he loses all track of time, and he glances at the clock. Just past two. He hasn't eaten lunch. He can't remember if he had breakfast.

The rumbling gets closer. Tiller waits. Two large bodies appear in his doorway, blocking out the illumination from the corridor. Now only his desk light shines, casting the men's faces with menacing shadows. Behind them he can hear Diane's frantic tones.

'Andrew isn't in today,' she squeaks to Tiller. 'I've been calling him.'

The men ignore her.

'Mr Hamilton?' one of them asks. He nods. 'We need you to stand up slowly and raise your hands above your head.'

He does as he's told. The cop is large and broad-shouldered, dressed all in black. His stab vest prominently displays a bright yellow taser.

'Please,' Tiller says. 'What's this about?'

The cop steps forward. He has a pair of silver cuffs ready to go. He roughly turns Tiller around, pulling his hands down and behind his back. He feels the metal, cold and tight against his skin. He feels his heart rate flutter.

'Teàrlach Hamilton,' the cop standing in the doorway begins. He pronounces it phonetically – Tear-Lack. 'We are arresting you on suspicion of grievous bodily harm. You do not have to say anything. But it may harm your defence if you do not

123

mention, when questioned, something you later rely on in court. Anything you do say may be given in evidence.'

The cop's still talking, but Tiller's dazed, barely listening. He's turned round again, facing the doorway. One cop behind him, one in front.

'Do you understand?' the cop finishes.

'But… who…? GBH?' he says dumbly.

'Do you understand?'

He nods.

'Come with us, please.'

The trio walk down the corridor. Heads pop out of their offices, blinking. Nocturnal creatures, afraid of the light. Tiller can hear whispers, exclamations of alarm as he goes.

The handcuffs pinch on his wrists. He's confused. Worried.

'What…?' he says, but it comes out in a croak. He swallows. 'What am I supposed to have done?'

'You can ask your questions back at the nick,' the cop replies.

They awkwardly negotiate the stairs. Tiller stumbles, and is quickly caught with a firm hand on his arm. The man's fingers almost go all the way round Tiller's bicep, he's that much of a beast.

Outside, a police car is waiting. A hand on the top of his head, and he's pushed inside. A grate in front of him. Secure. In case he… what? Tiller doesn't know what to think now. Arrested for GBH. It must be a mistake. Must be.

He hears himself make a tiny high-pitched squeak of panic. This can't be happening, it can't. His hands are shaking, and he grasps his lower arm tightly, as much as he can with the cuffs. It helps. A bit. Small breaths puff out of his chest; his head is light, not enough oxygen getting through.

The drive doesn't take long. He watches landmarks pass through the window, stunned into silence. They're heading towards the centre of town. Into Southampton. He knows the police station. A massive Lego brick of a building, he watched it go up, all those years ago, then the shiny outside dull from beige to streaky brown as pollution and rain took hold.

The car pulls in then takes a turn round the back. He's unloaded, no more than cargo, and escorted through the insignificant-looking side door. A policewoman waits behind the screens.

'Name?' she asks.

He gives it, the correct pronunciation this time. Then he spells it out for her.

'Time of arrest?'

'Fourteen-oh-five,' the cop says next to him.

'Offence?' she asks.

'GBH.'

'Necessities for arrest, please?'

A sheet of paper is passed across. 'To allow the prompt and effective investigation of the offence, and to prevent the person in question causing physical injury to another person.'

The cop talks robotically; the custody sergeant types. Tiller can hardly take it in. What person, what offence?

'Physical injury? What physical injury?' Tiller asks, but the cop blanks him.

'Do you understand why you've been arrested?'

'No. Yes. I mean… yes. I suppose so.' Tiller looks from the lady behind the screen to the cop next to him. 'Please – who's been hurt?'

The woman gives him a sympathetic look. 'I'm going to authorise your detention so you can be interviewed regarding the information the police have received. The detectives will be able to answer all your questions. Is that okay?'

He nods. He's searched, metal detectors run across his body and down his legs.

He's asked if he has any history of self-harming, told to stand against the chart on the wall.

'Five-nine,' the officer says.

'Would you like to have a solicitor?'

'Yes. But I don't know any criminal lawyers.'

'We'll call whoever's on duty.'

The rest is a blur. The mugshot photograph, the swab in his mouth. The endless questions. The indignity as they take his clothes, as he gets dressed in a shapeless grey tracksuit.

And then, finally, into his cell.

'Do you want anything to eat?'

His stomach feels like there's a block of lead inside. 'No,' he says. 'Thank you.'

The door closes.

He swallows. He takes in his surroundings. The blue plastic mattress. The smell of dirty protests and unwashed bodies that have been here before. The toilet area without a door.

His head swims; he's going to pass out. He bends down and puts his head between his legs, forces himself to take long, measured breaths. He feels like he's going to puke.

Thoughts whirl. This can't be real. It can't. It must be a mistake.

He can't suppress the nausea any longer; he clamps his hand over his mouth and stumbles, retching, as his empty stomach disgorges acid into the stinking toilet.

This can't be happening. It can't. And he falls to the floor, gasping, as the room swirls around him.

27

They start the clock. Robin mentally notes the time Tiller is booked into custody. 14:46. They have twenty-four hours.

Hamilton asks for a solicitor. Then a doctor's called; they wait. Mild panic attack; drugs are administered; the all-clear is confirmed.

In the meantime, they study the CCTV, put in requests for the traffic cameras, for the ANPR. Andrew Grace's car is brought back to the garage and the SOCOs begin their work, looking for foreign DNA, fingerprints. Any trace where their offender may have touched the bodywork and left vital clues behind. A fingertip search is carried out across the car park, looking for the weapon that struck Andrew Grace round the head, across the legs. They find nothing.

The search begins at Hamilton's house. Mina is briefed and sent out to supervise. They're looking for clothing, footwear, anything that might have blood.

Freya fidgets next to him. Then goes off to make coffee. Robin sits, tapping his finger idly against the desk, thinking.

What happened last night? Did Tiller ask Andrew to meet him – or was it the other way around? Did he go there to attack him, or was it on the spur of the moment – a crime of passion? His first impressions of Tiller weren't of a man prone to anger, but anyone can act out of character if the circumstances are right. If pushed to the edge. As Robin well knows.

Freya comes back and places his mug in front of him. The Little Miss Sunshine on the front mocks him.

'And why there?' he says out loud.

Freya slumps next to him, her own mug in her hand. 'Out of the way? Secluded?'

'Did he know about the black spot in the cameras, or was it just luck?'

The phone on his desk rings; Robin picks it up.

'They're ready for you,' the custody sergeant says.

–

Tiller Hamilton is pale. His eyes are raw and wide, his body language stiff. The moment Robin and Freya come into the room his expression changes.

'What's going on?' he asks.

Robin and Freya sit down in front of him, his solicitor by his side.

'We'll get to that,' Robin replies. 'How are you?'

'I'm okay,' Tiller replies quietly.

Freya goes through the formalities, switching the video on. They say their names in turn, and Robin waits, ready.

'Tiller – do you mind if I call you Tiller?' he begins.

'That's fine.'

'Tiller, last night, your friend and business partner, Andrew Grace, was attacked in the car park at Leisure World. He was hit round the head and the legs, then kicked and beaten as he lay on the concrete next to his car.'

Robin pauses. Tiller has gone ghostly white.

'I don't… I didn't…' he stutters, before he receives a stern look from his solicitor and abruptly stops talking.

Robin senses how this is going to go. He leaves a long gap, watching Tiller. He takes long gulps of air, his hands gripping the tabletop, his eyes blinking rapidly. Then, at last, he seems to regain control. He focuses on Robin, still pale.

'How is he?' Tiller asks quietly.

'He has a smashed-up face, damaged arm, a broken leg and one hell of a headache. But he'll be okay.'

Tiller visibly sags.

'This is your chance to tell us what happened. Why did you attack him?'

Tiller shakes his head quickly. 'I didn't...' Another warning look from his solicitor. 'No comment.'

'Why were you there?'

'No comment.'

'What did you hit him with? Because we have teams at the car park and at your house now. We'll find it.'

'No comment.'

'We'd like to hear a little more about the evidence you have against my client, please, Detective,' the solicitor interrupts. 'Since you've declined to share anything in discovery.'

'Okay. Fine.' Robin opens the file. He takes out the still from the CCTV of Andrew and Tiller, turns it around and pushes it across to Tiller.

'This is you, here,' he says, pointing to the smaller figure. 'And this is the victim, Andrew Grace. This is taken from the CCTV of the car park. CCTV which also shows your black Toyota driving in, and you getting out and walking across to Mr Grace.'

Tiller and the solicitor stare at the photo.

'This could be anyone,' the solicitor says, scornfully.

'The quality is much better on the video,' Robin replies. 'And ANPR caught your number plate on West Quay Road, heading in this direction, just before this was taken.'

'Again, Mr Hamilton could have been going anywhere. Even if this is my client, you can't prove he attacked him.'

Robin pauses. 'We also have a witness.'

Tiller's mouth drops open. He looks quickly to his solicitor.

'A witness to what?' the solicitor asks.

'To the attack. Someone saw a man that closely matches your description, driving a car with a plate similar to yours, attack Mr Grace and leave him bleeding on the ground of the car park.'

'But... I... I...' Tiller begins. Then he catches himself. 'No comment,' he says.

'If Andrew Grace dies, where does his share of the company go? To his family?'

Tiller shakes his head. But then replies, 'No comment.'

'To you?'

'No comment.'

'That's a lot of money. A good few million.'

Tiller's face has completely drained of blood. His lips and his complexion are grey.

'What were you arguing about, Tiller?'

'No comment.'

'Was it something to do with the sale of the company?'

'No comment.'

'I get it, Tiller, I do. Your solicitor has advised you to keep quiet. But that's only advice. It will work in your favour if you tell us what's going on. Juries and judges are inclined to go a lot easier on people who tell the truth. Who don't waste police time. Who explain exactly why they beat up their business partner and left them bleeding in a car park.'

'No comment.'

'Because things are only going to get worse from here. We're calling it GBH now, but what if we find something else that makes us think you were trying to kill him, Tiller? You have the motive. That's attempted murder. That's life.'

Robin stops, watching as Tiller battles with his emotions. He looks like he's going to cry. Then he stops, and his eyes widen.

'You need to call Chloe,' he says.

'Chloe Somerset?' Tiller nods. 'Is she involved?'

'No, but... Please. Call Chloe. Make sure she's okay.'

'Have you done something to Chloe?'

'No... no. Not me. But someone. Someone might have hurt her.'

Robin sits forward in his seat. 'Who?'

Tiller presses his lips together. Then he says quietly, 'Call her. Make sure Chloe is safe.' He looks up, making eye contact for the first time in the interview. 'Then I'll tell you everything you need to know.'

28

Freya peers through the window, her hands cupped against the glass.

All their phone calls have come to nothing so here they are, outside Chloe Somerset's house.

'Try the bell again?'

Robin does as he's told; Freya listens to it ring in an empty hallway.

'Can you see anything?' Robin comes up and joins her.

'Not much.'

Next to each other, they peer through, but the lights are off and they can't see inside. Robin steps backwards, then moves off to the side of the house. Freya follows.

The gate opens without opposition, both trailing through into the small, neat garden. Grass and mud underfoot, small well-tended beds of pansies, wood poppies and hyacinths. But a flash of light catches her eye and she turns; to her left, a window is smashed; sun reflects off the shards of glass remaining in the window frame. She catches Robin's look, both of them tense as they carry on their journey through the garden.

The back door is gaping, the lock smashed. Robin goes first, calling, 'Police,' as he slowly pushes it open. Freya follows, senses on alert.

There's no noise from inside. She can only hear their heavy breathing, the crunch of broken glass. Freya flips a light switch, and the extent of the devastation is revealed.

The house is trashed. Broken crockery and glassware crack under her feet as she walks through the kitchen. The living room is a mess of feathers and foam from the slashed sofa cushions. Every drawer has been pulled out, every book removed from the shelf and discarded on the carpet. While she stands there, assessing the mess, Robin has gone upstairs to continue the check of the house and now reappears by her side.

'Same there,' he says. 'The place has been destroyed.'

Freya looks at him for a moment, then follows the path last trodden out of the room. She takes the stairs slowly; behind her she can hear Robin on the phone, reporting the break-in.

She stands in the doorway of the bedroom. The wardrobe is open; clothes scattered in a mass of blue and white and purple and green. The mattress has been pulled from the bed, and a gentle white snow has settled on the carpet where the duvet and pillow have been ripped open. The mattress is the same – two large, long cuts down the middle, springs visible.

Freya gets a horrible feeling about Chloe. Where she is. Whether she's alive.

She goes back to join Robin. He's still standing in the wrecked living room, phone clamped to his ear.

'SOCO on their way,' he says, obviously waiting for Control to come back on the line. 'What does this look like to you?'

'Revenge?' Freya wonders. 'But it seems wrong for that.'

Freya's seen houses that have been trashed deliberately. A trail of gleeful mayhem – usually including spray paint and more than a few foul deposits. There's none of that here.

'They were looking for something?' she proposes.

'That's what I thought,' Robin replies, but turns away as someone comes back on the phone and he talks again.

Freya's ominous chill grows as she surveys the room. The coffee table is on its side, the drawer removed, and something next to it catches her eye. A small tin. Blue and white, that used to house fudge from a picturesque part of Cornwall. She picks it up in a gloved hand and opens it, taking out the baggie of weed.

So Chloe was a small-scale user. If it wasn't for the fresh air blowing through from the open back door they could probably have detected the smell as they came in. No wonder Chloe wanted to meet at the police station; she was most likely worried about them noticing. The least of her problems now, Freya thinks grimly.

Robin's off the phone, about to make another call.

'We're treating this as an abduction, right?' Freya says.

'Yeah,' Robin replies. 'I've called it in to the NCA, they're going to phone back.' He frowns, turning a full 360 in the mess.

'We do know one thing, though,' he continues. 'If they were looking for something, they didn't find it.'

'How do you know that?'

'This whole house has been destroyed. Not a single centimetre of space has been left. And if they'd found it, they would have stopped. Taken it and gone. No,' he concludes. 'They didn't uncover whatever they were looking for. And they were in one hell of a rage as a result.'

29

The wheels are turning. Robin updates DCI Baker on the possible abduction of Chloe Somerset; Response and Patrol have been briefed; SOCO are busy at the house looking for whatever trace they can find from her abductors. DI Ratcliffe has been called in along with his team, and Mina is scouring CCTV. Greg and Digital are pinging her mobile phone, traffic cameras and ANPR are being checked, although Robin already knows her car is sitting, alone, outside her house. They're doing everything they can – contacting known associates, family, hospitals, monitoring credit cards and bank accounts. So far, nothing.

Her handbag and purse have been found in the house, so wherever she is, she hasn't taken them with her.

There is only one person Robin wants to speak to.

Tiller Hamilton is escorted from his cell; his solicitor has been requested but Hamilton has agreed to talk without him. He sits opposite Robin and Freya in the interview room.

'She's missing?' he repeats, once Robin has passed on the news.

'Yes, and her house has been trashed. What's going on, Tiller?'

'Trashed?' Tiller's eyes are wide as he looks between the detectives. 'Have you found Max? Was Max there?'

Robin gets a jolt of fear. 'Max? Who's Max?' He imagines a small boy, young, scared. Or a baby. Snatched from a cot.

'Her dog. Wee black spaniel. He's a pedigree, potentially worth a few quid. She loves him. She wouldn't go anywhere without Max.'

Relief. 'We'll look for him,' Robin confirms. 'Tiller?' he pushes. 'I can't stress how important it is that you tell us what the hell is going on. Chloe's life might be at stake.'

'Oh, God.' His face crumples and he puts his head in his hands. 'You're right, we're trying to sell the company,' he says at last.

'And how is Chloe's abduction related to that?' Robin asks in disbelief.

'It sounds ridiculous, I know.'

He places his hands flat on the table and takes a long deep breath. Robin waits.

'At first we were just getting interest from fitness companies, from Google, even an approach from Facebook. Our software could help with Street View – that sort of thing. What we expected. It's very common – big predatory companies snapping up the minnows for their ideas and clever IP. Then another company came out of the woodwork, via a lawyer. Asking detailed questions but being vague about who their client was. Eventually the offer came – and it was millions.' He looks up, meeting their gaze. 'And millions. Nearly twenty-five per cent more than the value of the company. And they wanted it all.'

He pauses. 'Once software is written, it's frozen and it becomes vulnerable. Things change, bugs are discovered and it needs to be updated.' He lifts his hands to take a sip of tea; sweaty marks remain on the tabletop. 'So they wanted me.'

'You?'

'I'm the person who built it. I know it better than anyone. Contractually, they need me, otherwise the software becomes obsolete within years. They offered golden handcuffs – a compensation package that's boosted for every year I do with them.'

'But you didn't agree?'

'No. Not in the slightest. Their name is Parapet Holdings Ltd. It won't mean anything to you. These companies, they're just a front. A shell within a shell. But we guessed correctly – they're a private military contractor. Other defence primes were interested but we turned them down early on. They wanted the Hamilton Grace Software – and the algorithm specifically – to take out to the battlefield. To predict responses from enemy forces. To model how people, the public, a country will react.' He shrugs, wearily. 'Everything.'

'So you refused,' Freya says.

Tiller nods. 'That isn't why we started the company. We wanted to help people, not kill them.'

'But couldn't it save lives?' Robin counters.

'That's what Andrew argued. I didn't believe them – I didn't believe that they were British. This wasn't an offer from the UK government. This was a private contractor. They could have sold it to anyone. I didn't want to take that risk.'

'They've kidnapped someone, over a bit of software?' Robin asks, astonished.

'It's not *a bit of software*,' Tiller mocks. 'Coupled with the VR, it's an accurate real-life rendering of whatever landscape or building you want. But, as I said, it's the behavioural model that's priceless. Every day, the armed forces rely more heavily on drones and robots, controlled remotely by humans. If you can predict what a human pilot will do in the next second, not only can you provide feedback that isn't disorientating, but their actions are determined more quickly, and your drones and robots respond faster. Even a second's worth of advantage is a lot in a theatre of hypersonic missiles. People will die – British people will die – if they get this.'

Robin frowns. 'And – what? They haven't taken no as an answer?'

'It's worse than that. Andrew said yes. He started the due diligence. But I refused to sign. So they've obviously decided to steal it direct.'

Robin senses Freya shift next to him. 'But if that's the case,' she says. 'Why would they kidnap Chloe? She's not a managing partner. She was only the FD, and she left six months ago.'

Tiller puts his head in his hands again and howls. 'It's my fault,' he wails. 'I should never have involved her.'

'Involved her, how?' Robin asks. 'Is this linked to the attack on Laura Grace, and the theft of the laptops?'

'It must be. But stealing laptops is… amateur. Anyone who knows anything about software would know that all development is done in the cloud. And my algorithm – the behavioural model – isn't even in the same place as the company business as usual. I encrypted it, moved it off to a secret, hidden folder, disguised as a boring old debug dump file. And then I protected it with a key.'

'A key?'

'Aye, an eleven-digit encryption key. A combination of numbers and letters. Sometimes known as a passphrase, same thing. You can't hack it. Do you know how many possible combinations there are of eleven digits?'

'A lot?'

'Yeah, a lot. That's an understatement. If you have no knowledge of the character sequence it would take years to crack. You're talking multiple lifetimes.'

'And who holds this encryption key?'

'I used to. And then I got worried. I knew I was the obvious target.'

'So you gave it to Chloe,' Robin says slowly.

Tiller nods miserably. 'I upped the security by adding another level – my thumbprint. And then I left it to Chloe to enter the digits. I knew that if I had access to both, they could just kidnap me. And now they have her.'

'And they couldn't kidnap you—'

'Because I was in here. Arrested,' Tiller says miserably.

'How did they know? About Chloe?'

'I'm guessing they didn't. But a bit of surveillance and they would have known we were together.'

'She's your girlfriend,' Robin confirms.

'Not really. But as close as anyone is,' Tiller confesses with a shrug.

'Hang on...' Freya says slowly. 'If they only have Chloe, and you're in here...'

'They can't get in,' Tiller finishes for her. 'And that's going to be a bunch of very dangerous, pissed-off people.'

30

It's late, the sun setting, a fade of reds and yellows dissolving into black while they've been working. The team sits around the table, crammed into DCI Baker's office. Freya and Robin, DI Ratcliffe, Greg from Digital and Jess, the crime scene manager.

'We have nothing from her mobile phone,' Greg is telling them. 'Last known cell site is her house, when she called Tiller Hamilton at half one.'

'Just before he was arrested,' Freya says.

'We're getting nothing now, so it's either off or destroyed,' Greg continues. 'We'll keep trying,' he adds quickly.

'Have you found anything at the house?' Baker asks Jess.

'Multiple footwear marks from large utility boots. A type easily picked up at your local army surplus store.'

'And worn by military contractors?' Robin asks.

'Possibly. We're narrowing down the shoe sizes, but initial estimates show at least two different individuals. But that's it. No signs of blood. Fingerprints throughout the house, but nothing that's pinging on the database.'

'So they could be Chloe's?'

'In all likelihood, yes. And if your theory is correct, that she was abducted by these people, they were probably wearing gloves.'

'Witnesses?' Baker asks. 'Mouse?'

DI Ratcliffe takes over. His moniker would suggest a small man, toothy and fidgety, but police nicknames don't need much to get traction. He's large, over six feet tall, and bulky. But with his chubby cheeks, narrow eyes and fine, fur-like hair, he has the look of a dormouse or hamster, and that was all it took. He's never seemed to mind.

'That's where we came up trumps,' Mouse says now. 'Neighbours were at work until lunchtime, arrived back at three when they heard loud crashing and breaking glass. Looked out of the back window to see a white van drive off.'

'And they didn't call the police?'

'They called 101 but got put on hold so gave up.'

'Great,' Baker grumbles with a frown. 'Plate or distinguishing marks?'

'No, nothing. Couldn't even give us a make. But we're searching CCTV and traffic cams in the area.'

'Not much to narrow it down,' Robin comments. 'How many white vans are out there?'

'A lot,' Mouse admits. 'But we might get lucky.'

'They took her in broad daylight?' Robin says. 'That's bold. Or stupid. We're still getting zero interest from the NCA?' Robin directs to Baker.

Baker sighs, the frustration clear on his face. 'Because there's no ransom, no evidence of foul play—'

'Except for a broken window, a vandalised house and multiple footwear marks?' Robin says sarcastically.

Baker shakes his head. 'You don't have to tell me. This is a clear tiger kidnap in my opinion, one that's live and ongoing, but they're saying she could have come home, seen the mess and run. The white van might belong to a friend. And they don't believe this story about the encryption key. Unless someone gets a call from the abductors demanding money, or we get sent a severed finger or a phial of blood, they're treating her as a misper. And that's ours.'

'We're monitoring Hamilton's phone?' Robin asks Greg.

Greg nods. 'Home, mobile and office. Grace's too, even though he's in the hospital and they're probably aware of that.'

'Do you think the attack on Grace was them?' Mouse asks.

'Could be. Even though we have a witness.' Robin frowns, then shakes his head. 'I can't make that line up either. It looks like Hamilton was definitely there – although he hasn't copped to that yet – but I just can't see him beating up Grace.'

'So if it wasn't him, who was it? And why beat up Andrew? And not Tiller, too?'

'A warning?'

'Maybe. I'd like to keep Hamilton in custody for the time being, boss,' he asks Baker. 'To keep him safe, if nothing else.'

'Agreed. Hold him for his normal twenty-four. How did the interview go with the PA? Diane something?'

'Davis went to see her at work,' Mouse replies. 'She was next to useless.' He flicks through the witness statement in front of him. 'She hasn't seen Chloe since she left the business six months ago, didn't like her when she worked for them, and knew nothing about Parapet Holdings, bar the fact there were meetings in the diary. All between Grace and their director.'

'Do we have the dates?'

'She told Davis to get a warrant.'

Baker smiles. 'Fair enough. Protective old bird. And you're interviewing this Giles Kepner guy in the morning?'

Robin looks to Freya and she nods. A call has been made to the man in charge of Parapet Holdings. A gentle approach, asking him in for a voluntary interview, reason given that he might have seen something on his visit to the office Saturday morning. Who knows what evidence they might have by then; Freya hopes they'll be able to arrest him the moment he walks into the nick.

'Do we think she's alive?' Freya asks.

The whole table goes silent. She's been watching the exchange, a hard ball of worry churning in her insides. She imagines Chloe sat at home, as large men broke down her back door. The dread, the fear as she was carried away, bundled into the back of the van. Then what? They don't know. Anything could have happened to her since.

'We didn't find any blood,' Jess reiterates.

142

'And they need her alive, for the key,' Robin says. His face is sympathetic, suggesting he's feeling exactly as she is – desperate, worried.

'Which they definitely don't have yet?' Mouse asks.

'No,' Robin replies. 'We've given Tiller Hamilton access to his laptop and he's confirmed that the key hasn't been breached.'

'So let's get on it,' Baker concludes. 'Mouse – take charge as SIO. Robin – 2IC. Everyone, keep both informed. However this ends, I need you all functioning. Mouse – Desai and Smith are in first thing, right?' DI Ratcliffe nods. 'Brief them as soon as they arrive and get them up and running. West, head home now—'

'But boss—'

'No. I need you fresh. Get some sleep. You too, Mouse. Robin, you'll be on call tonight.'

Baker nods, signalling the end of the meeting, and they all stand up.

'I'll call you if anything changes,' Robin says to Freya.

'I'll stay for another hour or so,' she replies. Robin gives her a disapproving look. 'And then I'll head back.'

'Fine. Get on the CCTV then.'

She follows Robin's gaze as he watches Baker and Ratcliffe talk in the doorway of Baker's office. 'That could be you,' she says.

'Hmm?' He turns to her.

'You.' She gestures to the senior officers. 'In charge. You're more than qualified for DI. This is your case. You should be SIO.'

He watches a little longer, without comment. Except for a slight lowering of his brows, she can't tell what he's thinking.

He turns back. 'What did we miss, Freya?' he asks quietly.

'We weren't to know this would happen,' she replies. 'Besides, we don't know she's in danger yet. We haven't found the dog, have we? The NCA could be right – she could have just taken off somewhere.'

143

'Without her car? Her purse or any credit cards?'

Freya stays silent. He's right. Things aren't looking good for Chloe Somerset.

31

Josh hums quietly to himself as he puts the key in the lock of the door and lets himself in. Freya's house – no, his house, he thinks with a small smile. He knows he should be concerned about Chloe Somerset – and he is – but it's been two weeks since he packed up his life and moved in with Freya, and he doesn't think he's ever been happier. Merging his life with hers – putting his books on her shelf, his clothes in his half of the wardrobe. He likes the commitment. This is what he's ready for.

He takes his coat and shoes off, then makes a cup of tea. He carries his mug upstairs to the bedroom and looks at the mess that remains. A few boxes in the living room, one or two here. Clothes that don't yet have a home.

He knows what's going on at the nick and should be getting to bed. Catching some sleep before he returns in the morning. He'll just put a few things away first. Finish unpacking.

He opens a few drawers then, finding them all full, calls Freya. She answers on the second ring.

'Is everything okay?' she asks. He imagines her at work, sat at her desk, a slightly harried look on her face.

'Yes, all fine. I was going to unpack, but you haven't cleared any space for me.'

'Oh, shit, yes. Sorry. Bottom two drawers in the wardrobe. Just take my stuff and put it in a box. I'll sort it when I get home.'

'No worries. Love you.'

'See you later.'

He smiles at the lack of returning affection. She doesn't like to show emotion in the office, says it interferes with her professionalism, whatever that means. But he understands. Whatever she wants, she gets.

He crouches down on the carpet and pulls out the two drawers she mentioned. They're full of clothes – tops and T-shirts he hasn't seen before; she obviously doesn't wear them much. Methodically, he takes them out, folding them carefully – not that she had – and placing them on the carpet to the side. He pulls the box of his own clothes over and empties them one by one into the drawer.

He puts on music, then sings along as he works. They've had their ups and downs, him and Freya, but he feels like finally things are starting to come together. Even Butler has a girlfriend. It shouldn't make a difference, but somehow it has. Like there's finally some distance between Freya and her sergeant.

He's never understood that relationship. He's had superior officers who were the opposite gender, but he's never got as close to them as Freya has to Butler. Every day they work together. While other pairings in Major Crimes shuffle and change, the two of them stay as one.

And in a way he feels sorry for Robin Butler. That his life is so empty he has to look to his DC for friendship. He knows Freya sometimes spends evenings over at his house, and he just can't understand why she likes him so much. Plus, there was *that* kiss. The one when they had just started working together that Freya dismisses as nothing. But why had it happened? Did they have feelings for each other? Maybe they still do...

Josh frowns and shakes his head. No. That isn't what this is. Freya is committed to him – he's here, isn't he? And things are going so well.

Having replaced her clothes in the now empty box, he turns his attention to the bottom drawer. More items he hasn't seen her ever wear, and he places them on top of the others. Maybe she'll take them straight to charity, he idly wonders, maybe...

146

But then he stops. In the bottom of the drawer is an envelope. White, A5. He turns it over – the front is blank, but the flap is open. He frowns. He should just put it in the box with everything else, but curiosity threatens. One little look, he thinks. It's open, and she told him to clear the drawer. It's not like he's snooping.

He opens the flap and pulls out what's inside. They're photographs – and they're all of the same man. Sometimes Freya is in the shot with him, her arms round him, sometimes he's alone. Josh flips through them slowly. There are around eight or nine, and they all seem to be from the same day. The man is wearing the same blue shirt; he has wavy blond hair, curling around his ears. A broad smile. In one, he's laughing. It's a selfie, Freya's lips pressed against his cheek.

And then he realises. This is *him*. Jon. The man she was seeing before Josh. The one she won't talk about, who died before he and Freya had even met. Josh looks at the photographs closely. He's felt like a ghost for so long – and here he is. It's strange.

He couldn't look more different to Josh. Untidy, where Josh is always neat. Blond where Josh is dark. But they both have blue eyes, and they both clearly adore Freya.

But then Josh stops. He frowns. Something about this man – he seems familiar. Did he know him? But how could he? While he was alive, this man lived here, in Southampton, while Josh was in Newcastle. How could their paths have possibly crossed?

The sound of Freya's car on the driveway diverts his attention, and he quickly puts the photographs back in the envelope. But before he does, something jars. He has seen his face before. Not smiling, but serious. On a police file.

Jon. Jonathan. *Jonathan fucking Miller.*

Oh, shit.

His hand flies to his mouth. That's why he recognises him. Jonathan Miller was the husband, murdered by his wife. When was it? October 2020. A few months before Josh moved down, but detectives were still talking about the case when he arrived. He'd read the file out of a desire not to miss out on juicy gossip: his wife had killed him, and then she'd died in a tragic accident before they could properly charge her. But… but… His wife?? Freya had been seeing a married man? And hadn't she…? Hadn't she and Butler been working on this case?

Suddenly everything makes sense. Her reluctance to talk about it. Why he'd never seen any photographs before. Why there was no fucking mention of a mistress in the case files.

A figure appears in the door. He jumps, then looks up, not able to prevent the guilty look slathered across his face. And he's still holding the envelope of photos.

Freya's gaze shifts from his face down to the envelope. She meets his eyes and her smile disappears.

'You know,' she says, simply.

32

Freya's stomach lurches when she sees the envelope. Her breath catches. She'd forgotten they were there. Others she keeps safe. Properly hidden away.

And the look on Josh's face – anger. Confusion. Maybe even some love.

'You know,' she says.

'The man… the man you were seeing. That was Jonathan Miller.' He says it as a statement. She's always known that Josh isn't stupid – that the slightest clue to Jon's identity and he'd work it out. Now here they are.

'Yes,' she confirms.

'But how… but what…?'

Freya sinks to her knees next to him. He won't look at her. 'We met at a barbecue. Mutual friends. I didn't know he was married. Not at first.'

'And when you found out?'

'I loved him,' she says. She shrugs, weakly. 'That's all there was to it.'

'And then he died.'

'She killed him.' Freya's surprised about the anger behind the words, even after all this time.

'And you worked on the case. With Butler.'

There's no point in lying now. 'Yes.'

A long pause. He stares at the envelope, turning it over in his hand. 'Did Butler know?'

'Did he know what?'

'Just tell me, Freya!' Josh suddenly shouts, his face contorting with rage. She jumps. 'Enough of this shit. Tell me what happened.'

Freya bites her lip, trying to hold back the tears. 'Yes. Robin knew. But not straight away. He worked it out. And by the time he confronted me about it… it was too late.'

'But the protocols you breached? The procedures you ignored. Why didn't he report you? It was his duty to report you.'

'Robin… Robin understood.' Freya looks up, and for the first time she meets Josh's blue eyes with hers. She can see the hurt she's caused. 'He knows about grief. And the crazy things it can make you do.'

'But what if you'd charged his wife with murder? What if you'd gone to court and someone had found out? What then? The whole conviction could have been in jeopardy.'

'But it didn't, Josh, did it?'

'Only because she died.'

Freya can see his jaw tightening, muscles clenching. He takes a long breath in.

'So that's it? That's what you've been hiding all this time?'

'Yes.'

'And that's all? No more secrets?'

'No. I promise.'

She's still lying, but she's not going to tell him about Amy Miller, and how she died. About Robin – and the circumstances around the death of the man who killed his sister. She reaches out to Josh, but he pulls away, wrapping his arms around himself.

'I'm sorry for not telling you, Josh. I am,' she pleads. 'But I didn't know how you would react. I was worried you would report me. That I'd lose my job.'

'Not that you'd lose *me*?' Josh spits.

'Of course I was worried about losing you! That you'd see me as this… I don't know.' She can't help the tears now, all her worries from the last few years coming to the surface. 'Someone… not good enough.'

'Maybe you're not.' Josh gets to his feet now, and Freya does the same, slowly. She desperately searches for something to say to make it better. 'Maybe you aren't the person I thought you were. What you did – with that investigation. Everything you put at risk.'

She reaches out to him, but he takes a step back.

'You've lied to me, over and over again. When I asked you at Christmas, and you refused to tell me, did Robin know?' Freya nods. 'Were you two laughing about me behind my back?'

'No! Of course not. Josh—'

'You and Butler, you've always been the same. I've always felt like I was on the outside. That there was something you weren't telling me. I convinced myself you were having an affair.' He laughs now, short and sharp. 'That you were in love with Robin Butler.'

'I… I love you, Josh.'

'Do you, though? If you couldn't trust me to share this pretty fucking important part of your past? I would have understood, Freya.'

Freya nods, mute. There's so much she could say. That no, she hadn't trusted him. That she still doesn't. That he shouldn't be so dismissive of Robin, and her complicated feelings towards her boss. But she knows her relationship with Josh is hovering on the edge.

She watches her boyfriend. He's looking down, at the discarded envelope of the photos of Jonathan.

'You loved him, this man?' he says, quietly.

'Yes.'

'Then I understand.' He looks up again. 'Why you lied. Why you stayed on the case. Because I would have done the same. For you, Freya.'

She tries to take his hands but he pulls away.

'But the lying to me. That I can't take.' He shakes his head, then pushes past her towards the door.

'Please, Josh. Don't leave.'

'I have to. I can't... I can't be around you at the moment. I need to think.'

He walks quickly out; she hears his footsteps on the stairs, the front door open and close.

Her throat is tight, her eyes hot. 'Fuck,' she whispers as his car drives away. 'Fuck.'

33

Midnight. The hospitals have come up a blank, all bank accounts and credit cards are quiet. If Chloe Somerset is lying low, she's doing a good job of it.

Robin sits back in his seat, closing his eyes for a second. They have three interlocking investigations: the break-in and attack of Laura Grace and her son, the assault on Andrew Grace, and the apparent abduction of Chloe Somerset. Thierry Durand is now languishing in HMP Winchester having been denied bail for GBH; could they assume he was acting under the orders of the same people who have taken Chloe?

The priority has to be finding Chloe, but Robin knows there is more to be done on the other cases. There are too many unanswered questions. He doesn't believe that Tiller Hamilton attacked Andrew – even with this eyewitness – so who was it and why? Nothing was stolen. Was it a threat? A warning shot – sell the company to us, or else?

And on the subject of the eyewitness, if he is mistaken, why had he led them so convincingly to Hamilton's door?

'DS Butler?' A PC appears by his desk and immediately Robin is shocked awake. Two fluffy black paws appear on his leg, quickly followed by a hard head nuzzled into his arm. A long pink tongue protrudes from the black snout and licks his face. He recoils.

'DS Butler?' the cop repeats.

'Yes?' He pushes the dog off him, who leaps up again immediately, tail wagging.

'They said to bring him to you.' He gestures to the dog, who now bounces enthusiastically at the end of the lead. 'This is the spaniel you were looking for. The one belonging to Chloe Somerset? They found him about a mile away, running along the road.' Robin stares at the dog. The uniform mistakes his hesitation for fear. 'He's friendly.'

'I can see that. Why haven't you taken him to the pound?'

'Pound's shut.'

'Well, can't a dog handler take him?'

'He's not a working dog, Sarge. He's evidence.'

'He's not going to identify the offender. This isn't *Turner and Hooch*.'

'Turner and what, Sarge?'

'Tom Hanks film with a dog? Big slobbery thing?' The PC still looks baffled; he can't be older than early twenties. Robin rolls his eyes. 'Never mind.'

The radio on the cop's shoulder buzzes. 'Sarge? I'm needed.'

'Yes. Fine. Go on then.'

Robin frowns. The lead is thrust into his hand and a bin bag dumped by his desk. The dog jumps up again. Robin pushes him off.

'Sit,' he says. The dog sits, panting, tongue lolling over bright white teeth. 'Max?' Robin says. 'Is that your name?' He leans down and pulls at the collar, looking at the tag. *Please return me to my family*, it says, and then a phone number. He turns it over. *Max. Microchipped*.

'Max it is then. Lie down.' The dog ignores him. 'Down,' he says more firmly. The dog drops to his haunches. 'Shit,' he grumbles under his breath.

His mobile rings; the dog instantly springs up on him again. He holds it down with one hand, while awkwardly answering the phone with the other.

'What do you know about dogs?' he says immediately.

'Dogs?' Jo replies. 'Not much. Why?'

'I've… acquired one. It belongs to a victim and the pound's shut for the night.'

'Dogs Trust? RSPCA? Some sort of shelter?'

'They'll be closed too.' The dog rests his head on his lap, and Robin looks down into his beseeching brown eyes. 'Maybe I'll keep you tonight,' he mutters. 'What are you doing up?' he directs to Jo.

'Suspected floater in the river. Turned out to be a bag of clothes. On my way home again and I thought I'd say hello.'

'Hello.' Robin smiles.

'Hello.'

There's a pause, and he knows why.

'I'm sorry,' he begins. 'But I've been busy. I haven't had a chance to think.'

'Okay.' Another beat. 'I spoke to Holton again today. She needs to know by Friday.'

'This Friday?'

'Yes.' She stops. He can hear her sigh. 'Is this… is this too much, Rob? Are you trying to tell me something?'

'No, no. I'm not. I like the idea, I do. It's just…' He screws his face up in exasperation. 'Could you say yes and then we see how it goes for a bit? Do the long-distance thing?'

'We're doing the long-distance thing now. Don't you find it annoying? All that driving to and fro. Plus, this would be further. It's… what? Two hours to Exeter?'

'And the rest.'

'And I've done it before with my ex. It didn't end well. I want us to do this together, Robin.'

'Just give me some time. Please. I'll think about it.'

'By Friday?'

'By Friday. I promise.'

They talk for a while longer – their cases, the headlines of their investigations, sharing a moment of connection through the frustrations of the job. Eventually their conversation comes to a natural end and they say their goodbyes.

Robin places his phone down on the desk with a sigh. Next to him, the dog finally settles under his chair, lying down on Robin's feet with a contented groan. Robin doesn't know why he's been putting the decision off. It's like he's waiting. For a sign, for something to happen that will make his mind up one way or the other.

His brain says yes. Moving closer to Finn and Josie. The chance of a promotion. And a future with a woman he really likes. *Likes*. And there it is. The reality.

Neither of them has said the L word. It's been four months, their relationship trotting along nicely. They spend weekends together, the odd weeknight if their schedules align. He enjoys her company; she makes him laugh. Regular sex. Good sex. Getting to know each other. She doesn't mess around, like other women have in the past. He knows exactly what she's thinking about him, and he's tried his hardest to be nothing but honest with her every step of the way. But something... It feels like something's missing.

To distract himself, he turns back to the CCTV. Freya made some good headway before she left. She'd been working on footage from Monday night at Leisure World and had managed to track both Tiller Hamilton and Andrew Grace. It was clear Grace had gone nowhere near the now closed cinema. He'd arrived just after eight and walked straight in the direction of Ikea and the main dual carriageway, where he'd been stopped by Hamilton. Tiller had parked closer to the entrance and the two argued for twenty minutes before Tiller stormed back to his car and left. So there was no way Kurt Cook had seen Tiller attack Andrew that night. He hadn't gone anywhere near the Audi, and had left hours before he was attacked.

He sighs and rubs his eyes. The CCTV blurs. He needs to think about glasses; he's not getting any younger. It's time to call it a night. Someone can phone if they need him.

He stands up; the dog jumps to attention in a nanosecond.

'Come on,' he says. 'Bedtime.'

He takes a quick look into the bin liner – someone's helpfully collated a bed, a few bowls and a heavy bag of dog food – then slings his bag over his shoulder and picks up the dog's stuff, the lead in his other hand. The dog trots happily next to him as he makes his way to the car park.

Maybe this is the sign, he thinks, as he coaxes the dog into the footwell and throws the bag on the back seat. The frustration of playing second fiddle to another DI. Freya happily coupled up with Josh. And Jo asking him to move.

Maybe this *is* the sign he's been looking for.

34

At night, Tiller's custody cell takes on a different life. The lighting changes: an artificial omnipresent yellow. Footsteps echo in the corridors; the pretence of concern as eyes periodically appear at the hatch in his door; shouts and catcalls from the disgruntled other residents.

Sleep is impossible.

He worries about Chloe, the guilt gunning his imagination into overdrive. Her broken body, dead in a ditch. A black fabric bag over her head, bright lights shone in her eyes. Just tell them, he wills her silently. Please.

He should never have involved her. But who else could he have asked? Laura flashes into his head. Andrew's wife, too close to be trusted with this. They've got friendlier again recently, but any chance of a romance between Tiller and Laura faded into hopelessness years ago.

They came near, once. In the early days, pre-Andrew. A drunken night out, alcohol lowering Tiller's inhibitions and social awkwardness. A pub, open late, a band singing over guitars and drums; Laura dancing, laughing, her hair framing her face in sweaty tendrils. Tiller had watched her feeling a mixture of awe and lust, and when she'd come to sit back with them in the busy pub, she'd chosen to sit on his lap.

'Aren't they fantastic?' she'd laughed.

'You're fantastic,' he replied, but his words were lost over the hubbub of the music. She'd taken the pint out of his hand, had a swig, then wobbled.

'I need to go home, Tiller,' she said. 'Will you take me?'

Internally, he'd sighed. Always friend-zoned; women described him as 'safe' and 'reliable'. But then Laura had passed his pint back and said, 'Will you stay?'

He had. And in the morning, lying next to her, he'd felt both excited and overwhelmed at the thought of the potential life with her. Until Andrew met her. Andrew, with his confidence, and height, and broad grin. Tiller saw how Laura responded to him – with a giggle and a hand on his arm.

Tiller was no match for Andrew, so when he was asked by his best friend, 'What's going on between you and Laura?' Tiller could only reply, 'Nothing serious.'

That was it. Laura and Andrew got married; Tiller was best man. Two kids, big house.

And Laura in the hospital.

Was that his fault too?

The people who want his algorithm will stop at nothing, that much is clear. But even given everything that's happened, Tiller knows protecting it was the right thing to do. And soon, nobody will have it.

He hasn't told the whole story to the police. Knowing how valuable the algorithm is, he made sure that without him it wouldn't exist at all. An extra level of protection. A bargaining chip. A last resort.

He wonders what time it is. It must be Wednesday now, and mentally he calculates how long he has left. Two days. Forty-eight hours.

11.59 p.m. on Friday night.

And all of this will have been for nothing.

WEDNESDAY

35

At six o'clock, Robin gives up on sleep.

'Get the fuck off,' he growls again to the dog, who's sitting on the bed next to him. Max ignores him, panting happily, hot doggy breath merely centimetres away from Robin's face.

When they'd first arrived back, Robin had let Max out into the garden, filled the bowls up with food and water, put the bed down in the kitchen and closed the door. He assumed the dog would be fine, but then, as he cleaned his teeth, he heard the noise. A whine at first, escalating to a tortured howl. A noise so full of despair and loneliness it almost punctured his soul. Robin thought that if he ignored it, the dog would get bored and go to sleep.

But no. It hadn't stopped. Thirty minutes turned into an hour, and Robin started to worry about his neighbours. The moment he opened the kitchen door, the dog raced past him, into his bedroom and onto his bed; Robin was too tired to protest. And there it stayed, trying to lie as close to Robin as possible, shoving his cold wet nose into Robin's ear.

Robin assumes he must have dropped off from sheer exhaustion, because at five a.m. he heard a bark, and looked over through his half-closed eyes to the door. The dog was stood there, waiting.

'Fuck,' Robin had cursed and got up in his boxers, shivering, to let the dog into the garden.

And that had been it. In Max's eyes the day had begun.

Robin has a shower and gets dressed, the dog supervising his every move. He pours more food into the dog bowl and eats his own breakfast next to the spaniel. Why do people get dogs? he thinks as he spoons Weetabix into his mouth. If last night was anything to go by, they're nothing but an absolute pain.

Max rides to the police station sat in the front seat of Robin's Volvo, happily looking out of the windscreen. As soon as he gets in, he'll make some calls. Max will go to the pound today; he won't have to worry about him anymore.

Robin parks up and walks into the station, Max receiving admiring glances as he goes. When they get to Robin's desk, he quickly slumps underneath with a grunt. Robin looks at him.

'Don't make yourself too comfortable,' he says.

'Who's this?' Freya appears at his side, then crouches down at Robin's feet. Max jumps up immediately, enthusiastically greeting Freya with licks as she rubs his head. 'Is this Chloe Somerset's dog?'

'Yes,' Robin grumbles. 'He stayed the night with me. Howled the place down.'

'He's gorgeous.' She plonks herself on the floor and the dog curls himself into her lap. She laughs and massages the dog's ears.

'You can have him.'

Freya sits there for a moment longer, her face buried in his fur. Robin regards her with curiosity.

'Are you okay?'

'Mm-hmm,' she replies, but she doesn't look up. 'What's on today?'

'We're seeing Giles Kepner in three hours and still have nothing on him or his company. His record is squeaky clean. Background in the army, but that's all Intel can find. Tiller was right – Parapet Holdings is a shell within a shell, no doubt with accounts in the Caymans and no discernible history.'

'Have we managed to find the van on any other CCTV footage?' Freya looks up for the first time, and he notes she looks like she's been crying.

'Are you sure you're okay?'

'Yes. Fine. Have we?'

'No, but—'

They pause as Josh approaches Robin's desk. Freya's sat out of sight, on the floor with the dog, and as soon as Josh sees her he stops short. The two stare at each other for a second, Josh's mouth open slightly. Robin watches them, confused.

'Josh?' he says at last. 'Can I help you?'

'Yes. Er... Mouse said to come and see you. What do you need looking at this morning? Related to the Somerset abduction?'

It's annoying. DI Ratcliffe should know what's going on, it shouldn't be up to Robin to allocate resources. But Freya and Josh's response to each other is so bizarre, he's too distracted to complain.

'CCTV?' Robin replies. 'If you could look at the footage of the roads around her house?'

'I'll get on it.' And he leaves again, without comment to Freya.

'Frey—?'

'What do you want me to do?' she says.

'Laura Grace has been given the all-clear to interview. Someone needs to go down there.'

'I'll go,' Freya replies quickly.

'I'll come with you,' he starts, but she's already on her feet, grabbing her coat.

'No, you should stay here. You need to find Chloe. Plus,' she adds, as the dog strains on its lead, desperate to go with her, 'you have this one to look after.'

Without another word, she hurries out of the office. But Robin's not the only one watching her go: Josh's eyes also lift, then he gets up quickly and follows.

What's that all about? Robin wonders. But before he can think, DC Lee Davis is standing at his desk.

'Mouse said—'

Robin rolls his eyes. 'ANPR,' he replies, and allocates a task to yet another one of the team.

36

Laura Grace is lying alone, scrunched up in her hospital bed. The nurses told Freya to go ahead, but she pauses before she goes in, composing herself.

Josh hadn't come home last night. Freya had lain awake until the early hours, jumping at every noise, waiting to hear his car return. But he hadn't. Her phone was similarly silent. And in the cold light of the early morning, her dismay turned to anger.

Last Christmas, when Josh first mentioned wanting to know more about Jon, Freya agonised over whether or not to tell him. To share the truth would risk Josh being appalled by her blatant disregard of protocol and procedure – plus the danger that Robin would be brought down in the process. In the end, she'd kept quiet – a decision that Josh accepted.

At the time, in her grief-stricken haze, she'd done the only thing she could: she'd lied so she could stay on the case. Finding Jonathan's killer was more important than anything, and she knows that if she had her time again she would act in exactly the same way. How dare Josh be angry at her? Why should she have told him? This was personal. It was before they had even met, and had no impact on her feelings for him or their future together.

And now the truth is out. She's being ignored and judged – and she doesn't like it.

She arrived at the nick agitated and tired, a feeling only calmed when she sat on the floor and buried her fingers in the spaniel's soft fur. Her parents' dog has the same effect on her. A pampered Cavalier King Charles, Barnaby is often an understanding ear for her problems, either sitting on her lap or a companion on a walk to clear her head.

Just seeing Robin helped too. He had never blamed her for lying – and the events that followed. And his career had been put at risk at the same time.

What right did Josh have?

So when Josh caught up with her in the corridor as she was about to leave, she didn't want to wait.

'Frey, please?' he said. 'Can we talk?'

'Where were you last night?' she snapped.

'I stayed at Adam's. I'm still angry with you, but—'

'But what, Josh? I'm sorry I lied. But everything with Jonathan, everything that happened then. It makes no difference to you and I.'

'It does. If you lied about that, what else have you been lying about?'

And with that Freya walked away. Before she said something else. Before her feelings of disappointment and anger and – something else she can't quite put her finger on – made her say something she'd regret.

–

Freya approaches Laura Grace's bed quietly. She can see she's awake, but she's staring ahead, lost in thought.

'Mrs Grace?' Freya begins. The woman looks at her. 'DC Freya West. From Hampshire Police. I'm here to ask you a few questions.'

Laura Grace smiles gently. There is a painful-looking line of bruises round her eye, now faded to a mottled purple and blue in the days since the attack. A scabbed and stitched cut above. But the psychological scars are invisible, and just beginning to surface. What will it feel like for Laura to go back to that house? Freya wonders. To live there again?

'How is Andrew?' Laura asks. 'The nurses try to keep me updated, but they're busy, I don't like to disturb them.'

'He came out of surgery yesterday. The bone in his leg's been pinned, but he'll have to stay in for a few weeks while it heals.'

'It wasn't Tiller.' She gestures towards the iPad resting on the table. Freya knows that they've managed to keep Chloe's abduction out of the press, but Andrew's attack has been widely reported. 'I read that you'd arrested someone – "a thirty-seven-year-old man, known closely to the victim"? That can only be Tiller, right? But there's no way he attacked Andrew.'

Freya doesn't confirm her assumption, but asks, 'How can you be so sure?'

She shakes her head firmly. 'I know Tiller. No way. Is he okay?' she asks again. 'He won't cope with being locked up. He has…' Freya waits, but she doesn't elaborate further.

'He's being well looked after,' Freya replies. 'Do you mind?' she asks, pointing to the seat next to her bed.

'Please.'

'Could you tell me what happened? On Friday night?'

Laura Grace's face clouds for a second, then she slowly recounts the events of that fateful evening, while Freya takes notes. The ring of the doorbell; the confusion, the terror as the man pushed his way inside. Her worry for the kids, the need to protect them and the impotent rage when she realised she couldn't.

'Had you seen him before?'

'Never. Andrew said you've caught him.'

'Yes. Although we believe he wasn't acting alone.'

'There's someone else involved?' The fear is visible across her face. 'Who?'

'That's what we're trying to find out. Have you any idea?'

Laura stops. She thinks for a moment, then her jaw clenches, her eyes narrow.

'Mrs Grace?' Freya prompts.

'Where was Andy? When he was attacked?'

'Down at Leisure World. Near the old Odeon cinema.' Laura nods slowly. 'Why?'

There's a long pause. Laura chews nervously on her bottom lip; it's already red raw.

Then, 'Check our bank account,' she says. 'HSBC.'

'Mrs Grace?'

'Just do it. I haven't logged on for years. I manage all our finances from a different account, but this one...' She meets Freya's eye. 'I can give you access, can't I? It's a joint account. My name is on it too.'

'Yes, I'll get the forms sent across. You can sign them now. But why?'

'I don't want to be the one to tell you. Unlike Andrew, I keep my promises, but this has gone on too long. Have a look,' she says, finally. 'And you'll see.'

Freya nods and moves away from Laura's bedside to make the necessary arrangements. She'll get the forms signed, she'll call HSBC and get their bank records.

And as she does so, she wonders. What secrets is Andrew Grace hiding? What are they going to find?

37

If Giles Kepner had joined a line-up of similarly dressed, fifty-year-old men, Robin would have been able to pick him out as ex-army in a second.

He sits in the interview room, ramrod straight. His shoes are polished to a sheen, his checked shirt done up to the top, his tie in a plump Windsor. Double-breasted jacket in dark green tweed. His arms are crossed, and he regards Robin with a look of barely disguised superiority.

'Thank you for coming in today,' Robin begins, feigning a civility he doesn't feel.

'My pleasure.' Kepner shifts his gaze to Freya and gives her a leer. Freya forces a smile.

Freya had returned from the hospital interview with Laura a bustle of determination, passing the forms to Mina to process with the bank, and following Robin quickly into the interview. They haven't had the chance to exchange more than a few words, but Robin is as curious as she is to know what those bank records have in store.

But for now, it's Giles Kepner. Robin reads out the preliminary warnings of a voluntary interview; Kepner declines any need for legal advice.

'What do I need a solicitor for? This is a friendly chat, right?' His voice is private-school-educated polished steel.

'A request for information,' Robin confirms. 'Unless you want to make a confession?'

Kepner gives him a sarcastic smile. 'Fire away, DS Butler. Let's hear what's on your mind.'

'Could you start by telling us about your meeting on Saturday with Andrew Grace?' Robin begins.

'That's commercially sensitive information.'

'You're looking to buy the company?'

Kepner tilts his head to one side, appraising him. 'Yes. But as you also probably know, the sale has now been rejected.'

'How did you take that, Mr Kepner? You don't strike me as the sort of person who is used to being told no.'

'We tried to negotiate, of course. But Mr Hamilton had made his mind up.'

'And who is "we"?'

'My business partners and I.' Kepner smirks. 'And how is Mr Hamilton adapting to life in jail?'

Robin notes his tone, but ignores it. 'How do you know about Mr Hamilton's circumstances?'

'The news. It's not hard to work out.'

'Can you account for your whereabouts on Monday night?'

'This Monday? I was at home with my wife.'

'And Tuesday? At about fifteen hundred hours?'

'At work. My office.' He names a well-known building in the centre of town. 'As many people and a fair few cameras would be able to confirm.'

'What did Parapet Holdings plan to do with Hamilton Grace Software?'

'That's commercially sensitive.'

'Were you going to sell their technology on?'

Kepner doesn't answer, but tips his head to one side, patron-isingly.

'Do you work for the British government?' Robin continues. 'Or any other government?'

'That information is way over your security clearance, DS Butler.'

'Will you give us permission to access your mobile phone records?'

'No.'

'Will you give us permission to access your bank records?'

'No. What am I being accused of here?'

Robin smiles sweetly. 'Nothing. As you say, a friendly chat. Do you know a woman called Chloe Somerset?'

'No. Should I?'

'She's gone missing.'

'That's unfortunate.' The smirk again. 'But I know nothing about that.'

'So you haven't seen her?'

'I'd never even heard of her before today.'

'Are you sure? Because she used to be the FD at Hamilton Grace Software. You would have seen her name on the company accounts.'

His smile wavers for a moment. 'My money man deals with that side of things,' he recovers smoothly. 'I'm more about strategy. Business development. Top-line information. I don't read *company accounts*,' he adds with disdain.

'When were you in the army, Mr Kepner?'

'From 1986 until 2012. I was a colonel when I left in my mid-forties.'

'And what did you leave to do?'

'Set up Parapet Holdings.'

'But Parapet Holdings wasn't incorporated as a company until 2021. You must have done something before then?'

Kepner pauses. His left eye twitches. 'Get to the point, DS Butler. What exactly do you think I've done?'

Robin stays silent. He wants to stand up, grab this guy by the throat and pin him against the tired magnolia walls of the interview room. He wants to accuse him of paying Durand to break into the Grace household. Of beating up Andrew Grace. Kidnapping Chloe Somerset. But no, he tells himself as he gets his temper under control, nothing will be gained from showing his hand.

Instead, he turns to Kepner with a sarcastic smile, 'Just information gathering. As you said at the beginning. No more than a friendly chat.'

38

The dog is passed from detective to detective, amid squeals of laughter as the little spaniel licks faces and demands love. Robin still hasn't phoned the pound; every time he goes to look up the number he feels a twinge of guilt. Max clearly loves company; he'd be unhappy by himself in a cage. And besides, while the focus is always on finding Chloe Somerset, Robin knows a bit of levity can help maintain motivation at times like this.

The incident room is abuzz. A new whiteboard has been acquired and DI Ratcliffe's small, neat capitals direct the team's attention.

But they haven't found anything to help. Her mobile phone is still off; no contact with family or friends. There have been no demands for a ransom; no body parts pushed through a letter box. The CCTV is coming up a blank: all the cameras round Chloe's house are inundated with traffic, too many white vans to narrow down. Without a plate, it's hard to focus.

Freya disappears down to custody with the dog. The clock on Tiller Hamilton has run out; they need to release him without charge. Robin had argued for requesting an extension, but Baker had been clear.

'We provide protection through the proper routes, Butler,' he'd said. 'Rather than making up spurious reasons and blocking up custody.'

Robin had to acquiesce. Plus, Tiller agreed to take the dog, and Robin had no desire to spend another night with the bloody spaniel.

Freya volunteered to drive Hamilton home. An unnecessary trip, and something that makes Robin wonder if she's avoiding him. Or – with a quick glance towards where Josh is working – maybe someone else.

He hasn't got time to worry. Robin has faith in his theory that the attacks on Andrew and Laura are connected. That something thrown up from those investigations will give them a lead.

The forensics team have come back on the Audi. The blood on the car definitely belongs to Grace, but no other biologicals have been found. No fingerprints, nothing to show who else was there that night. And then there's this – the telemetrics from the car's tracking system. Robin scans the data quickly. Trips to the Hamilton Grace office, a few to the local Tesco, and the one to Leisure World on Monday night. But there are more. Journeys to that same car park, almost two or three times a week. Robin frowns, runs a highlighter across the lines, then pushes it to one side as his computer announces a new email.

HSBC have responded quickly following the request for access to the Graces' joint bank account, especially when Robin had pointed out the gravity of the situation. Three years' worth of statements are here, and Robin prints them out, tired of squinting at the screen.

Long lines of numbers. Credits and debits. Payments to credit cards that make Robin's eyes water – at one point an amount is paid to a Capital One credit card equivalent to a year's worth of Robin's mortgage. He can't comprehend having this much cash to throw around.

And there is money going in. A regular salary from Hamilton Grace on the first of every month, equating to well over a hundred grand a year. A few one-off payments of tens of thousands – dividend payments, maybe. But everything stops nearly a year ago.

The salary disappears, and so do the bonuses. There are no more debits from Tesco or Costa Coffee or John Lewis – none of the regular outgoings you expect to see from a family of four. Now only random amounts remain. Cash paid in – varying amounts, from fifty quid to a few thousand. And payments going out. Always different values, seemingly haphazard in frequency.

Robin looks at the names on the transactions, and then the dates. He recognises a few, but others – the ones that fall mainly on a Friday or a Saturday night – all have the same description. HW Properties Ltd.

Robin turns to his computer and types the name into Google. And everything becomes clear.

39

Andrew's starting to feel better. Slowly but surely, the physical wounds are mending, scabs forming, bones knitting together. Breathing isn't as painful as it was.

But the guilt. The stomach-wrenching, mind-numbing guilt – that stays.

He sees the detective arrive. That same old black coat, the shoes that have seen better days. As Andrew watches, he refastens the top button of his shirt and pulls the tie up. He talks to the nurse for a moment, then he looks down the ward towards Andrew.

He walks slowly, taking his time. His head is bent to the floor; he looks like he's thinking. Why is he here? Surely Andrew was clear on Monday night? He was telling the truth when he said he didn't know who hit him. The blows came thick and fast, he hadn't had time to turn around.

But he could make an educated guess.

The detective stops. He pulls the curtain round the bed.

'How are you feeling, Andrew?' he asks.

'Like I've been hit by a truck. Or an iron bar.'

Butler takes a seat next to him. 'I thought you didn't know what hit you?'

'I don't. It's a joke.' He smiles, but the attempt is painful as scabs stretch and crack.

'I won't keep you long. I have a few follow-up questions, if you don't mind.'

'Of course.'

The detective doesn't hang around. 'Are you aware that Chloe Somerset has gone missing?'

'Missing? Is she?' No, he wasn't bloody aware. How could he be. He's been stuck in here.

'She was abducted yesterday. Her house trashed. Tiller tells us he thinks whoever took her was looking for the encryption key to access the algorithm.'

Andrew shakes his head slowly. They know about the key. What else has Tiller told them? 'Chloe doesn't have that.'

'Tiller says she does. He locked it with a thumbprint from him, then an eleven-digit key she inputted.'

'Shit,' Andrew whispers. He looks at the detective. 'I didn't know.'

'You did know what Tiller had developed though, right? And you wanted to sell it?'

'Yes, but… as part of the company. In a normal business deal.' Andrew's confused. 'They wouldn't abduct Chloe. Not over that.'

'Who?'

Andrew's too tired to lie. Besides, the police probably already know. 'Parapet Holdings,' he says. 'They've offered us millions. It will change our lives.'

'Particularly yours. Isn't that correct, Andrew?'

Butler rustles in his bag and pulls out a few sheets of paper, a recognisable logo on the top. Andrew can barely look at them as they're put in front of him.

'This is your bank statement, Andrew.'

'How did you get this? Don't you need a warrant?'

'Your wife gave us access.'

'Laura… she…' He's speechless.

Butler points at a line on the sheet. 'Here, here and here. Almost every few lines, we have payments out and money in from a company called HW Properties Ltd. I looked them up. Could you tell me who they are?'

Andrew shakes his head, but of course he knows.

'They run a chain of casinos across the UK. But particularly one situated next to the Odeon cinema in Southampton. Outside which you were captured on CCTV arguing with Tiller Hamilton. Near where you were attacked.'

'There's nothing illegal about going to a casino.'

'No. But it says a lot about your current state of mind. You're in huge amounts of debt, aren't you?'

He nods. 'Yes,' he admits, his voice breaking.

At first it was the odd quid here and there. At university, it was a fun place to go after a night out. Spank a few quid on blackjack, have a drink, then go home. Better than a dirty kebab or getting into a fight.

But then he won. To a poor student, two grand was a king's ransom. The rush. The euphoria of victory, the shouts of jubilation from his mates. So he went back the next night. And the next. He didn't win like that again. In that first week of gambling he blew his entire student loan.

He knew he could win it back, so he went into his overdraft. Credit cards, a tenner here and there from friends – chasing his losses. He was one big win away from being sorted, he told them.

In those days it was just the casino. As long as he stayed away, as long as he didn't drink, he was fine. He'd seen the old men at the betting shops and felt pity for them, watching as they fed pound coin after pound coin into the slot machines, losing every penny. He would never be that desperate. That beaten. So what if he bought a few scratch cards? So what if he lost a few mates? It wasn't a problem; it was just a bit of fun. Fuck them if they took offence when he forgot to pay them back. Again.

But then came the apps. The smartphone games, the free bets, the online bingo. The flashing lights and the bright colours and the screaming congratulations telling him he'd won, even when he knew he'd just lost another hundred quid.

He would stay up all night, losing thousands at the click of a button. He came in tired to client meetings, where all he could think about was getting these people out of his office so he could open his phone and have another go. Win back what he'd lost.

But he never did.

Laura told him to stop, like it was that easy. With Tiller's help, she downloaded software that blocked gambling sites; she sent him to Gamblers Anonymous. Another bunch of losers, these people weren't the same as him. He had it under control. But still the envelopes came through the door. The bank, asking for money. The payday loans wanting repayment.

He tried to remortgage the house, and that was her final straw. Laura left him, taking the kids, but he drove to her mother's to find them, begging. He agreed to transfer his salary into an account just in her name. He pleaded to keep his smartphone; Tiller made sure he was barred from the apps. Tiller paid off all his credit cards – the shame of that. That Tiller, who could barely communicate if it wasn't via his computer in C#, had come to his aid.

But by then, it was impossible to ignore. Adverts were everywhere – on the shirts of the footballers, on the television. Ladbrokes, Coral, William Hill. Emails, tempting him back. So he'd go for a walk. To the bookies, the very place he'd scorned at the beginning. Lose a hundred on the horses, then walk back, his head down. Defeated.

He is controlled by his addiction. Beaten. With every bet, every pound lost, he feels like he is destroying himself, but there is nothing he can do to stop. He finds no pleasure in other things. It talks to him. A tumour in his brain that can never be removed.

'Was that what you were arguing about?' Butler asks. 'With Tiller? On Monday night?'

Andrew nods miserably. 'He wanted to talk, to make things better between us. But he tracks my phone. He guessed I was going to the casino. He tried to stop me.'

'How much do you owe?'

Andrew shakes his head. 'I don't know.' He sees Butler's disbelief. 'I don't. I don't dare look. That's the horror of it.'

'And you need the money from the sale of the company.' The detective pauses. Andrew feels him studying his injuries. 'You borrowed money from the wrong people, didn't you,' he says quietly.

'Yes,' Andrew whispers. 'I'd started taking money out of Hamilton Grace. But Chloe noticed and said she'd report me for fraud. And then what? Hamilton Grace is all I have.'

He didn't want to go to prison, but where could he get it from? His credit score was ruined; no loan company would go near him. He needed it, and he needed it fast.

He starts crying now. He had warnings. Burly men appearing out of nowhere, threatening him. With a broken nose, broken legs – the injuries he has now. The time before, they broke his fingers; just grabbed his hand and pulled. He heard the sickening crunch; he felt the acid rise in his stomach as he looked at his destroyed hand. Fell over, he explained to the doctors in the ED, to Laura and Tiller. And they all believed him. But what else could he say?

That's how it wins – the gambling. The silence and the secrecy isolate you. The shame renders you mute.

He is alone.

'Where's Chloe?' Butler asks.

'I don't know.'

'What happened to your wife?'

'That has nothing to do with this.'

'How can you be so sure, Andrew?' the detective asks.

But he just shakes his head. Everything he has worked so hard to build is falling around his ears. His marriage, his best friend. Soon, even his company will be at risk. And there's nothing he can do to change it.

40

Tiller is silent for the whole journey from the police station to his house. The dog sits happily in his lap in the front seat; Freya watches his hands methodically working the dog's fur, seeking comfort.

They've released him without charge, no further action. He'd emerged from the cell, tired and emotional, and the first question he'd asked was, 'Have you got any news about Chloe?'

Freya sadly shook her head. The dog pulled on the lead, anxious to get to Tiller, almost choking himself in the process. Tiller bent down to say hello, his face drawn.

'Are you happy with me taking Max?'

'Oh, yes. My sergeant had him last night and he howled the place down.'

'He is a bit highly strung. But that's spaniels for you.'

'We still need to set up protection—'

'No,' Tiller interrupted.

'But Tiller—'

'No. I don't want anyone in my space. I can't have anyone in my space.'

His tone was steady and certain. Freya accepted his decision, knowing he'd been through hell in the last twenty-four hours and the last thing he must have wanted was more cops.

They walked together to the pool car, Tiller reticent as she turned the ignition and drove.

'Tiller?' she asks eventually. 'Are you okay?'

He nods, his eyes set on the road in front of them. The dead air yawns. Freya's never been one comfortable with silence, so she fills the space, telling him about her parents' spaniel, the whole story from puppyhood to now. He doesn't say a word. Not even a polite smile.

The dog pokes his head up the moment they pull into the driveway of Hamilton Grace and the old manor house comes into view. In the sunshine of the spring day, the rustic brass letter box shining in the bright blue front door, it looks beautiful.

'I can see why you like it here,' she says.

Tiller just nods, then opens the car door. The dog jumps out and starts doing frenetic laps on the grass, legs a blur. Outside the only noise they can hear is birdsong, and the quiet rustle of the wind in the trees.

'Will you need to include the manor house?' Freya asks from the driver's seat. 'If the company is sold?'

He pauses for a moment, looking towards the house, one foot out of the car. On the lawn, the spaniel has paused, panting, looking expectantly at his new owner.

'I guess so,' Tiller replies. 'It's counted as an asset.'

'But it's your home.'

He shrugs, dispassionately. 'Then I'll need to find somewhere else to live.' He picks up the bag of the dog's belongings and gets out of the car. 'Thank you for the lift,' he finishes.

She watches him trudge towards the huge front door, put a key in the lock and push it open. He shouts towards the dog; it charges inside. The door closes, and he is gone.

She goes to start the engine again, but Robin calls. She answers it.

'Tiller home?' he asks. She hears a buzz of conversation in the background, an echo of an empty corridor.

'Safe and sound,' she replies. 'Plus dog.'

'Thank fuck for that,' he mutters, and she laughs.

'Where are you?' she asks. It's odd for Freya to be working and not be with Robin, and she feels a fresh pang of despondency at his possible departure.

'The hospital.'

He fills her in on Andrew's confession: the secrets revealed in the bank statements and the telemetry from the car.

'There's no law against gambling,' Freya says, once he's finished. 'He's done nothing wrong.'

'Except withhold information from us. And I'm sure he still is.' Robin sighs at the other end of the phone. 'I'm heading back to the nick now. See you there?'

Freya agrees and hangs up. But something niggles.

She looks up at the big old house. Behind the empty windows, she notices lights turn on, Tiller returning to normal life, whatever that is for him. She feels a pang of sympathy for the guy, combined with worry. There are so many unknowns; so much unsolved.

If Andrew's injuries were all inflicted at the hands of some thuggish loan shark, what of the witness statement?

It's plausible that Kurt Cook had seen Tiller's car – they know he had been there, even though he parked at the other end of the car park hours before Cook claimed to have arrived. But the man beating Andrew up was unlikely to be short and slim – the description given that perfectly matched Tiller.

Freya sits back in the loan car, then picks up her mobile and calls Mina.

'Come back, please,' Mina says straight away. 'I need help with all this bloody CCTV.'

'I will,' Freya laughs. 'I just need to follow something up first. Can you do a search for me on the PNC?'

'Sure. Fire away.'

'Kurt Cook. Southampton address.'

'Kurt with a U? Cook – no E?'

'Yep.' She hears tapping at the other end. 'You could have got Control to do this,' Mina notes.

'But then I wouldn't get to talk to you,' she replies. After her argument with Josh she wants to speak to a friend. Ideally, she'd have sat down with a coffee and told her best mate all about it – the parts she could, at least – but now wasn't the time. Just hearing her voice has to do.

'No trace,' Mina replies at last.

Freya frowns. 'Try Kurt with a C? Cooke with an E?'

'Already have. There's nothing here. A guy who lives in Basingstoke, but that's not right, surely? He's IC3.'

'No. My guy is definitely white.'

'You could try Intel? They might be able to find something else?'

Freya thanks Mina and hangs up. She weighs her car keys in her hand, then picks up her bag and digs out the paperwork. *Kurt Cook*, it says, then his signature. She looks at the address. It's not unusual that someone wouldn't be on the system, but why go to all that effort to incriminate a man? To get him arrested?

She puts the keys in the ignition and starts the engine. Time to find out.

41

The address Kurt Cook has given is a tall, ugly tower block in Southwood. She knows it well: site of many a call-out in her PC days. Fights, dealing, domestic abuse. Grey pebble-dashed concrete, rusted iron railings.

Freya walks across broken paving stones to the double doors at the bottom of the block. There are no security measures here. No CCTV, no entry buzzer, nothing to stop anyone just walking in. She pulls the doors open and slowly goes inside. It smells of urine and neglect; inner-city multistorey car parks. Graffiti tags scrawl the walls. There's a lift, but she doesn't trust it so she chooses the stairs, walking quickly up, pulling her coat tightly around her. She has no place being here – and being here alone. On the drive over her phone had rung but she'd ignored it; now she wishes she'd answered and brought Robin with her. She pauses. She should call him, but he needs to be back at the nick, directing the search for Chloe. She'll just have one conversation and leave.

As she climbs, she feels her anger growing. She'd believed Cook, she'd even felt sorry for him, and as a result they'd wasted precious hours arresting Hamilton. She reaches the third floor, out of breath, her heart beating hard, and pulls the door open at the top. They reveal a narrow balcony, iron railings on one side, doors on the other. She counts along, looking for number thirty-seven, then stops. She can hear the *thump thump* of a bassline coming from a neighbour; shouting; a baby crying. But nothing from the door in front of her.

She knocks. Hard. Three times. She waits. She knocks again. This time she hears shuffling footsteps, and the rattle of a security chain. The door opens a fraction, and a wrinkled face pokes out.

'Yes?'

'Does Kurt Cook live here?'

'Who?' The eye narrows. 'Who are you looking for?'

'Kurt Cook? Maybe your son, grandson?'

The wizened mouth puckers. 'Who's asking?'

Freya takes her warrant card out of her pocket. 'DC Freya West. Hampshire Police. I need to speak to him.'

'Don't need no police here,' and the door starts to close.

'No, he's... he's not in trouble.' The door pauses, and the eye pokes through again. 'He's about five-ten, skinny, blond hair. Red birthmark on the left-hand side of his face.'

The old woman stares at her for a moment.

'A young 'un?' she asks.

'Mid-twenties?'

'Number fifty-three,' she replies. Her eye looks skyward for a moment. 'Fifth floor. And don't say I told you.'

The door closes, and Freya frowns. A false address? The bad feeling about Kurt Cook grows.

Freya turns, about to go back the way she came, when a man in low-slung baggy jeans and a puffer jacket appears. He stands in the middle of the walkway, blocking her exit.

'You police?' he says. He has a cigarette in his hand. He takes a last puff then flicks it over the balcony into the darkening sky.

'Can I help you?' Freya says, with more confidence than she feels. She touches her phone in her pocket; her car keys find their way between her fingers.

'Me?' He grins, showing a missing tooth. 'Nah.'

He takes a step towards her. She doesn't move. She debates her options. She could brazen it out, hoping he's more bark than bite. She could knock on the old woman's door, get somewhere safe while she calls for assistance. She glances back over her shoulder. Can she run?

'Nuffin' back there,' the man says. 'This your only way out.'

Freya takes a step towards him. 'My colleagues are a floor down. Let me through.'

'Nah. They ain't. I been watching you.'

She feels adrenaline flow. Shit. *Shit.* She shouldn't have come here alone. How could she have been so *stupid.* She's three floors up. A cop in a bad neighbourhood.

The man walks towards her. Freya doesn't move. She fingers the metal of her keys, wishes she had her CS spray or baton. Something with a bit more kick. She could go for his face. Try to get some ground back.

'What you doin' here? A pretty girl like you?'

He's so close now she can smell him. The sickly-sweet scent of a methadone user, teeth rotted to stubs in his mouth.

'Let me through,' she repeats. But she can't stop the quaver in her voice.

'What you gonna do if I don't?'

'Get out of her way. Now.' The voice is loud and assertive. It echoes off the walls, down, out into the courtyard. The man jumps as if hit and looks behind him. A man comes charging through. Six foot, perpetual frown; Freya couldn't be more pleased to see him.

Robin repeats the words, his face like thunder. 'Get out of her fucking way or I will throw your useless pile of bones off this balcony.'

'Okay, okay, guvnor,' the man says. He raises his hands above his head in surrender then takes two steps so his back is against the wall. Freya quickly scrabbles along to Robin, who roughly pushes her behind him.

'Now fuck off,' he growls. 'Before I do something you'll regret.'

The man scuttles away. A door slams, and he's gone.

'Robin, I—'

'What were you thinking?' Robin snaps. She's never seen him look like this before. Angry, upset, but something else too. Fear. 'Coming here alone?'

'I didn't… How did you know I was here?'

He points to his phone in his hand. 'Find my iPhone. We knew it would come in handy one day.' He takes a long breath in, looking up to the inky sky. 'Shit, Freya. Why didn't you answer your phone? I would have come with you.'

'I thought you were busy.' Freya feels stupid now. Police don't come single-crewed to areas like this for a reason.

'Never too busy for you.' His face softens. 'Mina called me, she was worried. She said you're looking for Kurt Cook?'

'Yeah. He must have made it up. I was…' She shrugs. It sounds silly now, that this is the line of enquiry she chose when Chloe is still missing. 'I was pissed off,' she finishes.

Robin nods, accepting her explanation. 'We're here now. Let's find out. This the address he gave?'

'He's not here. It's false. But the woman who lives there recognised him. Number fifty-three.'

'So he was smart enough to give a false address, but not with enough imagination to think hard.' Robin smiles. 'Come on then.'

–

They head up two more flights of stairs, the wind whistling through the concrete stairwell as they go. Freya feels more confident with Robin at her back, hearing his steady trudge behind her.

She pushes the door open at the top, and a gust whips through the doorway, nearly pulling it out of her hand. She holds it open for Robin and it slams shut behind them.

Again, down the open balcony. Two more floors up – and Freya feels vertiginous. She notices Robin shuffling and glances behind her; he's walking close to the wall, as far away from the drop as he can get. She smiles knowingly.

He catches her look and frowns. 'Shall we get on with it?' he mutters.

Freya knocks on the door. It opens a fraction; a face is revealed before he swears and tries to close it again. Robin jams a shoe in the gap, then opens the door into a dark narrow hallway. Kurt takes a step back, his face pale.

'Fuck,' he says again.

'Fuck, indeed,' Robin replies. He glances to Freya. 'Would you like to do the honours?'

Freya smiles, and Robin passes her a set of handcuffs. 'Kurt Cook, if that is your real name, I am arresting you for wasting police time. You do not have to say anything, but it may harm your defence if you do not mention when questioned something which you later rely on in court. Anything you do say may be given in evidence. Do you understand?'

Kurt nods, his hands now behind his back. She fastens the cuffs round his wrists.

'Now, if you'd like to accompany us down the station, you have a lot of explaining to do.'

42

A patrol car brings him in. They drive in convoy: Freya in the pool car behind, Robin bringing up the rear in his Volvo. When Mina had mentioned Freya's call he knew he had to go after her; now he thanks his lucky stars he did.

'He cried the whole way back,' the PC complains after 'Kurt' is booked into custody. 'I don't like the ones I feel sorry for.'

He gives his real name as Ricky Hall and asks for a lawyer; they wait for a duty solicitor to arrive.

'So Andrew Grace is up to his ears in debt,' Freya says as they wait.

'Looks that way. And he's got himself in with some pretty shady people. He needs the money from the sale to keep himself above water.'

'Do you think the attack on Laura is related?'

Robin frowns. 'Maybe, but it's hard to see how. If Durand was there on behalf of the loan sharks, why didn't he take anything of higher value? It seems to me it's more likely he was after the encryption key and the same people that paid him are behind Chloe's abduction.'

Freya looks back to the room where the duty solicitor is currently talking with Kurt-slash-Ricky. 'And you think this guy's going to shed some light?'

'We can but hope. Listen, Freya—'

'I'm sorry about going there alone,' she interrupts, holding her hands up quickly. 'It won't happen again.'

'It's not about that. I mean, yes, don't do that again. But I was going to ask if you're okay. Things seem… weird. Between you and Josh.'

She glances around. They're surrounded by cops. 'Now's not the time,' she says, and he gets an inkling of what's going on.

'Detectives?' the solicitor shouts.

They go in. Robin starts the tape; he nods to Freya to begin. He feels the burn of anger and annoyance, that their time has been wasted in this way, and knows she's feeling the same.

'Ricky,' she begins. 'Were you at Leisure World on Monday night?'

Robin enjoys being able to sit back and let Freya lead, safe in the knowledge she knows exactly what she's doing.

Ricky glances to his lawyer, then sniffs wetly. 'No.'

'Did you see the attack on Andrew Grace?'

'No.'

'Have you ever met a man called Tiller Hamilton?'

He sniffs again, but not before a drop of snot lands on the table. 'No,' he admits.

'So why on earth,' Freya says, somewhat exasperatedly, 'did you say that you were there?'

Another glance to the lawyer. 'No comment.'

'Ricky, do you know the name Chloe Somerset?'

His eyebrows knit together in confusion. 'No.'

'She's missing, and we believe it's connected.'

His head jerks up. 'What do you mean?'

'She's been abducted. We're concerned for her safety. And we think you might know something about it.'

'I don't know nothing,' Ricky says quickly.

'Why should we believe you? From where we're sitting, you put in a spurious witness statement about two men that are connected to her, and then she goes missing. You're saying the two aren't related?'

'I haven't hurt no one.'

'Then tell us why you gave us that statement.'

He leans over and whispers to his solicitor. The lawyer mumbles something back.

'What will you do for me, if I tell you what I know?' Ricky says.

Freya sighs. 'We won't arrest you for kidnap or breaking and entering. Worse, if she doesn't show up soon.'

He stutters nervously, then starts crying again. Robin has to use all his strength not to roll his eyes at Freya.

'I met this bloke, down the pub,' he begins. 'Monday night, just before closing.'

'What bloke?' Freya asks.

'I dunno his name. Tall. Smart, like. Asked if I wanted to earn some money. And all I had to do was go to the police. Mention this bloke that had been beaten up.'

'Andrew Grace.'

'Yeah. He gave me details about it. The time and the place. The beginning of a number plate. Said I had to describe the guy hitting him just right. Said I could even use a false name and address so if the police did get suspicious, they wouldn't be able to find me. Except you did.'

'It wasn't exactly rocket science,' Robin mutters. Freya gives a small smile but keeps her focus on Ricky.

'Did he say why?'

'Nah.'

'And you didn't ask?'

'He gave me three hundred quid! You don't ask questions when some bloke offers you that much cash and doesn't want something kinky in return. I'm not going to go to prison, am I? I swear I know nuffin' about this girl. They didn't say nuffin' about a girl. Oh fuck…' His voice trails off with a fresh onslaught of tears.

'Give us a full description of this bloke,' Robin says. 'Help us produce an E-FIT so we can get a picture of what he looks like, and we'll see what we can do. If you're lucky, you might just get away with a night in the cells and a bit of community service.'

'Yeah. Anything. Please.'
His eyes look up, beseeching and desperate.
'Tell us everything you know.'

43

Back upstairs, the team are going full tilt. Robin greets DI Ratcliffe, who's plotting a timeline of Chloe's disappearance on the whiteboard.

'You're back – good,' the DI says. 'Perhaps you could shed some light on why this encryption key is so bloody important.'

Robin explains what he knows – that those eleven digits unlock an algorithm, and without that algorithm the whole company is worthless.

'And she didn't tell Hamilton what it was?'

'No. He says he didn't want to be tempted.'

'Instead, he put his girlfriend at risk. What a gentleman.'

'You haven't come up with any other explanation for her disappearance?'

'No, nothing. We've been interviewing her friends, old workmates. Family. Nobody's seen her. Still nothing from her credit cards or phone. Hospitals have come up a blank. We have every uniform searching a parameter, but nothing.'

'CCTV?'

'Nah. There are no good cameras near where she lives. We're checking the plates for all traffic on the ones nearby, but there's a lot. It's going to take weeks.'

'Time we don't have,' Robin says grimly.

'Exactly.' The DI crosses his arms and stares at the board. 'What would you do?' he asks. 'If this was your case?'

It bloody well *was* my case, Robin thinks. And once again the prospect of that DI promotion in Devon pops into his head. He pushes it away.

'There are two theories,' Robin begins. 'One, that Chloe has been taken because of this encryption key. By people who know what they're doing. They know about police methods – about cameras, and ANPR, and forensics – so my guess is they're smart enough to avoid it all.'

'Great,' Mouse says sarcastically. 'And the other?'

'That the NCA are right, and she's a misper who's gone into hiding.'

'So what do we do? Which angle do we go with?'

Robin frowns. 'Fucked if I know.'

The DI laughs. 'You look a state, mate. Take yourself home, get some sleep. And call me if you think of anything. We've got detectives working round the clock. I'll swap out West, Smith and Desai, get the next lot on it overnight.'

Robin goes to protest, then feels a ripple of tiredness. 'Yeah, that would be good. Thanks, boss.'

He heads over; as always Freya is sat at the desk next to his. She has Andrew Grace's bank statement open on the screen.

'Leave that for now,' Robin says. He slumps down in his seat, shoving a few belongings in his bag. 'Mouse says you can head off.'

She doesn't look away from the screen. 'It's just… these withdrawals.' She points to a few lines. 'What does that say to you?'

'He was taking cash out to gamble? I don't know, Frey. Addicts will do anything to feed their compulsion.'

'Yeah, I suppose.' She frowns. 'Don't you think there's something odd about the kidnapping?'

He leans forward, interested. 'Like what?'

'See here? The search. It's messy, like someone went round at speed.' She pulls the crime scene photos from Chloe's house up on her screen. 'They made a lot of noise, attracted a lot of attention.'

'Okay. And?'

'And the fact they did it in broad daylight. Smashed a window. Brought a massive white van. If you were ex-military,

193

if you'd been trained in covert operations, as they probably had, is this the way you'd do it?'

Robin looks at the screen. She has a point. 'You'd go at night. In and out. Pick the locks, silent. So what are you thinking?'

She sighs then pushes back on her chair, running her fingers through her hair. 'Fuck knows,' she replies, and he laughs, hearing the echo from his own comment just minutes earlier. 'Sorry,' she says with a smile. 'I didn't get much sleep last night.'

'Frey? Is everything okay?'

'Yeah.' She glances towards the other detectives, then back to him. 'It's Josh. He found a photograph. Of Jonathan.'

'Shit. He guessed?'

'Yes. And he knows you knew. But nothing else, don't worry.'

'I'm not worried about me,' Robin replies, and he realises that that's the truth. He's more concerned about Freya. 'What did he say?'

'He wasn't happy. He's pissed I lied about it. That I didn't trust him. He stayed at his mate's house last night.'

'And…?' Robin's tentative. 'How are you?'

'I don't know. I was upset at first. But now? Now I can't be arsed. I don't have the energy for this shit. Not today. Not while Chloe's missing.' She pushes her fingers into her eyes and sighs. 'I should try to get some sleep.'

'Do you want to come back to mine?'

She stares at him for a moment, a questioning look on her face.

'I just mean… watch some TV, get a takeaway. That chilli beef you like from the Chinese?' He feels hot for a moment, embarrassed at how she might interpret his offer.

'That's okay. I'll wait until Ricky is done with his E-FIT downstairs, then head home.' She smiles. 'Thank you.'

'Any time.'

'And for rescuing me earlier.'

He laughs. 'I was shitting myself. I wasn't in the mood for a fight.'

'You couldn't tell.' She turns back to the screen. 'See you tomorrow, Robin.'

He murmurs a goodbye and heads quickly away. He feels that same flush, ridiculous when the conversation is the same as one that has happened a million times before. But this time it felt charged. Like something different passed between them.

I need some sleep, he mutters as he heads back to his car. Just some fucking sleep.

44

Josh watches the exchange between Robin and Freya from the other side of the office. He'd been in the kitchen, making coffees for the team, and when he'd come out they'd been there. Talking, but Robin is leaning into Freya and their heads are close, almost touching.

He feels a rush of jealousy. They're always like that, always have been. He watches as they converse, smile, then Robin puts his jacket on and heads off.

He carries his coffees over to his bank of desks and sits next to one of his colleagues.

'I've been doing this for two hours,' DC Davis complains, taking the coffee with a grunt. 'And not a single plate has come up with anything interesting. Just a few unpaid parking tickets. Not one red flag.'

'Lee?' Josh begins.

'Yeah?'

'DS Butler. And Freya. Before I started, was there anything going on? Between them?'

Davis pulls a face and glances over at Freya. 'Butler?' he scoffs. 'Before they started working together they barely knew each other. So, nah.' He studies Josh's face. 'And you have to be kidding. Top-class woman like Freya? No offence, mate,' he adds quickly. 'But Butler? I mean, he's been better lately, but for the few years before you came along he was an absolute mess. Once he even turned up with a broken arm and collarbone. Bust his ribs up too. Had fallen down the stairs blind drunk.

And,' he lowers his voice to a whisper. 'He even spent time in the Priory.'

'What? The local nut house?'

'Yeah. If the rumours are to be believed. So, no. There's never been anything going on. Why would you worry? You two are solid, right?'

'Yeah, yeah,' Josh says quickly. 'Solid.'

He picks up his coffee, but as he does so he notices Freya stand up and put her coat on. She doesn't even look in his direction as she grabs her bag and heads towards the door. He runs quickly to catch up.

'Freya! Frey.' She stops in the corridor, waiting. 'Are you going home?'

'Yeah. Robin said I could.' She indicates her laptop slung over her shoulder. 'Although I'll probably do some work for a few hours.'

'I won't be far behind you. And we can talk.'

'What about?'

Her bluntness surprises him. 'The photo. And... you know. Your ex.'

'What is there to discuss? You know what happened. You know what I did. What happens next is up to you.'

'Freya, don't be like this. It's a lot to process. You lied to me—'

'With good reason, it seems,' she snaps. 'This was all before I knew you. I'd never do something like that again. I'm a good cop. I was then, despite the fact I knew I should have recused myself from the case.'

She turns and he grabs her arm. She pulls away abruptly. 'Freya—'

'Look. I don't want to talk about this now. I want to go home. Maybe have a bath. You can stay at Adam's. Or don't. I don't care anymore, Josh.'

And with that, she walks away. He stares after her, shocked. She lied to him. *Lied*. How can she not see that she's in the wrong? Why isn't she apologising, begging for forgiveness?

He's not used to her being like this. To any woman being like this with him, for that matter. Normally his charm and his good looks work in his favour, and his own indiscretions are forgiven quickly.

Suddenly, he feels bereft. He doesn't know what to do. This? This is new. But he loves Freya. He doesn't want to lose her.

He needs to make things better. And there's only one person who will know how.

45

Robin has barely taken his jacket off when the idea hits him.

He pauses in his hallway, one arm half out, and quickly dials Ratcliffe's number.

'Go public,' he says the moment his DI answers.

'And there was me thinking you'd left, Butler,' Mouse replies. 'What are you talking about?'

'With Chloe Somerset. The NCA are claiming she's a misper, so let's treat her as one. We put appeals out on social media. We get people to retweet it, publicise it to the *Chronicle* and Missing Persons. Make her too hot to handle.'

'She's not a stolen puppy.'

'Same principle.'

'And what if whoever has her then decides to get rid of her? In the way *we don't want*,' Mouse stresses.

'Well, that is a risk.' Robin pauses, thinking for a moment. 'But Freya's right. The kidnapping doesn't bear any of the hallmarks of a carefully planned and meticulously executed operation, which you'd expect from a team made up of ex-military.'

'Go on...'

'Broad daylight, a lot of noise. The search wasn't quick and efficient – it was someone going round with a box cutter, smashing and ripping. And they've had her for... what? Over twenty-four hours? I hate to say it, but a military team could have easily tortured information out of a civilian by now. How long would you last for?'

'I'd tell them the moment they took the bag off my head.'

'Exactly,' Robin says.

Ratcliffe is quiet at the other end of the line.

'Maybe she's dead already,' he says softly.

'Then it won't matter, will it? Put some detail in about her being diabetic, or some other lie,' Robin continues. 'Really get the public's attention. I bet someone will have seen something – and if not, it'll stir the kidnappers up.'

'So if it's not this military lot, who has her?'

Robin stops. He has a point. If it's not Kepner and his Parapet goons, they don't have a clue.

'And what if they do then kill her? This is my career on the line, Butler, I'm the SIO.' Robin hears a loud exhale of breath. 'What would you do?'

'Have you got any other lines of enquiry? Any other way of finding her?'

'No. CCTV and ANPR are blank. No other witnesses. Nothing.'

'Then I'd do it.'

'I'll call Baker,' Mouse says, then hangs up.

Robin feels that niggle of frustration again – that he's not the one in charge, in the centre of it all at the nick. He's at home, being told to get some sleep while the investigation rushes on in his absence.

He finishes taking his shoes off, then goes through to the kitchen. He'll get something to eat, do as he's told, then head back first thing in the morning. They need to make some progress. It'll be two nights now that Chloe Somerset has been missing. Locked away, tied up. He imagines the fear, the pain the poor woman is going through – and that's at the pleasant end of the spectrum. She could be enduring far worse.

He's just contemplating beans on toast for dinner when the doorbell rings. He walks back through already smiling, hoping it's Freya having reconsidered his offer. He almost recoils when he sees it's Josh.

'What are you doing here?' Robin says abruptly, surprise overtaking a more socially acceptable response.

'I'm sorry, Sarge. It's just…' Josh pauses, his voice cracking. He looks like he's going to cry.

'Bloody hell, Josh. Come in. And don't call me Sarge. I think turning up at my house at…' He glances at his phone. 'Nearly nine p.m. dispenses with all the usual niceties.'

Josh mumbles a thank you and steps inside. He treads on the heels of his shoes, pulling them off without undoing the laces, then stands in his socks and coat, waiting.

Robin frowns. 'Take your coat off. And come through. Do you want a drink?'

'Are you having one?'

'Beer?'

'Yes, please.'

'Go and sit down.' Robin points through to the living room and Josh silently obeys.

Robin opens the fridge and pulls out two bottles of Peroni, twisting both caps off. For a moment he pauses, debating whether to message Freya. He assumes it's related to Jonathan – and the discovery of the photo – so whatever Josh wants to talk about can't be good.

He decides to hold off. Until he knows more.

He goes through to the living room, passing one bottle to Josh and taking a seat on the sofa opposite him.

'I'm sorry to turn up like this. You must be wondering why I'm here.'

Robin stays quiet.

'I assume Freya's told you about me finding that photo of her ex. She tells you most things.'

'She mentioned it, yes,' he replies, ignoring the dig at their friendship.

'You know who it is.'

Robin nods, the bottle half to his lips. He takes a swig. He swallows.

'Jonathan Miller,' Josh continues. He spits the name out. 'She didn't tell me her ex was Jonathan Miller.'

'Perhaps because she knew you'd react like this.'

Josh stops in surprise. 'I've just found out my girlfriend was dating – no, having an affair with – a man whose murder she then investigated.' He glares at Robin. 'How am I supposed to react?'

'With patience and understanding?'

'When did you know?'

'Not until later.'

'And you didn't take her off the case? Report her?'

'I knew reporting her would put her career at risk. And as she'd already lost the man she loved, I wasn't going to take anything else away from her.'

'The man she—' Josh stops and gapes. Then he runs both hands down his face. 'I just don't know what to do.'

Robin sighs. Josh looks awful. His skin is grey, dark shadows below his eyes. It wasn't fair he found out in that way, and Robin has no doubt about his love for Freya.

'You know her,' Josh continues. 'The two of you spend all day together. I know nothing's going on between you.' He laughs, as if mocking the idea, and Robin's sympathy towards him wanes. 'But you know her. What should I do?'

'Go home,' Robin says. 'Speak to Freya. Let her apologise. Then drop it.'

'But how can I? She lied to me. She compromised a murder investigation. She's not the woman I thought she was.'

Robin feels a surge of anger. 'You stupid twat,' he snaps. 'If anything, after finding this out, you should have more respect, more love for Freya as a result. Yes, she lied, but only to protect you. She didn't want to put you in a position where you knew what she'd done. Where you might have to lie for her one day. What she did for Jonathan – it just shows how loyal Freya is. What lengths she'll go to to protect the people she loves. She solved his murder – how many women do you know could do that?'

Josh sniffs, then laughs. 'None.'

'Freya is an incredible woman. She's fearless, and smart and beautiful, with more integrity than anyone you'll ever meet. She walks in a room and… It's like the sun comes out—'

He stops swiftly as Josh stares. 'Well, I'm just saying,' Robin continues quietly. 'You should think yourself fucking lucky she loves you.'

'I do,' Josh replies.

'Good. Then stop wasting your time with me and go and see her.'

Josh tips the last bit of beer into his mouth. Robin holds out his hand to take the bottle but instead, Josh grabs it and shakes it firmly.

'Thanks, Robin.'

'It's fine.' Robin pulls his hand free.

'No, really. Freya's always going on about how wonderful you are, and I've never seen it before.'

'Thanks,' Robin says sarcastically.

'I mean, you're a good bloke. And you're good to Freya.'

Robin nods. He's not sure how to respond to Josh's praise. He makes a move towards the front door and Josh takes the hint.

Robin shows him out.

'See you at the nick, Sarge,' Josh says with a smile, then heads out to his car.

Robin watches him go, then closes the door with a slump of his shoulders. Josh seems much happier following Robin's pep talk; there's every chance their relationship will be back on solid ground once Josh has stopped being an idiot. But Robin regrets his words.

Everything he said about Freya, he meant it. And saying it aloud only cements what he's known all along. He wants to be with her – and not just as her colleague. As something more.

But she's with someone else. A man who has to be told how amazing she is. A man not worthy of her. But the man she loves more than anyone else.

46

Freya's in the bath when she hears the front door open, the clatter of Josh putting his keys down, the rustle of him hanging his coat on the hook. She imagines him abandoning his shoes where he left them, in a messy pile by the door.

After their argument at the police station, Freya stormed away, getting in her car and driving home, doing her utmost not to apply her right foot to the pedal in frustration. Her head battled a muddle of emotions. Worry and frustration for Chloe Somerset. Anger towards Josh. And the confusing mess associated with Robin.

Robin showing up at the tower block this afternoon had only confirmed what she'd already known: he was the one person that always had her back. Who wondered where she was. Who knew she would need him before she even realised herself.

Robin would never doubt her.

She ran the bath, still thinking. Left her clothes where they fell and climbed into the almost scalding hot water. She lowered her head under, muffling her hearing, enjoying being lost in the echoey silence.

All she'd ever wanted as a child was a normal life. A nice house, a job, kids. A happy marriage, like her parents. But the closer she moves towards it, the more she seems to be pushing it away.

Life as a PC was far from normal. Irregular hours, night shifts, broken sleep. And then she moved to Major Crimes, and work as a murder detective is hardly conducive to an easy existence. Your day is defined by the case. You go home when the work is done – which it never is. But she loves it. She *loves* it. More so since she's been working with Robin.

And why is that? she wonders as she soaks in the hot water. Is it the freedom he gives her? The fact he listens, that he respects her opinion? That she feels like she's learning from him, benefiting from his quiet confidence in the job.

Or is it just that she likes being with him, every day?

She hears Josh's footsteps on the stairs, then a quiet knock on the door.

'Freya,' he says through the wood. 'Will you be long?'

'Give me five minutes,' she replies, and she hears him move away again.

What now? She washes her hair, then climbs out, drying herself off. She can't bear another argument, although his tone did sound more contrite.

She emerges from the bathroom in a towel, but he's nowhere to be seen. She gets dressed quickly in a T-shirt, tracksuit bottoms and a jumper, then goes downstairs.

Josh is sat on the sofa, waiting for her. His stillness, the quiet, is so out of character it's disconcerting. She sits down next to him.

'I've been thinking,' he begins.

'Okay...'

'I'm not happy. About the way you kept me in the dark about Jonathan Miller. Did you think I would report you?'

'I didn't know what you would do, Josh. But I didn't want you to have to make that decision – between me and your instincts as a police officer – so I didn't tell you. It has no bearing on us, or how I feel about you.'

'I know.'

'Do you? Because the way you've been behaving for the last twenty-four hours would suggest otherwise.'

'It was just a lot to get my head round. And Robin said—'

'You've been talking to Robin?' Her voice rises to a squeak, her hackles immediately up. 'You've been talking to Robin behind my back?'

'Yes, but hear me out. He seems to know you better than anyone else nowadays. You spend more time with him than you do with me.'

'That's not true.'

'It is. So I went to his house—'

'You did *what*? When?'

'Tonight. Just now. And he made me see sense.' Freya finds herself speechless. Stunned by this insane turn of events.

'What – exactly – did Robin say?'

'That you were fearless and smart and beautiful—'

'Robin said that?'

'Yes. And something about how the sun comes out when you walk into a room. And that I should consider myself lucky that I'm with you.'

Freya's mind is reeling. Robin said those things. About her.

'Frey?' Josh says. 'Say something?'

But Freya just stands up, goes to the hallway. She puts her coat and her shoes on. Then she picks up her car keys and walks out of the house.

47

At first, Robin thinks it's a dream. A knock, breaking through the haze of almost-sleep. He opens his eyes and stares at the darkened ceiling; a glow permeates the gloom, his phone jumping into life.

He leans over and picks it up. It's ringing, *West* on the screen. He quickly answers it.

'Robin? Are you awake?'

'I am now.'

'Can I come in?'

Robin scrambles out of bed, grabbing a jumper and pulling it over his head as he stumbles downstairs in his boxers.

He opens the door and Freya's standing there. In a jumper and tracksuit bottoms and trainers. Phone next to her ear. She lowers it as she sees Robin, then cancels the call.

'What's going on? Do we need to go in?' It's the most likely explanation for her being here, but it doesn't seem right. She wouldn't have just showed up. Not looking like this.

'No, nothing to do with work. Can I come in?' she repeats.

He can't describe the expression on her face. Something between confusion, fear and surprise. Her cheeks are pink in the chill of the spring night; her hair is damp, loose on her shoulders.

'Yes. Yes, of course,' he says, and opens the door wide. 'I just need to...' He gestures to his bare legs and feet. 'Wait a sec,' he says, and charges back up the stairs.

While he's putting jeans on, he wonders what's going on. First Josh, now Freya. Why does everyone feel the need to drop round tonight? Surely, after his chat with Josh, everything is sorted in their cosy little household?

He descends the stairs again, socks in hand, to find Freya stood in his kitchen. The kettle is boiling, her hand resting on two mugs in front of her. He stops, as she opens the cupboard above the kettle and takes out the box of tea bags, placing one in each mug. The action seems so simple, so normal, that it takes his breath away for a moment. Like she belongs here.

The kettle clicks off but she doesn't move. She's staring down, deep in thought.

'Freya?' he says tentatively, and she looks up. 'Is everything okay?'

'Yes, I think so.' She pours water into the mugs, then holds one out to him. He walks across and takes it. 'Was Josh here earlier?'

'Yes.'

'And you two had a chat? About me?'

'Yes.'

Robin's still baffled. Has he done something wrong? But she doesn't seem angry or upset. More… reflective. Deep in thought.

'Do you want to sit down?' he asks, and she nods.

She leads the way into the living room and goes to her usual spot on the sofa. Where she sits when they watch TV, when they chat and laugh, and take the piss out of whatever cop show they're watching. He sits down next to her, putting his mug on the coffee table.

Freya does the same, then sits back, looking down and picking at her nails. He waits.

'Robin,' she begins. 'What you said to Josh… Did you mean it?'

Robin frowns. 'Yes. I mean… I think so. Which part? What did he tell you?'

'That I was beautiful and smart and fearless. And that he was lucky to have me.' She looks unsure for a moment, then glances his way. 'Did you say that?'

Robin swallows. 'Yes. And yes, I meant it.'

'But… what does that mean?'

'Mean?'

'Why did you say it?'

'Because Josh needed to hear some home truths.' Robin pauses. 'But that's not what you're asking, is it?'

This moment has been coming for a while; everything that's gone unsaid between them, now threatening to push to the surface. Ever since Freya came with him down to Devon last June, ever since their argument at Christmas, he's felt differently about her. More than friends, more than colleagues. But he never even dreamed he'd tell her.

Until tonight.

Freya chews on her lip for a moment, looking down into her mug. 'Can we pretend, for one second, that I'm drunk?'

Robin's now more confused than ever. 'But you drove here. Didn't you?'

'Just pretend. Absolutely wasted. So that whatever I say next, if it doesn't go well, we can just laugh it off. Put it down to the alcohol and carry on with our lives like it never happened.'

'Okay…'

'Because when Josh said those things earlier, I got a little thrill. It made me happy. But not because Josh agreed with them – because you said them. About me.'

Robin stays silent.

'Robin, do you like me?'

'You know I do—'

'Not like that. More than that. Like…'

'Yes.'

The word comes out of his mouth unexpectedly, without thought. As if his brain is tired of the pretence.

'Yes, I do like you. Like that. When I'm around you, everything makes sense. I'm myself. A hundred per cent. And I never get that. Not normally.'

'Not even with—'

'No, not with Jo. Not with anyone. Except with Georgia. She knew me. Properly. As you do. And she loved me, despite all my...' He waves his hand vaguely. 'Issues.'

Freya gives a small smile.

'Issues?' she says. 'Is that what we're calling them now?'

'Whatever.' He smiles back, feeling awkward. 'There, I said it. What else do you want to know?'

'What would you say, what would you do,' she begins. 'If I did this?'

And she leans forward slowly and kisses him.

They've done it before. Kissed. Here on this couch. When they first met, when Freya was blind with grief from Jonathan's death. But tonight, nearly two years on, this is totally different.

He knows her now. She's not this new, pretty detective constable, assigned to his case against his will. She's his partner. His best friend. The person he wants to be around, who he can rely on when things get tough.

He feels the warmth of her lips on his, the light touch of her hand against his chest. She goes to pull away, but he stops her, his hand gently on her neck, in her hair. She returns his kiss, her tongue touching his.

It's everything he wants, everything he wanted. Everything he thought it would be. The thought of Jo flashes into his head; he pushes it away. This is Freya. *Freya*. Nothing else matters. This is where he should be, who he should be with.

He feels a soft hand against his face, another creeping up under his jumper. She's pressed up against him now, the warmth of her body next to his. But then he stops. He reluctantly pulls away; she looks at him quizzically, hands still where they shouldn't be.

'Freya, I'm sorry. I want this, so much.' *So, so much*, his body throws back. 'But... I don't know. I want it to be...' He feels his face flush. 'Perfect.'

'It's never going to be perfect, Rob,' she says quietly.

'No. But. What about Josh?'

'What about Jo?'

'I'll split up with Jo.'

'Just like that?'

'Yes,' he says without hesitation. Freya takes a long breath in and slumps on the sofa, moving away from him. He wants to pull her back towards him. Kiss her again. Do... other things. Instead, he says, 'It's not as simple as that with Josh, is it?'

She shakes her head slowly, and Robin feels his heart sink.

'I don't know, Robin. I really don't. You and me, we're... it's different. How would things work out, long-term?'

'I don't know, but I'd like to find out.'

'So would I... But...'

Her voice trails off.

'Freya, I'm not going to say anything to Josh. As far as he's concerned, you were never here. But please know that I want to be with you. And whatever happens with us, it's over between Jo and I.'

'Don't do that for me—'

'I'm not. She deserves better than this – me being unsure. She'll be fine. She'll go to Devon, get a promotion. Be amazingly successful.'

'And you?'

Robin shrugs. 'I'm fine.'

'And us?'

'You were pissed, remember. It's forgotten.'

Freya stands up slowly; she glances back to Robin. 'Unless it's not.'

He nods.

He watches as she leaves, waiting for the sound as the front door is opened. When the door closes, he sags back against the cushion.

Robin knows he should feel angry, even annoyed, at her turning up here in the middle of the night and kissing him, despite everything that's going on with Josh. But he doesn't.

He just feels unsure. And alone. And sad.

48

Freya's mind is reeling as she walks away from Robin's house to her car. She drives, just to get away, but without actually knowing where she is going.

She can still feel the scratch of his stubble on her chin, the taste of him in her mouth. Kissing Robin couldn't have felt more different to the first time, when it was rushed and weird and uncomfortable. She'd barely known Robin then.

This time, it felt soft and calm and hot and desperate – all at the same time. And… right.

She drives. She doesn't want to go home. Josh is there, and fuck knows what she's going to say to him. Instead she heads to the only person she knows will understand – to Mina.

Mina is less than sympathetic when she eventually opens the door.

'It's midnight, Freya. What the hell are you doing here?'

'I kissed Robin.'

'You… What? Come in, come in.' Mina ushers her through the door and almost forcibly pushes her into the living room. 'But be quiet, for God's sake. Last thing we need is you waking the kids. Do you want anything? To drink, eat?'

'A glass of water.'

Mina leaves Freya on her sofa and heads to the kitchen. The room is semi-lit, only a small lamp glows in the corner. Freya's surrounded by toys – a large plastic Bat Cave on one side, a car park on the other. She sits numbly, her hands resting on her knees.

Mina comes back and thrusts the water into her hands. Freya takes a sip, and then another large gulp.

'Go on then,' Mina prompts. 'What happened?'

'Josh and I, we were having an argument.'

'What about?'

'It doesn't matter. But then Josh went to see Robin—'

'Why did Josh go to see Robin?'

'To talk about me, I guess. Find out what was in my head.'

'Why didn't he just ask you?'

Freya shrugs. 'He doesn't ever believe me. Whatever I tell him. But then he came back and told me what Robin said... and...'

'And?' Mina is sitting forward eagerly.

'Robin said some things that made me think that maybe... he... I don't know. Liked me.' She looks up now, catching Mina's eye. 'More than just friends.'

Mina makes a frustrated groan. 'Of course he does. Fucking hell, Freya. I could have told you that. Robin's had a thing for you for months. Ages. Maybe even years.'

'He has not.'

'He has.'

'So why hasn't he told me? Done anything about it?'

'You've been with Josh. And he's your boss. And also, despite the confident image he likes to project at work, inside he's just as insecure and scared as the rest of us. Maybe more than the rest of us. He didn't want to say something and then lose you as a friend.'

Freya knew that, deep down, but had never wanted to acknowledge it. Because accepting that was the way he felt meant she had to confront feelings of her own. Feelings she was wrestling with now.

'So how did you end up kissing?'

'I went over there. And—'

'Was it just snogging? Or—'

213

'Just kissing, Mina. He stopped it. He said we couldn't…
With Josh and Jo.'

'Would you have?'

Freya feels her stomach turn – a fresh onslaught of butterflies.
'Yes,' she admits quietly.

Mina claps her hands loudly with excitement, then stops and
contains herself. 'What are you going to do?'

'I don't know,' Freya wails. 'He says he's going to split up
with Jo.'

'For you?'

'No. Just because. But that's easy for him. He's only been
with Jo four months. I've been with Josh for nearly a year. He's
moved into my house.' She starts to cry now, and Mina's face
falls.

She leans over and puts her arm round Freya. 'Oh, honey.
It'll all work out.'

'Will it?' Mina hands her a tissue and she dabs at her eyes. 'I
don't know how. I don't know what to do.'

'Do you love Josh?'

'That's just it. I do. We're good together. He's so perfect.
He's gorgeous, and everyone loves him. But Robin…' She
thinks for a moment, remembering how she felt when Robin
confirmed that he liked her. More than friends. The glow, the
smile she couldn't suppress. 'It's different. Being with Robin,
it's the feeling you get when you put on your favourite jumper.
When you get home and curl up on the sofa and it's raining
outside. I never worry when I'm with him. He's calm, and safe,
and…'

'You belong,' Mina finishes for her.

Freya looks at Mina. She has a serious look on her face.

'Yes,' Freya confirms.

THURSDAY

49

The call comes at five in the morning. It wakes Robin with a jerk; he rubs his eyes, bleary in the darkness. He answers his phone and listens.

'Understood,' he says.

He sits up in bed, switches a light on. Slowly, still half asleep, he puts on trousers, a clean shirt, a jacket. There is no time for a shower.

He picks up his phone, pulls up her contact and looks at her name.

What happened earlier that night – the strange conflicting feelings, the mess it may have caused – it will all have to wait.

He clicks the green button. He listens to the ringtone. She answers.

'Robin?' she says.

'You need to come in,' he replies. 'They've found her. They've found Chloe.'

Part 3

50

Chloe Somerset was found in an old caravan at the back of some disused allotments down by the river. Her bloodied unconscious body was still; they assumed the worst until an armed response officer put his fingers to her neck.

'She's alive. Get the paramedics in here, now.'

DI Ratcliffe tells Robin and Freya the events of last night, as they stand in the hospital corridor, waiting for the doctor. Robin has already checked social media on the way in – the feed is alight with appeals and requests for information.

To his satisfaction he saw that @HantsPolice had tweeted the request for information at ten last night, barely an hour after Robin made the suggestion. The local news outlets responded quickly; Sky and BBC News picked up the story, followed by every single night owl on Twitter. #FindChloe is trending.

Since Robin arrived at the hospital, he's barely been able to look at Freya. Every time he does, he feels a mixture of worry and apprehension – coupled with such a surge of affection and desire he can hardly think straight. He tries hard to focus on Mouse.

'101 was flooded with calls,' Ratcliffe says excitedly. 'And most of them were crap, until one bloke told us about the caravan. Just said, "she's there" and gave us the location. Armed Response were on the ground in thirty.'

'There was no one else there? Just Chloe?' Freya asks, and Mouse nods.

'But we'll get them. SOCO are all over it now. Jess says it's covered with prints.'

They're interrupted as the doctor emerges out of the room next to them. She looks tired and harried.

Ratcliffe springs forward immediately. 'Can we speak to her?' he asks.

'How is she?' Freya interjects quickly.

The doctor pauses, her jaw tight. 'When she came in she was severely dehydrated, had probably been without food or water since she was taken.' Thirty-nine hours, Robin calculates. 'She has multiple bruises to her face, but no broken bones.'

Robin swallows down a swell of repulsion as he asks if there were any signs of sexual assault.

'Not that we can tell at this stage. But we'll have to wait until she's ready to talk.'

'And when is that?' Mouse asks again.

'We've given her something to calm her down. When she woke in the ambulance she was severely distressed. Could barely remember her own name.'

'We think the people that did this to her are nasty, brutal mercenaries,' DI Ratcliffe says to the doctor. 'We need to catch them – fast.'

Robin throws a look his way. Do they still think that? He's not so sure. A disused caravan filled with fingerprints? Yet another aspect that doesn't fit with highly trained professionals.

The doctor turns to Mouse with a hard stare. 'I have my patient's well-being to think of, DI Ratcliffe. She's traumatised. Give her another few hours. We'll let you know, Detectives.'

They thank the doctor and she leaves them, standing helpless, in the corridor.

Robin looks through the glass into the room where Chloe Somerset is lying. The lights are down low; he can just see a small figure under the blankets, an assortment of machines by her side.

Ratcliffe's face is grim when he turns back. 'It was a good shout, Robin. Who knows what might have happened if we hadn't got there when we did. And you think this is all to do with a bit of bloody software?'

Robin shakes his head in disbelief. 'I don't understand it either. Even if it is worth millions. The main thing is she's safe now.'

'I'll get a guard on her door. And ensure they call us the moment she's able to talk.' Ratcliffe runs his hands down his face. 'There goes another night's sleep.'

'Have you been up this whole time?'

'Yeah. Not like you lucky pair.' Robin feels Freya's glance.

'You go home, boss,' Robin says. 'Get a few hours' kip. I can keep everything going.'

Ratcliffe thinks for a moment, then nods. 'Yeah. I will. But shout if you need me.'

They move to the side of the corridor, and Mouse updates Robin. SOCO, house-to-house, Intel finding out all they can about the caravan and the allotments.

'Oh, and Greg wants to talk to you,' Mouse concludes. 'Something about Andrew Grace and the telemetry on the car.'

'He's still working on that?' Robin replies. 'I told him we had all we needed on Grace.'

Mouse shrugs. 'He didn't say. Just give him a call. He said it was important.'

With a final nod of thanks, Ratcliffe heads off, leaving Robin and Freya alone in the corridor. They stand in an uneasy silence, the bustle of the hospital around them.

'Are you okay?' she asks after a moment.

'We need to head back to the nick,' he replies, dodging the question. 'Mouse has already called in reinforcements. We're going to have a full team to work with once we get there.'

'Including Josh?'

He nods. He notes her awkwardness, and wonders what it means for him and their future.

'Did you get any sleep?' she asks. Robin spots a uniform heading towards them: the guard to stand sentry over Chloe's hospital room.

'Not much.' He tries to smile, but it comes out as an apologetic wince. 'Freya, I know we need to talk. About what happened last night. I meant everything I said,' he quickly adds. 'I did. But with this case—'

'I get it,' she replies. 'This is more important.'

'For now,' he finishes softly.

51

They head back to the police station in their separate cars; Freya's glad of the space. For a while she tracks the Volvo, but then loses Robin in rush-hour traffic.

Robin looks as bad as she feels. She thinks she got an hour, maybe a bit more before his call. Mina had gone to bed about two, leaving Freya with a blanket on the couch. Freya hadn't wanted to face Josh; her head was no clearer and seeing Robin this morning only confuses her further.

After his call at five, she'd rushed home, quickly changed her clothes to whatever she could find without waking Josh, then driven to the hospital. The world had been slowly coming to life – sun touching the tops of the houses, birds starting to wake. It gave her a burst of sudden optimism. She would work out what to do. She would.

But when she saw Robin, the conflicting feelings returned. The horrific news of what had happened to Chloe, coupled with what they had done last night. A desperation to talk – to *kiss* him again, oh God, get a *grip* – but also knowing they had a job to do, and nothing could get in the way of that.

She parks up at the station – and notices Josh's VW Golf is already here. She remembers the early days of her and Josh's relationship. Seeing his car and feeling the buzz of nerves in her stomach. Wanting to be with him. And now? It's not that she doesn't love her boyfriend – she does. That's the confusing part.

As she's staring at Josh's car, the Volvo pulls up alongside. Robin gets out awkwardly, two Costa coffee cups balanced in his hands. She joins him; he hands her one wordlessly.

'You stopped?'

'At the drive-thru. Thought we would need it.'

She takes it gratefully.

They walk together to the conference room. They're overly polite, Robin holding the door open for her, a smile and a thank you as they go through. Everyone's going to know, she thinks.

She notices Mina's stare, but she tells herself the quietening room is because of where they've just come from. Who they've been to see. The detectives all stop as Robin moves to stand next to the whiteboard.

'So, Chloe Somerset is alive and recovering at the General,' he says, and a chatter of relief ripples around the room. 'But I wouldn't say she was well. Mina – have SOCO sent across the crime scene photos?'

Mina nods and brings her laptop to the front, connecting it to a projector. Someone dims the lights and sharp images dominate the room. A squalid interior of a caravan. Tatty curtains drawn, a slither of dark down the centre. Food containers, half-filled plastic bags, empty bottles of Coke. Freya remembers what the doctor said about Chloe's lack of food and water, and wonders who had been consuming this. The photos move forward. A muddy floor, multiple footwear marks. A dirty sleeping bag, covered in rust-red stains. Pieces of discarded duct tape, cigarette butts, a porn mag. Wrappings from medical equipment, left by the first responders.

Mouse said Chloe was found on the floor, her wrists bound behind her, her feet taped, a strip over her mouth. Freya can't help but imagine her there, for nearly two days and two nights. Cold. Scared. Alone. Not knowing what was going to happen.

Next – the rest of the caravan. A small toilet, filthy and soiled, with what looks like a patch of vomit to the side, missing the bowl. A kitchen – a few spoons and dirty mugs in the sink. The exterior shots show a patch of overgrown grassland, long aban- doned. Only a few run-down sheds and broken fences remain of the allotments. The caravan is old – the type you rarely see on the road nowadays. Beige shows through in patches; it leans drunkenly to the left.

The photographs end and the room is plunged into darkness. Someone snaps the lights back on and the detectives wince.

Robin clears his throat. 'It's not a pretty sight,' he begins. 'All the more reason to find the people who did this to Chloe. Where are we on the traffic cams?'

DC Lee Davis sits up straight in his seat. 'Now we know where they were going, we're tracking all the routes from Chloe's house to the caravan. We're hopeful we'll find the van soon.'

'Brilliant, thank you. And Mina, have you managed to get in touch with Hamilton?'

'On his way in.'

'Good. Freya and I will speak to him when he arrives.'

Robin moves on to the next line of enquiry and Freya watches him as he takes charge of the incident room. He's confident, commanding the team with an ease that well exceeds his sergeant rank. He shouldn't be doing this, she thinks with a sting. He should be a DI, doing Ratcliffe's job – exactly the same way as he is now. Mouse left with barely an argument, knowing he was leaving the investigation in more than capable hands.

Josh is talking now, taking Robin through their efforts to track down the owner of the caravan. All his attention is firmly fixed on Robin, but when he stops talking, he glances across to Freya. She can't read his expression. He looks tired, but is he angry? She hadn't told him where she was going last night, and when he eventually texted, at three a.m., she just replied she was at Mina's. Can he guess? she wonders. Can he tell something happened between her and Robin?

The briefing concludes, and everyone moves away to their desks. Freya does the same, but soon notices Josh heading her way.

He crouches down next to her desk; her gaze flickers to Robin, who's talking to a DC on the other side of the room.

'You didn't come home last night,' Josh whispers.

'I told you, I was at Mina's.'

'But you didn't say why. I apologised, Freya. And if you want me to, I'll do it a thousand times more.' He frowns at her continued silence. 'What's going on?'

'I...' But she doesn't know what to say. 'I just need time to think.'

'About what?'

Freya notices Robin turning and coming back over.

'Josh, not now. There's too much going on here.'

'Later? You'll come home later?'

But before Freya can answer, Robin is next to them. He looks at Josh quickly, no more than a micro-expression, then points to the door. 'Tiller's here,' he says.

52

'Everything okay?' Robin asks under his breath as they head towards the interview room to speak to Hamilton.

'Yes, fine,' she replies quickly, then looks away.

Robin gets that feeling, that well-trodden burn of self-doubt and defeat. There is no way this will work out; he won't get the girl.

But they haven't got time for his pessimism now.

Tiller's waiting for them in the formal interview room, the door open, a uniform waiting outside. He's dismissed as Robin and Freya go in and sit opposite Hamilton.

'How's Chloe?' Tiller asks.

Robin jumps as a cold wet nose is thrust into his crotch. 'I didn't realise you were there, Max,' he replies with a smile. He leans down and strokes the dog's fur.

'Sorry,' Tiller says. 'But I couldn't leave him. With Chloe gone he's a bit clingy.' Robin pushes his chair out so he can properly say hello to the dog; Max responds by trying to climb onto his lap. Tiller glances around. 'You're recording this?'

'We are,' Robin replies. He pushes the dog off then rubs his fluffy ears. Max licks his hand. 'We just want to make sure that everything's captured on tape. You're not under arrest, although I will need to caution you.'

The video is started. Robin reads the standard warning for a voluntary interview, and Tiller nods, then signs the forms.

'How is Chloe?' Tiller asks again. He pulls the dog away from Robin and coaxes him under his seat. The dog lies down with a grunt. 'The officer that came to pick me up was vague.'

'We're waiting for an update from the hospital, but she's stable.'

'What happened to her?'

'She was beaten up. We don't know any more than that.'

Tiller curls his hands into fists. 'Shit,' he whispers. 'This is my fault. I should never have got her into this. Should never have given her a key.' Then, remembering why he's there, he picks up the laptop from under the desk. 'I've checked already. They haven't got in.'

'You're sure?'

'Yes. Look.' He opens the laptop. The screen lights up: a black background with a simple text box in green. He presses his thumb against the sensor and a second box springs up. 'If they had, this wouldn't be here. It would have been logged if either the key or the biometric had been used. And any techie worth their salt would have instantly taken the whole system offline. Moved it to their own platform. I wouldn't even be able to get this far.'

'But you can't get in either?'

'No. Multi-factored. Two levels of security. It was deliberate, so they couldn't access it even if they did… that… to me.' He puts his head in his hands. 'I didn't think for a moment they would go for Chloe.'

'What more can you tell us about Parapet Holdings?'

'Not much. I've been racking my brain, gone through all the files in Andrew's office. Trying to find something else about them. But they're sneaky. It's just PO box numbers, and companies within companies.'

'We found that too.'

'And Kepner, he's practically off the grid. I can't find any trace of him on social media or Google.'

'Who else might have been after the algorithm? Any competitors?'

Tiller shakes his head, slowly. 'Nobody that would go to this extent. We've had plenty of interest, but from big reputable companies. Ones I would be willing to sell to. I only said no to Parapet. Where was Chloe found?'

'In a caravan, at the back of some allotments near the river at Millbrook. Why?'

Tiller pauses, thinking. 'It's just…' He shakes his head. 'Don't worry.' He looks up again. 'No, I'm sorry, I can't help. I wish I could.'

'Do you want police protection?' Robin offers.

'No. As I said before, I don't want anyone at my house. I'll be fine. I have a guard dog.' Tiller offers a weak smile, gesturing to Max. There's a knock on the door and the dog eagerly jumps to his feet and stands, tongue lolling in a wide grin as Davis pokes his head round the door.

'Sarge?' Davis says. 'I thought you'd want to know as soon as possible – Chloe's awake. She wants to speak to the police.'

Robin nods his thanks and Davis disappears again.

'Can I see Chloe?' Tiller asks.

'We can ask.'

'Yes, please. The thing is…' Tiller pauses; Robin notes a look of panic pass across his face.

'What, Tiller?'

'If nobody logs on to our server on the cloud where the algorithm is kept by 11.59 p.m. on Friday night, the system will autodelete.' He says it in a burst, the words coming out almost incomprehensible with his broad accent. 'I set a scheduled task to run a cloud-saved batch script to delete everything at a predetermined time.'

Robin looks at him with astonishment. 'What? The whole thing will go?'

Tiller nods. 'Years of work, gone in a second.'

'What about backups? Couldn't the company in charge of your… cloud thingy… resurrect it?'

'I thought of that. The batch script acts like a virus. It attacks the backup servers and wipes the lot.'

Robin is gobsmacked. 'But why?' he stutters. 'You go to so much effort to protect it, and then you set up a kill switch?'

'A bargaining chip. Better that nobody has it than it falls into the wrong hands.' Tiller gives a quick flicker of a smile. 'I'm not so sure now.' His eyes plead. 'Please ask her. I hope she'll forgive me,' he adds in a whisper. 'For getting her involved in all of this.'

'I'm sure she will,' Robin says, but he's not so certain. Would he? he wonders as they end the interview with a final pat to Max. If Freya got him kidnapped and beaten up, would he forgive her?

He looks over at Freya, crouched down, saying goodbye to Max and laughing as the dog tries to lick her face. Her hair is tied back in a messy bun; she looks tired, her shirt creased. But yes, he thinks.

He would forgive her anything.

53

'I'll go,' Freya volunteers as they walk up to the incident room. 'You need to hold the fort here.'

Robin's phone beeps in his pocket and he pulls it out. He looks at the screen a little too long, then blinks and turns back to her.

'Yes, that's a good idea. Let me know if she remembers anything useful.' Mina waves to attract his attention. He throws a brief smile to Freya, then heads over to her desk.

Freya watches him pull up a seat next to Mina, then lower his brows in concentration as she starts to talk. Always so serious – a stark contrast to Josh, who she can hear laughing with Davis on the far side of the room.

She frowns, grabs her keys and heads off.

–

Chloe Somerset is looking better after a few hours' sleep. Even though she has tubes running to her arm, the oxygen mask has gone. She's sitting in her hospital bed, propped up by a few pillows.

Chloe sees her coming; Freya forces a smile.

Up close, Chloe's injuries look awful. Her face is swollen out of all proportion, a mess of red and purple and black. Freya feels a pulse of anger; too many women have been beaten up this week. Too many women lying black and bruised in hospital, all because of this. And what is it? A software algorithm. A model, whatever that is. A way to make money for already rich men.

Looking at Chloe, she doesn't care if the whole thing does get erased at midnight on Friday. What good has it done?

'How are you feeling?' Freya begins.

'Where's my dog?' Chloe asks straight away, ignoring the question. 'Did you find Max?'

'Yes. He's with Tiller.'

Chloe slumps in relief. 'He'll hate that,' she says. Freya's not sure whether she's talking about the dog or the man.

'Do you feel up to answering some questions?' Freya asks. 'I won't be long, and then you can rest.'

'Take as much time as you need. I want you to catch these bastards.' Chloe speaks slowly, every word measured from her bruised face. 'Have you got any idea who did this to me?'

'Nothing definitive, but the team are working flat out. Anything you could tell us would be a great help. What can you remember?'

She closes her eyes for a moment, and takes a long slow breath in. When she opens them again her gaze is steady and determined.

'I don't remember much. It all happened so fast. I was at home. I heard something smashing in the kitchen, and next thing I knew I had been punched in the face, a bag put over my head and my hands were behind my back.' She frowns. 'Tape round my wrists. Then they hauled me into the back of... Must have been a van.'

'Did you manage to get a look at them?'

'Not really. They had that bag over my head when they weren't asking questions. But there were two of them. Young.'

'How could you tell?'

'The way they moved. That swagger, especially the bigger one. And their jeans – tight. No older bloke wears jeans like that. They were both wearing black ski masks, I couldn't see their faces.'

'And you say they questioned you?'

Chloe nods. 'Most of the time they left me on the floor. I was lying on something softer, not sure what. But occasionally they pulled me up and sat me on the sofa. Took the tape off my mouth.' She pauses, and tentatively licks her chapped lips. 'Can you pass me the water?'

Freya reaches across and pours a beakerful from the plastic jug. Chloe takes it, drinking through a straw.

'I was so thirsty. I asked for a drink, but he just said, "When you give us the code." That's all he said. "Give me the code, give me the code."'

'Code?'

'Yeah. Like he didn't know what he was asking for. I said I didn't have it, and then he punched me in the face, over and over again.' She screws her eyes shut. 'I thought he was going to kill me.'

Freya's heart goes out to the woman. 'I'm sorry to put you through this, Chloe.'

'No. No. You need to know.' She opens her eyes again, then thinks for a moment. 'That was the bigger bloke. The other one, he was skinny. More Tiller's build? But much taller.' Freya nods in acknowledgement. 'He didn't have a clue what he was doing. The other bloke goaded him at the beginning. Said "punch her, you pussy". Or something like that. He wouldn't at first. And then, when he did, it was more... scrappy. Like he'd never hit someone before. It made the big guy angry. So he took over. And he...' Her voice trails off. The bruises speak for themselves. 'But he was furious. That's when I got really scared. I thought he'd kill me there and then. Or rape me... or something.' She screws her eyes shut. A tear creeps out and runs down her battered cheek.

'But he didn't?'

'No. Just the...' She raises her hand to her face, touching it tentatively. 'I kept on telling him it's not like that, you can't just memorise an encryption key, but he wouldn't believe me. "Give me the password." Password this time. Like anyone who knew anything about software would ever call it a password.'

'Why didn't you tell him where it was?'

'Because...' She pushes her lips together. 'I didn't want to take the risk.'

'What risk, Chloe?' But she just shakes her head and takes another sip of water.

'Where is the key?' Freya asks again, to no avail. Freya can't understand why she's being so loyal. 'Tiller wants to visit,' she says in the face of Chloe's silence. 'I said I'd ask you—'

'Fuck him,' Chloe spits, her voice full of anger. 'This was his fault. His stupid encryption key. We were never together, not properly. Never in *love*.' She says the word, slightly mocking. 'I left that company for a reason. I shouldn't have got involved.' Then she frowns. 'Unless he brings Max. Then he can come.' Her face relaxes into a smile at the thought of her dog, and she closes her eyes. 'Make sure he brings Max.'

'I'll let him know. Get some rest,' Freya whispers. But Chloe's already asleep. Freya creeps away, no more the wiser as to the location of the key.

The key at the centre of this whole mess.

54

The incident room is alive with noise. The babble of leads coming to fruition, of lost sleep and neglected marriages finally yielding results.

Robin's sitting at his desk, coffee in hand, digesting the latest bit of news. Land registry records on the patch of old allotments have come back to a man called George Freeman, but Intel are scrabbling to find anything useful about him, bar the fact he's dead.

His phone rings, distracting him from the mess.

'Freya? How is she?'

'Fucking bastards,' she spits. He hears the echo of a large corridor and the background noise of the hospital. 'Her face is a mess. The arseholes,' she reiterates, and then fills him in on Chloe's assessment of her kidnappers.

'They're looking less and less like trained military,' Robin says. 'Did she tell you where the encryption key is?'

'No. And I got the distinct impression she wasn't keen to tell Tiller either.'

'Can't blame her.'

Freya agrees, then confirms she's heading back; he hangs up and stares at his phone. He selects the last text message received and types in, *See you tonight*.

It sends. The tiny confirmation appears: *Delivered*. He puts the phone down, then feels Mina watching him from the next desk.

'Was that Freya?' she asks.

'Yes. She's on her way back. So how did this guy die?'

'Lung cancer. In 2015.'

'Former address? Dependants? Living relatives?'

'We're working on it.' Mina gives him another look. 'Are you sure it's relevant? Or are you just looking for a way to occupy that big brain of yours?'

Robin glances at her; she's staring in a way which clearly tells him she knows something.

'Spit it out, Mina.'

'You kissed Freya,' she hisses in a low whisper.

He glances round, but Josh has already gone home to have a shower and some food before taking over for the evening.

'She kissed *me*. She told you?'

'She came round to mine after. And?'

'And what?'

Mina makes an exasperated noise. 'Are you two getting together?'

'That depends on Freya. And what she decides to do about Josh. I told her how I feel.'

'You told her you loved her?'

'Not exactly.'

'Well, don't you think you should?'

Robin feels like he's back at school, being told off by a grumpy teacher for not doing his homework. He puts his fingers in his eyes and rubs them.

'I need to hold onto some shred of dignity, Mina. I'm not going to beg.'

'I'm not saying you need to beg—'

'We both know which way this is going to go.' Robin shrugs, and apathetically sips his coffee. 'Freya will see last night as a momentary lapse in sanity. Mr Incredible will come out on top. And then somehow we're all going to have to carry on working together.'

'Give her time, she just—'

'Sarge?' Davis appears by their desk. They look up guiltily. 'Sarge,' he repeats. 'There's something you need to see.'

Robin gets up but feels a tug on his arm. He looks back to Mina.

'This isn't over, Robin,' she says quietly.

'I think it is.'

He follows Davis over to his desk, where CCTV footage is up on the screen. They sit down and Robin watches as Davis scrolls it forward.

'Josh made some good headway this morning – we tracked the van from Chloe Somerset's house, all the way down Winchester Road to Millbrook. But the angles were wrong and we couldn't see the plate. Until here.'

He points to the screen and presses play; a white Transit van progresses through traffic lights and over the roundabout, street lights reflecting off the yellow plastic on the back. Robin feels a jolt of excitement.

'Have you run it?'

Davis smiles. 'Comes back to a twenty-one-year-old called Stephen Dolan. Lives on Cotswold Road, Millbrook.'

'Bring him in,' Robin confirms.

55

Stephen Dolan has hair like a teenage pop star, but that's where the resemblance ends. It's thick and long and flops into wide, bloodshot eyes that dart nervously round the room. His hand trembles; his left leg jiggles constantly under the table. He's tall – towering over Robin as he showed him into the interview room – but doesn't look like he's eaten in weeks.

'And you're sure you don't want legal advice?' Robin repeats. Next to him, Mina waits quietly.

'Nah. Last guy I had got me locked up for three months.'

Handling stolen goods; conviction at eighteen. Robin's already had a read of his record – he was lucky he hadn't got more. But Robin's not going to argue. The video is rolling, the caution has been read. Time is ticking and the day's already been long.

'Can you begin by telling me where you were on Tuesday, at fifteen hundred hours?' Dolan looks confused. 'Three p.m.,' Robin clarifies.

'No comment,' he replies. Then he pauses. 'Isn't that what you're supposed to say?'

'The truth would be a better way forward, Stephen.'

'No comment, then.'

Robin nods. He smiles for a moment, then takes a photograph out of the file in front of him. He turns it round and lays it on the table. The kid gawps at it.

'This is your van,' Robin begins. 'You can clearly see the number plate, here.' He points to the photo. 'We have your van now. We've towed it to our garage where our forensics team are currently going over it with a magnifying glass. And what do you think they'll find, Stephen?'

The kid shakes his head, his mouth open.

'I think they'll find hair and skin cells from a woman called Chloe Somerset. Do you know who that is?'

It's like a switch is thrown. At the mention of her name, the kid starts sobbing. His body folds to the table and he covers his face with his hands.

Mina leans forward. 'Stephen, are you okay?' she asks gently. 'Do you want a break?'

'No. I don't want to go back to that cell. I don't want to go to prison again.'

'What happened, Stephen?'

'Is she okay? Is she dead?'

'No, she's fine. She's in hospital.'

'Because when those coppers showed up and arrested me, I thought for certain she were dead.'

'We arrested you for kidnapping and false imprisonment, Stephen,' Robin says. 'Not murder. But that's a serious charge. Tell us what happened and maybe we can help.'

'I didn't know.'

'Didn't know what?'

'When he called. He just said he wanted to borrow my van. He didn't say he was going to beat up a woman and drag her away in it. I didn't know what to do. She was there, and he said I was... I dunno. Like I was to blame too.'

'Culpable?'

'That's it. I dropped them at the caravan and he said to get rid of the van then come back with some food. So I did, but he was beating her up. Punching her in the face. I was brought up right. You don't hit women. Made me sick. I vommed in the bathroom, but then he got me one in the gut for making a mess.'

His words come out in one long string, Dolan barely pausing for breath. Robin lets him talk, not wanting to disturb his train of thought.

'I told him to let her go. She was crying, blood coming out of her nose. But he said no, not until he got what he needed. He just dumped her back on the floor, tied up with all that tape. It looked like… like I see on TV.'

He stops now, sniffing back snot. Mina hands him a tissue and he smears it across his nose.

'What's his name?' Robin asks carefully.

'Nah-uh,' Dolan replies. He shakes his head. 'I saw what he did to her. I've seen him go for people outside pubs. He's a nutter. I ain't going to dob on him.'

'But Stephen,' Robin says gently. 'You have already, haven't you?'

'Nah-uh,' he repeats.

'The call to 101. That was you. We have your number. You were worried about Chloe and you called us.'

Dolan stares. Then he says quietly, 'I thought she was going to die.'

'You did the right thing, Stephen. Just give us his name. He won't know it came from you.'

He shakes his head again. 'No way.'

Robin rests his elbows on the table, then leans forward towards him. 'Stephen, I'm sorry to tell you this, but you're going to prison.' The boy's eyes widen again. 'But how long you go for, that's up to you. We're going to find your fingerprints and DNA in that caravan. We're going to find evidence of Chloe in your Transit – the same one we have on CCTV clearly making its way from Chloe's house to the caravan. We know you were there, and we know you helped kidnap her. What we don't know is the rest, and unless you give us a name we'll have to assume you were there alone. And you were the one beating the living shit out of her. Battery. Assault. GBH. Making threats to kill. Whatever. And if you're afraid of this nameless bloke you say was also there, imagine what your cell mate's going to do to you in prison.' Robin leans back in his seat, contentedly. 'You have no idea what they do to skinny kids like you in jail.'

The kid starts trembling again. His knee twitches so hard under the table Robin can feel the vibrations through the floor.

But he shakes his head, over and over.

'Nah-uh,' he repeats. 'I'll take my chances. Those guys – I survived them before. But him? I *know* he'll kill me.'

56

Freya has absolutely no idea what she's going to say to Josh. Her hand shakes as she puts the key in the door, her gut churns. She hasn't been able to eat all day.

She knows he's here; his car is in the driveway. And Mina wasn't taking any shit when she returned from her interview with the suspect.

'You can't hide at mine,' Mina said, as they put their coats on. She'd glanced at Robin as he stood talking to Ratcliffe and DCI Baker at the whiteboard. 'You need to make a decision.'

'I don't know what to do,' Freya whispered back.

Mina gave her a look. 'You can't have them both. If it's not Robin, then let him go. Once and for all. It's not fair on the poor man – to leave him pining after you all this time.'

'And if it is Robin?' Freya said quietly, and Mina had given her a small smile.

'Then you need to sort everything out with Josh. Be honest. It's only fair.'

Freya had glanced back to the whiteboard, where the men had been talking.

'We've put him back in the cell overnight,' Robin was saying. 'Hopefully a shitty night's sleep will help him see sense.' He'd lifted his hands over his head and stretched, rolling his head from one side to the other.

'You go home, Butler,' Baker said. 'Mouse can take over. Bloody good work. One out of two, and our victim alive and well.'

'But we don't know—'

'Butler. Home. Now.'

Freya had watched as Robin accepted defeat, grabbed his coat and bag and headed out. For a moment, he had glanced in her direction and met her eyes, but she couldn't tell what he was thinking.

She'd done her own handover and been sent home.

Freya knows Mina is right. But she still has no idea what to say. She pushes the front door open. She can hear the radio on in the kitchen. She takes her coat and shoes off, then slowly makes her way in.

Josh hasn't heard her over the noise of the music, and for a moment she stands in the doorway, watching him. He's singing along, slightly out of tune, while he's cooking at the hob. Mess covers the surfaces: a chopping board, the skin of an onion spilled onto the floor. An open tin of tomatoes, speckles of red around the saucepan. He glances her way, then jumps.

'Freya! How long have you been there?'

'Not long.'

He reaches over and turns the radio down. 'I'm cooking. Chilli, if that's okay?'

'Yes, thank you.' But she doesn't think she can stomach it.

He pauses, watching her. 'Are you all right? I'm glad you're home.' He puts the wooden spoon down and comes over to her, putting his arms round her. 'I'm sorry. I shouldn't have reacted like that, when I found Jonathan's photo. It was just a shock. Do you forgive me?'

He grins and wheedles his face round so she looks at him. She can't help but return his smile. This is what Josh does. The charm, the self-assurance. There is no doubt in his mind that he will be forgiven. That all it will take is a home-cooked meal and a kiss and everything will be back to normal.

His manner is so opposite to Robin's, Freya wonders how she could have fallen for both men. This scene captures Josh perfectly – the noise, the mess, the confidence, his happiness. While Robin is more contained, more hesitant about life.

But that's not Josh's fault. He had a perfect childhood. Two parents, one sister. He was popular at school, played sports. Never bullied. Never even had to try, really.

Unlike Robin, he didn't have a mother who died young, a father who struggled. A best friend who was far smarter than him. A sister and nephews who died horribly at the hands of a drunk driver. And secrets. Secrets Robin would take to his grave. For her, too.

'Josh,' she says, slowly. 'Why are you here?'

'Here?' He looks around, confused. Then he spots the chilli bubbling on the stove and releases her to go back to stir it. 'What do you mean?'

'Why did you join the police force?'

'Excitement. And to do something good. A detective came in for a careers day when I was about ten and he seemed like the coolest guy in the world. Solving murders! I couldn't think of anything else I wanted to do.' He glances back to her. 'Why?'

She ignores his question. 'And why are you with me?'

'Because I love you.' He frowns for a second. 'What's brought this on, Freya?'

'It's nothing, don't worry.'

'It's clearly something.' But he's distracted as the beeper goes and he drains the rice. 'Sit down. Eat dinner with me. I've got to go back to the nick after this.'

'Tonight?' Freya says, surprised.

'Yeah. Mouse wants me to follow up on some of the other tips from last night. Someone might have seen the second guy. And I need to pull my finger out, make a good impression, if I want to get promoted.' He grins. 'Especially if I have you as competition.'

He puts a bowl of steaming hot chilli in front of her. She tries to smile back, but it feels strained.

'Now what's up?' he says, as he shovels a forkful of dinner into his mouth.

She stirs the chilli, then takes a mouthful, giving herself time to think. It's delicious. Why is she rushing to end this? she wonders. Josh is perfect in every way. Her parents love him, everyone at work loves him. He's happy 95 per cent of the time. He can cook, as this meal shows. He's gorgeous. What is her problem?

'I can't explain it,' she says at last. 'I look at the people around us, and they're all married with children. I mean, take Mina. She has two kids and a husband and a mortgage and...'

Josh frowns. 'And she's always complaining how tired she is.'

'I know. It's just...' Freya sighs. 'Oh, I don't know.' She forces a smile, her cheeks tight. 'I'm just tired. Ignore me. Tell me about your day.'

And Josh does. He cracks straight on, telling her about the progress he's made on the case, some compliment DI Ratcliffe had given him, while finishing off his plate of chilli. When he's done, Freya is barely halfway through.

He checks his watch, then stands, the empty plate in his hand.

'Are you sure you're okay? I can stay if you want?'

'No, go. They need you at the nick.'

He places a hand on her shoulder then bends down to kiss her. 'Get some sleep, Freya,' he says. 'And I promise everything will be okay in the morning.'

She listens as he bustles about in the hallway, then a shout of goodbye and the door slams shut. She exhales slowly and pushes the plate of food away from her.

She needs to make a decision. And soon. She can't carry on like this. It's so unlike her.

Up until this week, everything was clear. She wanted a successful career in a job she loved, and a family. The whole package – that society expects, that everyone else has. That apparently makes your life complete.

She thought that was with Josh. But Robin... But what about Robin? her head screams.

What about the man she's worked every day with for the last twenty months? The man she trusts with her life, to always have her back. Who she can count on without hesitation? Who has seen her at her worst, and didn't bat an eyelid?

Who, if she's really being honest, is her closest friend. Who she kissed, and felt a rush of desire and longing and connection so powerful she never wanted to let him go. What about him? she thinks as she sits in her empty kitchen.

What about *him*?

57

Andrew doesn't get many visitors. Every day he watches loved ones arrive for the other patients on the ward, clutching magazines and chocolates and books. He lies here alone. Bored, with nothing but his thoughts to occupy him.

Diane breaks up the monotony. She arrives with a binder under her arm, paperwork for him to sign. Purchase orders, invoices, payroll.

'We need to keep the business running,' she says, twitching with efficiency.

'What for?' he asks, despondent, and she starts, looking at him with disapproval.

'I'll not have you talking like that,' she snaps. 'Hamilton Grace is your home. Yours and Tiller's. You boys have had your disagreements before, you'll make up soon enough.'

If only it were that simple – like kids arguing in the school playground – but he signs the documents anyway. She fusses around him, straightening his blanket, plumping his pillows, but then Andrew spots a familiar figure in the doorway. Diane follows his eyeline as a nurse points; slowly his wife makes her way down the rows.

Laura stops at the end of his bed. Her bruises have faded in the days since he last saw her; this is the first time she's visited him here. She's wearing blue jeans and a checked shirt; her hair is neat; she has small silver studs in her ears.

She regards Diane frostily. 'Some space, Diane. Please?'

Diane grumbles under her breath, but she gathers the paperwork back up and leaves.

'You don't need to be like that,' Andrew says. 'She's just doing her job.'

'She babies you. It's pathetic. Hasn't she got children of her own to look after?'

Andrew ignores the question. 'When did you get out of hospital?' he asks.

'This morning.'

'How are the kids?'

'They're fine. We're staying at Mum's.' Her answers are short; she's not inviting conversation.

'That's good.'

'Is it?' She snaps this time. 'We don't dare go home. Not just because of… what happened, but because I'm worried someone will come back. How much do you owe, Andy?'

He looks down to his hands, feeling the surge of shame and guilt.

'You don't know, do you? Bloody hell.' Laura's nearly shouting and she catches herself, glancing around to the eyes now trained on them. She pulls the curtain round his bed, then leans forward.

'I just came to tell you that it's over.' She's quieter now. A controlled calm. 'I can't do this anymore.'

'Laura, please—'

'No. I warned you. Last time. When we agreed no more casinos, no more apps on the iPhone. But I knew where you were going. Every time you went for a *walk*.' She spits out the last word. 'I knew you were going to the bookies. All those friends we've lost – because of you borrowing money. All those nights I've laid awake, wondering what you would sell next. How we could afford to pay the mortgage. When the police would arrest you for fraud.'

'How did—'

'Tiller told me. You've been stealing from the company!'

'I borrowed it.'

'It doesn't matter,' she hisses. 'All those times I've pulled you out of casinos. When you sold your car — your fucking car, Andrew!'

'I got it back.'

'That's not the point!' She catches herself again, then stands, hands by her sides in fists. 'You need to admit you have a problem. You need to get help.'

'And then you'll stay?'

'No. For your own benefit. Me and the kids — we'll find somewhere else to go. I'll sell the house. Get a job. I can't be responsible for you anymore.'

Andrew starts to cry. 'I'm so sorry,' he manages, his voice thick. 'Please, Laura. I can't do this without you.'

'No.' She takes a step back. 'No more emotional blackmail. No more lies. I'm a victim too. Me and the kids. The worry, the shame of what you do. I never feel secure. Always waiting for the day when someone will show up and take our home away. And instead, someone pushed into our house and traumatised our children.'

'That wasn't to do with my gambling.'

'Wasn't it? How can you be so sure? The police don't know who paid that man. You're a rotten blueberry in the box, Andrew. You make everything bad, and I can't take it. Once you get out of here, you'll need to find somewhere else to go. Because you're not welcome with us.'

And with that she turns on her heel, pushes the curtain to the side and strides away.

He watches her go, tears drying on his cheeks. He wants to go after her and he tugs at his broken leg in frustration, feeling the ache of the healing bones. He has his company. They can still sell. He can pay off his debts and get her back.

He collapses onto his pillow. He feels the familiar shake in his hands; the restlessness in his brain. Despite the knowledge that it has put him in hospital, destroyed his marriage. Lost him his family. Despite all that, he's still thinking: I can win her back. I can win it back.

Just one last time.

58

Robin is not skilled in the art of ending a relationship; his previous girlfriends have always got there first. He would begin well in his role as boyfriend, but eventually work and general apathy would mean he forgot birthdays and missed weekends, and the poor women would dump him in despair and frustration.

Now, he sits in front of Jo, dinner eaten, his wine drunk. He should have done it when she'd first arrived, because now the tension is awful. She's been quiet too – they've managed no more than small talk over dinner, quick snippets of discussions about work.

'Robin,' she says at last. 'I need to talk to you.'

He instantly relaxes. Oh, thank God, he thinks, she's going to dump me first. He looks at her. She fiddles with the stem of her wine glass; she's barely touched the contents.

'You might have noticed I've been a bit distracted these past few days.' He hasn't, but he makes a non-committal noise, waiting for her to continue. 'I've felt a bit out of sorts. Not my normal self. And I wasn't sure why.'

She looks at him now. She's smiling slightly; a reaction that doesn't feel right, given the words he's expecting to come next.

'I'm pregnant, Robin.'

His eyes widen. He sits back in shock.

'You're... what?'

'Pregnant.' She grins, then the smile fades to uncertainty in the face of his reaction.

'Well... fuck,' he manages.

'It's a shock. I get that. And I don't expect you to say anything now, but I thought you should know. Sooner, rather than later.' She pushes the glass of wine in front of her away.

'Yes. Right. How far along are you? I thought... but... we were... being careful. You know.'

'Yes, so did I. But obviously condoms weren't enough. And six weeks. I think.'

'You're sure? You've done a test?'

'I've done about five tests, Robin.'

'A baby. Shit.'

He blinks again, then leans forward and pours himself another glass of wine.

'Are you...' Jo begins. 'Are you happy about it?'

'Yes! Yes, I am.' And weirdly, now he's had five seconds for it to sink in, his immediate thought is joy. Complicated by a thousand other things, all Freya-related. But this? This is what he's been wanting for a while. 'Shit,' he mutters again. *He's going to be a father.* A smile creeps onto his face. 'Fuck me.'

His brain is conjuring up tiny fingers and toes. A boy or a girl, which would he prefer? He doesn't care, he realises, because this child is his. A part of him. No more than a few cells, but something he already feels a bond to.

'How long have you known?' he asks.

'A few days. I thought I was hung-over, after that meal out with Josh and Freya. But then the sickness didn't go away, so...' He's still stunned and silent in front of her. 'I know we haven't been together for long,' she continues quickly. 'And if you don't want to be involved, that's fine. But I'm not getting rid of it—'

'No. Absolutely not,' Robin interrupts. 'As long as this is what you want?'

'Yes,' she smiles, then reaches over and takes his hand. 'Yes, I'm very happy.'

'Then I am too.'

She leans over and he kisses her.

'How will this work with the potential move?' he asks. 'The promotion?'

'I'll take six months off, then hire a nanny. Or something. I don't know. We'll work it out. That's if… Have you given it any more thought? I know you've been busy with the case, but tomorrow's Friday. This has to take priority now.'

'Yes, yes, I know. I'm sorry. It's a lot to take in. Can I… Tomorrow?' He's stuttering, barely making sense. 'Just give me until tomorrow? To process it all.'

'Of course. But you're happy? With the news?'

'Yes. Yes, I am.' Robin thinks about everything that's happened in the last twenty-four hours. A flush of guilt as he remembers the kiss with Freya — his promise to her, that he would end things with Jo. The conflicting feelings he's now facing.

But one thought remains, that makes the silly grin reappear on his face.

'Fuck,' he repeats. 'I'm going to be a father.'

FRIDAY

59

The sun catches the edge of the windowsill, sending a perfect triangle of light across the dusty floorboards. Tiller looks up from his desk and peers at the clock: 5.52 a.m. A whole night lost in a whirlwind of numbers and letters.

He types without needing to look at the keyboard – to the onlooker it would seem incomprehensible, but to Tiller it's a language as natural as English.

This is how he communicates. To machines. To networks and servers. As long as there's Wi-Fi, he can connect.

The dog snores quietly at his feet. Max has wheedled his way slowly out of his bed and now the spaniel sprawls among the cables and connectors under his desk. He twitches and yelps; Tiller imagines a doggy dream of squirrels and birds and tender roast meat.

He's enjoying having the dog here now. Max isn't low-maintenance; he's not the sort of dog who sleeps all day and is comfortable with a mere scratch under the ear. But his lust for life is contagious, and Tiller has found himself laughing more than he has in weeks as the dog hurls himself with abandon at every puddle and body of water on their walks.

Tiller turns his attention back to his computer. He hasn't worked this way in years. As a kid he tried a bit of hacking. Nothing complicated. His parents' computer at first – child's play, the password written down in the book kept in their desk drawer. Servers at school, downloading test papers.

His nemesis's personal laptop, embarrassing photos somehow finding their way to everyone's inbox.

At university he joined a club. An undergraduate project in white hat hacking next. A different discipline, a bit of fun. He liked learning quick dirty code to get a job done, so different to the precision he employs now.

In his spare time he explored. Public infrastructure. The national grid. Traffic and travel information centres. He exploited poor passwords, found security flaws in programs. He downloaded hacking tools from the communities and forums, even straying onto the dark web for tricks and tips. Never breaking anything, just having a snoop around. Knowing that he could. It was much easier back then.

But it scared him. The thought that he could go to prison made him stop.

And now? Now the stakes are far higher.

It's not just the guilt that's driving him forward. He knows it's his fault that Chloe's in hospital, but it's more than that. A burning rage – that someone would try to take his baby from him.

This algorithm, this company. It's everything. Other people have children and friends and fully functioning relationships with people they love. Tiller has this. It's his life's work – and they wanted to *steal* it. Fuck, no.

Earlier in the evening, he'd driven around, parking outside residential houses, looking for vulnerable Wi-Fi. The wardriving of old. He'd negotiated home CCTV systems, networks so badly configured he could log in from the road. He'd downloaded footage from places near to where Chloe had been held, looking for something, someone that would make sense.

Back at home, hours passed. He found himself lost in the work, oblivious to anything going on around him, until now he notices something strange on the screen. It's a camera from someone's Ring CCTV system, much like the one he knows Andrew has on his own house. But unlike Andrew's, expertly configured and installed by Tiller, this one's kept all the default passwords. It's footage from the road that leads to the allotments where Chloe was found, and he squints at the screen. He rewinds it; stares at the car again. He recognises it – but from where?

He moves on, logging onto to the ANPR system that monitors the road network around Hampshire. He writes a simple script, looking for a backdoor – a test function that some absent-minded developer has forgotten to remove – and exploits it. He writes a program, searching for the number plate he's seen before, then he glances at the clock.

It's nearly eight. Visiting hours at the hospital begin soon; he needs to get there to see Chloe. Leaving the program running, he stands up and heads for the shower.

60

Robin's still smiling when he wakes up in the morning, and for a moment he lies in bed, taking it all in. He's going to be a father. Where once the thought terrified him, now he only feels excitement.

Jo left last night, the demands of an early start providing him with a much-needed reprieve from her scrutiny. She could tell something was up – his joy at her news was real, just tempered by thoughts of Freya.

He picks up his phone, then frowns at the lack of messages. Normally she'd be in touch, first thing, with whatever was on her mind. Thoughts about a case, a rant about the news, sometimes even the dream she'd had that night. He misses her, and a ball grows in his stomach as he wonders if this absence will become permanent once she knows Jo's news. How will this complication change things? Or does none of it matter, decision made, as he imagines her lying in bed with Josh?

He sighs and pulls himself to a sit, swinging his legs out of bed. Jo needs to know about Devon today and he has no idea what to tell her. But he knows one thing for certain: this baby – *his* baby – has to take priority.

–

The drive to the nick is clear and he makes it in half an hour. He parks up, then walks to his desk, one coffee in each hand. Freya is already there and working, but before he can say anything to her, his phone rings. He puts the coffee in front of Freya and answers it.

'I'll be right down,' he says, and picks up his cup again. Freya looks up with interest.

'It's Tiller,' he says. 'He's at the front desk.'

Freya follows Robin down, both of them swigging coffee as they go. Through the small glass panel in the double doors, Robin can see Hamilton is agitated, pacing one way across the foyer then the other. When he sees Robin he heads straight over.

'She won't give it to me,' Tiller barks.

'Pardon, Tiller?' Robin asks sweetly.

'Chloe. She won't tell me where the encryption key is.'

Robin sighs, then escorts him through to the small interview room close to the double doors. He gestures for Tiller to sit down; he does so reluctantly. Freya stays standing, while Robin takes the seat opposite him.

'You need to get it from her,' Tiller starts up again. 'She says it's my fault she got kidnapped and now I can fuck off. You need to tell her to give it to me.'

'And how do you suggest we do that?'

'It's blackmail. Or theft!'

'You told her to type in the key. To keep it secret from you.'

'But only temporarily. Go down to the hospital and arrest her.'

'You want us to arrest a traumatised woman recovering from being beaten and kidnapped?' Robin articulates it carefully, hoping that Tiller will see the error in his thinking.

Luckily, it does the trick. 'Well, maybe not that. But please, somehow? You need to get her to tell you.'

'Can't you just crack it?' Freya asks from behind Robin.

Tiller pulls a face. 'No, I can't *just crack it*,' he mocks. 'It would take me years. Multiple lifetimes to break a key like that. Why do you think it was set in the first place?'

'There's no need to be rude, Tiller,' Robin says. 'What if you wrote it again?'

'I could, but…' Tiller's face falls and for a moment Robin thinks he's going to cry. 'It took me years. Years of development and testing, and that was just to write the initial algorithm. That code is now deep within the weightings of the vast spider's web that is our machine learning model – and that model has learned from various users over many years. The data that it used is gone. No one can recreate it. Even the way it learned is unique. The weightings, the values of those silks in our web are encrypted, neuromorphically – it can make the predictions but can't be copied. So no, I can't just write it again.'

He puts his head in his hands for a moment. Then he quickly looks up. 'Have you caught the people that did this to her?'

'We have one in custody. Stephen Dolan. Does that name ring any bells?' Tiller shakes his head. 'We're hoping to get a lead on the second man shortly.'

'What if I help you?'

Tiller has an expression on his face that tells Robin he isn't going to like what comes next. He takes a swig of his coffee. 'How?' he asks slowly.

'You have access to the traffic cameras across the city, right?'

Robin glances back to Freya. She looks as confused as he is. 'Yes. But there's so much footage we haven't found it helpful.'

'What if I could give you the camera locations and timestamps for a car going back and forth to the caravan?'

Freya moves forward and sits down next to Robin.

'How exactly have you come across this information, Tiller?' Robin asks.

Tiller grins. 'Do you need to know? Can't you just say it was luck and hard work that led you there?'

'We could.' He looks across at Freya. Her eyes narrow for a moment, then she gives a small nod.

'Go on then,' Robin says.

61

Robin and Freya wait as Tiller pulls his laptop out of his bag and opens the lid. It springs to life, showing a box of scrolling code.

'Don't pay too much attention,' Hamilton says as he types, his fingers a blur on the keys. Then he grabs a piece of paper and writes a series of numbers on it, followed by a number plate. 'Camera location, timestamp,' he says, pointing to the two rows of numbers, then pushing the piece of paper to Robin. 'You're looking for a blue Renault Clio. With a body kit and lowered suspension.'

'Stay here,' Robin commands.

He leaves, Freya following closely behind. When they get to the office, they head straight to Freya's desk, and she pulls up the CCTV.

'Camera 022,' Robin directs, scooting his chair over to her. 'Tuesday the twenty-sixth, quarter past three.' They both lean forward towards the screen. 'There, there.' He points, one finger on the monitor as the Renault Clio comes into view. Robin checks the licence plate, then stands up, shouting across the office.

'Everyone, here!' Heads turn Robin's way. He writes the number plate on the board. 'We're looking for this car. A blue Renault Clio. Tracking from Millbrook, to...'

He looks at Freya, who's been typing in the rest of the timestamps.

'Lordswood,' she concludes.

'Who owns the car, Butler?' Mouse asks.

'Paul Freeman,' Freya replies.

That name again. 'The allotments where Chloe was found was owned by George Freeman,' Robin says.

'Twenty-two years old,' Freya adds. She has the PNC up and is reading through his record. 'Previous conviction for drunk and disorderly, ABH, class B possession. A regular charmer,' she finishes, but Robin is already at the door, heading back to Tiller.

When he gets to the room, Tiller is still sat at his laptop, staring at the screen. He looks up eagerly as Robin barges through the door.

'Paul Freeman,' Robin says. 'Do you recognise the name?'

Tiller's eyes widen. 'That's why I knew the car! I've seen it. At the office.'

'He works for you?'

'No. No, he doesn't. But his mum does. He comes to pick her up sometimes. Diane. Diane Freeman. She's Andrew's PA.'

62

Freya and DI Ratcliffe watch through the remote video feed as Robin and Mina interview Diane Freeman. She fidgets nervously in the interview room, her hands constantly moving in tiny jumps and shakes. Her eyes dart to the solicitor next to her, then back to her interviewers.

She'd been at work when she'd been arrested. Diligence or a desperation for an alibi, Freya's not sure, but yet another yellow and blue patrol car had arrived at Hamilton Grace. Freya can only imagine the gossip going around that office.

Mina's talking, taking the role of good cop to Robin's bad. And so far the interview's not going well. The solicitor has read a brief statement; all follow-up questions have been answered with a quiet 'no comment'.

'How did Paul know about the encryption key, Diane?' Mina is asking. Freya feels usurped, but the allocation was Ratcliffe's choice – nothing to do with Robin.

'No comment,' she replies. It's almost a whisper, her eyes fixed on the table.

'Because it must have come from you. Did you tell him?'

'No comment.'

Mina glances to Robin; Robin opens the beige file in front of him. Freya gives a small smile; she knows what's coming next. Grumpy cop, with the nasty stuff.

Robin takes a photo out of the folder, turns it around and pushes it towards Diane. Diane flinches.

'This is what your son did to Chloe Somerset,' Robin says. The photo is swapped for a different one. The left side of her face this time, bruises rendering her almost recognisable. 'You worked with Chloe, didn't you? Did you know her well?'

'No comment.'

'Would you have considered her a friend? Before your son punched her repeatedly in the face?'

Diane starts to weep, her hands over her eyes.

'I think my client would like a break, Detectives,' the solicitor says, disapproval dripping from his words.

Mina announces the suspension of the interview and she and Robin move out of the room.

Freya and Ratcliffe meet them in the corridor. Robin's face is grave.

Mina sighs and leans against the wall. 'She's saying she knew nothing about what Paul had planned.'

'We're not going to get anything out of her,' Robin adds. 'Except a complaint for mental distress if we're not careful.'

Ratcliffe nods. 'Stick her back in her cell. We'll have a go at the son.'

Freya's seen this guy already. Watching from a distance as he was escorted through custody in cuffs. Biceps bulging, chest like a lump of timber. He couldn't look less like his delicate mother.

He'd barely grunted as he was booked in, kicked off when they tried to get him in his cell. Freya doesn't relish the thought of sitting opposite him in a confined interview room; it's a fraction of what Chloe must have felt, tied up and locked in a caravan with this guy.

Little wonder Stephen Dolan didn't want to talk.

Freya and Ratcliffe wait as Freeman is escorted from the consultation room, the duty solicitor in tow. They all sit down at the table. Freeman glares at Ratcliffe, then switches to a leer once he sees Freya.

They start the video; they say their names.

'Shall we begin?' Ratcliffe asks with a slight smile.

'My client has prepared a brief statement,' the solicitor replies.

They look to Paul; he stares at the piece of paper in his hand, words written in neat capitals. By the solicitor, Freya assumes.

'I have never met Chloe Somerset. I did not abduct her on Tuesday the twenty-sixth of April. On this date, and the subsequent days, I was working at the Critchlow Building Merchants as a builder. I have loaned my Renault Clio to a friend. I have no more to say on the matter.'

He looks up with a sarcastic smile.

'That's it?' Mouse says. 'You're claiming you knew nothing about the kidnapping?'

'No comment.'

'Where were you when you weren't at work? You couldn't have been there twenty-four seven?'

'No comment.'

'Has your solicitor shared the footage of your Renault Clio travelling to and from the place where Chloe was held? What do you have to say about that?'

Freeman taps a sausage-like finger on the statement. 'I lent that car to a friend.'

'What's your friend's name?'

'No comment.'

Mouse glances to Freya. Freya leans forward.

'Paul, are you aware that we have your mum next door?' she says quietly.

At that question, his entire expression changes. The façade slips, and he glances in the direction Freya is indicating.

'Why do you have my mum?'

'She's been arrested for conspiracy to kidnap.'

'She's got nothing to do with it. You let her go.'

Freya had taken a long look at the file they had on Paul Freeman: his record on the PNC, and all the available information Intel had been able to gather at such short notice. Up until a year ago, Paul Freeman's registered address had been his mum's place. An only child. His father had died seven years ago, leaving son and mum together. Mum never remarried. Regular payments from Paul's bank account to Diane's. A dutiful son who picked Diane up from work when he was needed.

A man built like a brick shithouse, with one point of vulnerability.

Freya pulls a piece of paper out from the file. She lays it on the table in front of them.

'These here, Paul, are the mobile phone records for your number.' She takes another sheet out. 'And here is the same, for your mum's. Do you know what we found when we compared the two?'

Paul glares; the solicitor leans forward and tries to decipher the highlighted sections.

'Chloe Somerset was abducted on Tuesday at around three p.m., and at that point calls between you and your mother go nuts. At least six an hour. Not talking for more than a few minutes at a time. Sometimes, it seems, you don't answer and she leaves a message on your voicemail. Do you know, Paul, that we can recover voicemails, even when you've deleted them?'

His head jumps up. He blinks rapidly, like he has something in his eye.

'Shall we listen to a few of them?'

Freya pulls the laptop forward and presses play on the clip she has loaded. There's static, then a voice.

'Paul, answer your phone. You need to promise you won't hurt her, Paul? Please?' A pause and a stifled sob. 'Please?'

Freya looks up at Paul. 'There are more, mostly along the same lines. This is a good one.'

She presses play again. 'I should never have told you. Why did you do this? Let the poor girl go, Paul. Please.'

'She told you about the encryption key, didn't she, Paul?' Freya says. 'Perhaps she overheard Tiller talking to Andrew, but somehow she found out. And then you conspired to steal it. Your mum's going to go to prison. Is that what you want?'

'She had nothing to do with it,' he growls.

The solicitor interrupts. 'I need to speak to my client.'

But Paul carries on. 'It was all me. She didn't know. If I tell you what happened, will you let her go?'

Freya glances to her DI.

'There are no promises, Paul,' Ratcliffe says. 'But it'll certainly help.'

Freeman pauses for a moment, as if considering his options. Then he sits forward. 'That bastard locked that company up tight – that was her retirement fund. She doesn't have a pension, she never set one up. Grace said he'd see her right. She's been with them from the beginning – that company is as much hers as it is theirs.'

'But then Hamilton refused to sell.'

'The prick! I knew that if we got the password off that girl and gave it to Andrew that he could go ahead with the sale. Mum had heard Hamilton on the phone to his woman, something about a code, so we knew she had it. Then all I had to do was follow him one day to hers so I knew where she lived.'

'Then abduct her?'

'I knew Steve would let me use his van. Thought he'd help out, but he was useless. No stomach for it. But she was no problem. Shoved her in the back, drove her to Dad's caravan. No one would disturb us there.'

'Did Andrew Grace know what you were doing?'

He shakes his head. 'Nah. That pansy twat wouldn't have the balls to do something like this. But I knew he'd be grateful. Then Mum would be sorted.'

'But Chloe wouldn't give you the key.'

'It's her fault, stupid bitch. If she'd just told us where it was, she could have been out of there within hours. No problem. But she refused. What could be so important she wouldn't fess up?'

'So you punched her in the face. Repeatedly.'

His nose wrinkles in defiance. 'Yeah. Stupid bitch. She should have told me.'

His solicitor slumps back in his seat, his arms folded across his chest. His work is done. There is no more to add here.

63

News travels fast; there are cheers and whistles as Freya and Mouse arrive back in the incident room. Mouse raises his hands to calm the applause.

'Good work, all of you,' he says. 'Now crack on. There is a case to build.'

They need to gather the evidence, pull it into a compelling file for the CPS, although with his confession he has already been charged with false imprisonment, kidnapping and GBH, and plonked back in his cell.

All the same, Freya feels disappointed they haven't managed to pin anything on Giles Kepner and Parapet Holdings. She would have loved to have slapped that smug git in jail.

She sits down next to Robin; he gives her a grin that makes her stomach flip.

'Robin,' she begins. But before she can get any further, Greg is standing at their desk.

'Thanks for your quick work on those mobile records,' Robin says.

Greg nods. 'I'm always amazed how stupid people are. Mobile phones are just tiny surveillance devices. I'm waiting on the cell sites, but once we get those we'll have him tied up nice and tight. And on the subject of cell sites...' Greg points to Robin's screen. 'I emailed you the data from the burner phone. Do you remember? Our 897 number that was messaging our French friend, Durand?'

Robin turns back and pulls up the information.

'What am I looking at here?' he asks. Freya looks over; she can't make sense of it either.

Greg sighs in mock exasperation, then slumps in the seat next to them.

'Headlines?'

'Yes, please.'

Greg grins. 'I can tell you've been busy, because if you'd looked at this sooner you'd have been on the phone to me straight away. Calls from 897 were made from a variety of locations across the city. But the majority come from two places.'

Greg pauses for effect; Freya nudges him with a finger.

'Greg. Come on.'

'A lot of the calls were made via this mast – 2291. Out in the sticks, so it covers a large area. Sherfield English, West Wellow. Maybe even down to Bramshaw. So it's hard to be certain.'

Freya glances to Robin. He meets her eye and smiles slowly. She knows what he's thinking.

'But couple that with the location of the second mast, and you start to see a compelling picture.'

'Where's that one?' Freya asks. But she already knows the answer.

'2265. Only covering a narrow band of houses in—'

'Chilworth,' Robin finishes.

Greg points a confirmatory finger at Robin. But Robin is already on his feet.

'Freya, grab your coat,' he says. 'We're going to see Andrew Grace.'

64

All along, Robin's had the feeling that Andrew Grace has been lying to them. And he's sick of it. He strides towards Grace's ward, Freya at his side. The gambling addiction is only the beginning.

The nurse stops them at the entrance, but Robin explains the severity of the situation and she lets them through. It's lunchtime, food is slowly being distributed down the ward; the smell makes Robin's empty stomach rumble.

Grace has been moved to the end, and he sees them coming. His fork pauses in mid-air; his mouth opens.

Robin closes the curtain with a decisive swoosh. He places the small recording device on the table next to them. Switches it on; tape already in.

'Andrew,' he says assertively. 'We need the truth.'

Grace points to the box. 'What's that?'

'We're recording this conversation. The doctor has cleared us to speak to you. Are you happy to be interviewed voluntarily?'

'Am I...?' Grace seems stunned. 'Yes.'

'Thank you. You are under caution.' And Robin recites the words all cops know by heart. 'Do you want legal advice?'

'Why do I need legal advice? No, no, I don't want a lawyer.'

'Sure?'

He shakes his head.

'For the benefit of the tape, Andrew Grace has declined legal representation.'

'I heard you found Chloe. I told you everything I know.'

'It's not about that.'

269

Robin takes a sheet of paper out of his bag and slams it down on the patient table in front of Grace. The water glass wobbles and spills.

'This shows the cell sites for calls made from a mobile phone number ending 897. A mobile phone that was used to contact Thierry Durand. The guy who broke into your house. Who assaulted your wife and your son. And do you know where these calls were made?'

Grace's face goes pale.

'Your office, Andrew. Your house.' Robin feels tension in his muscles, a hot burn of anger in his veins. All along Grace has played the victim. Robin felt sorry for him, has done his best for him. And all along he'd known.

Robin forces himself to calm down. 'But that alone isn't definitive, Andrew,' he continues. 'Cell sites are broad, it's hard to know precisely where calls are made. But coupled with the data from your car?'

Jess has the Audi in the garage. They called her once they were on the road. 'You're right, Robin,' Jess had confirmed. 'He was there.'

'You drove to Southwood. The telemetry from your car puts you outside Durand's house. Early that Saturday morning. Why did you go? So you could take him this cash?'

Freya places Grace's bank statements down in front of him. The same ones she'd been closely studying, two cash withdrawals of fifteen hundred pounds highlighted. One Friday morning, before the break-in. And one just before the visit to Southwood on Saturday morning.

Grace gawps at them, his mouth opening and closing like a suffocating fish.

'Laura was lucky. Tim was lucky!' Robin snaps. 'You paid a hired thug to break into your house. Who knows what he might have done. Three grand, Andrew!' His voice is rising with astonishment. 'You know we have that cash, don't you? You know we'll find your fingerprints. Three grand!' he repeats.

'That's all your family was worth to you. They're traumatised for life. For what?'

Robin suspects why, but he wants to hear it from Grace.

The man's crying now, his head tilted towards his lap. He takes a laboured breath in, then puts his hands over his face.

Robin looks at Freya and catches her gaze, opening his eyes wide in frustration. She nods as if to say, leave it to me.

She leans forward and gently touches his hand.

He stops, staring at his quivering fingers.

'Andrew,' she says, gently. 'Tell us what happened.' Grace shakes his head, still crying. 'You couldn't have known what Durand was like.'

Grace looks up, blinking back tears. 'You have no idea. It was me. It was all me.'

Freya glances to Robin. He narrows his eyes, echoing her confused expression.

'Andrew?' Freya prompts. 'What do you mean?'

He looks up, his eyes red and watery.

'I told him. I told him to hit her. I told him to do it all.'

65

It was Tiller's fault. If it hadn't been for Tiller, none of this would have happened.

He was desperate for that money. Millions and millions. And to get the money he needed the key.

Why should it have been Tiller's decision? Why was it up to him? Hadn't Andrew also put late nights and determination and brain power into the company? Tiller's part was easy – he just had to write the numbers and squiggles, but he – Andrew! – had to grow the business. Persuade people that their idea could work, even when it didn't. That was the hard part.

And Tiller said no.

'No way,' he'd replied. They were going through due diligence and what they discovered, what little they could find, made for difficult reading. 'I'm not having my life's work help kill people.'

'They're not killing people,' Andrew had said, trying to keep the desperation out of his voice. 'They're protecting UK citizens.'

'And how do you think they're doing that?' Tiller replied, sarcastically. 'Gentle persuasion?'

Andrew needed that encryption key. He could forge Tiller's signature, sign over the company without him. But without the key, there was no sale.

Andrew had never understood the technology. He'd tried in the early days, but his eyes had glazed over and his brain hurt whenever Tiller tried to explain. So he learned enough to sell it, and on the rare occasions they needed a technical explanation Tiller would come along.

'We need the whole thing,' the man had said. 'Including the behavioural analysis model.'

But there was no way Tiller would give it up. 'I couldn't, even if I wanted to,' he replied. 'Someone else has it. Safe-keeping.'

Andrew's first thought was Laura.

The two had been close from the beginning. Andrew always suspected a burgeoning relationship between his awkward best friend and the pretty blonde, but when he got his sights on something, nothing would get in his way. But even after Laura and Andrew were married, Tiller and Laura would hang out together; they had private jokes, something to do with a book. He'd call her Artemis, she'd call him Parzival. Andrew didn't understand.

And now? Now, Laura didn't give a shit about Andrew. The gambling had ripped them apart; when they were together all they did was argue. Andrew suspected she had someone else, and one night he got hold of her phone, checking her messages. Long chains of conversations between her and Tiller. Never anything sexual or incriminating, but they talked about him. About his gambling problem. Ganging up.

He knew that if Tiller had given it to anyone, it would have been her.

He needed a way to get all their laptops, their tablets, without raising suspicion. If he took them, Laura would know. Tiller could change the password. Move the program, or whatever it was called. So he drove to Southwood. He asked around. Kids playing on street corners, their school uniforms dirty and worn. Who were the people that got things done?

A twenty quid note here and there, and he got a name and a number.

Thierry, they said, eyeing the Audi. A couple of grand and Thierry will do anything.

A couple of grand, he thought, and what else could this Rottweiler do? Scare them, so they sold the house? So they released the equity stored up in that mansion? They could make do with a smaller place. Maybe even go abroad, start again? The kids would like the sunshine.

The possibilities were clear. A fresh start. Money in the bank.

'Knock her around a bit,' he said to Durand. The bulldog stared.

'You want me to teach the bitch a lesson?' he said. Then he'd smiled, a row of stained uneven teeth. 'I know what you mean.'

'No. No. Just…' Andrew paused. 'Show her who's boss.'

The shock when Andrew heard what happened – as the ambulance took his wife and son away, as he'd seen the extent of the bruises. He'd felt the acid rise in his stomach. When he thought of what could have happened to Amber, the vomit couldn't be stopped.

Andrew met him afterwards as Thierry handed over the bin bag of electronics. He'd passed him the final fifteen hundred quid.

'How could you?' he said. 'You knocked her unconscious!'

Durand just shrugged. 'The bitch knows now.'

It was his fault. The laptops and the tablets were completely empty, Kepner confirmed. Andrew dumped them in the nearest bin.

He was wrong. There was nothing.

He deserved the kicking outside the casino. He deserved the pain and the blood. And now he deserves the handcuffs on his wrists, the caution the detective is running through again as they arrest him for conspiracy.

'I never meant it to go this far,' he says, tears running down his face. 'For Laura to end up in hospital. All over an encryption key.' Then he stops. 'Has Chloe got it? Where was it hidden?'

Butler looks at him. The contempt is clear, but something else flickers across his face. Confusion. Defeat. Hesitation.

'We don't know,' Butler replies.

66

A police guard is called to watch him; Freya knows the clock won't officially start until they take Andrew Grace into custody, and that could be days yet. In the meantime, Robin pockets the tape, safe with Grace's recorded confession.

'Do you think she suspects?' Freya asks, as they walk back to Robin's car.

'What? That her husband paid a man to break into their house? To beat her up?' He shakes his head, sadly. 'If she doesn't, she'll know soon. What an absolute shit.'

Freya couldn't agree more. How would that feel? Knowing that your own husband had paid a thug to attack you. She leans her head back in the seat and closes her eyes – savouring the quiet as Robin drives. The next thing she knows, Robin's gently rubbing her arm, encouraging her awake.

'Oh, bugger,' she mumbles. She wipes her mouth with the back of her hand. 'Was I snoring?'

'Loudly,' Robin replies with a smile. 'Nothing I haven't seen before.'

It's an off-the-cuff remark, but he turns away quickly. Freya knows he could be talking about any number of occasions when she has dozed off in his presence, but the thought brings up the image of beds, and being together, and— Oh, fuck.

They've come to a stop in the underground car park of the nick; the whole journey has passed while she's been napping. Robin pauses, the engine off, thinking.

'Jo came over last night,' he says softly, looking away from her to the car keys in his hand. 'I didn't break up with her.'

'Oh, okay.' Freya looks out to the empty car park. She chews her lip, feeling hypocritical at her disappointment. 'Did you tell her… about Wednesday?'

'No.' She hears a movement and when she looks at him, he's turned in his seat, facing her. 'Freya, she's pregnant,' he says.

The shock is almost physical. She stares at him for a moment, her mind blank. 'With your baby?' she manages at last.

'Yes, with my baby.'

'Well… fuck.'

'Yeah. That was my response too.'

'Was it planned?'

'No! Completely out of the blue.'

'And you're… happy about it?'

'About the baby, yes. About the rest?' He shrugs, apathetically. 'I don't know.'

'Are you staying together?'

'I think so, yes.' Robin pauses, running his hands down his face. 'Fuck, I don't know. I don't know!' he says, louder now, making Freya jump. 'You're all I've thought about since… then. Wondering what you're going to do. If you'll choose me, or him. But you're still with Bruce Wayne, right?'

'Don't call him that. But yes.'

'So, there you go. Neither of us is sure. Hardly the best way to start a relationship, is it?'

Freya doesn't reply, just opens the door and gets out of the car. Without looking back, she swings her bag over her shoulder and strides across the car park. A baby. Jo's having a fucking baby. Robin's baby. Fuck. *Fuck!*

She walks as quickly as she can, pulling the doors back and letting one slam against the concrete door frame before she runs up the stairs.

Getting as far away from him as she can before the tears spill, unabated, down her cheeks.

67

Robin mutters a few swear words as he watches her march away. That wasn't how he wanted it to go. But what else can he do? The idea of this baby, it's exciting. More than anything else has been for a while – his newly requited feelings for Freya notwithstanding.

Wearily, he climbs out of the car and follows in the same direction, back to the office. When he gets there, he scans the room, but she's nowhere to be seen.

Ratcliffe is talking to Baker on the far side. He heads over to Robin the moment he sees him.

'He confessed? What a shit,' Mouse says. Robin had called him on the journey back, filling him in on everything Grace told them.

'That's an understatement.'

'We can all go home early tonight then,' Mouse declares triumphantly.

'Except we still don't know where the encryption key is.'

'Oh, that.' Mouse shrugs. 'Chloe Somerset can keep it. Serves him right.'

Half of Robin agrees, but the unsolved mystery bothers him. In the face of all that violence, the threat of death, Chloe had kept quiet. Were her feelings towards Tiller so strong she would put him ahead of her own personal safety? Somehow, he doubts it.

As he's thinking, Freya comes into the office, Mina following closely behind. Her face is pale and she sits down at her desk without so much as a glance. Mina, however, is scrutinising the room and the moment she catches sight of him, her eyebrows lower. She meets his gaze, then points towards the kitchen with a slow finger. Robin obeys.

Once they're in the small space, Mina glances out, checks no one's nearby then turns to him.

'Robin, what the fuck?'

'What?'

'Don't play innocent with me. Jo's pregnant? You kiss Freya one night, and the next you find out Jo's having your baby?'

'I didn't plan it like that. I didn't know.'

'So that's it? You and Freya – it's over before it's even begun?'

Robin sighs. 'Mina, I honestly don't have a clue. I'm forty-three. I want a family. I'm not going to turn my back on Jo.'

'I'm not saying you ignore Jo—'

'So what are you saying? That I can be with Freya, and have a baby with Jo? What's the chance of me being able to have both? Unlikely, don't you think?'

'If you were just honest with both of them?'

Robin gives Mina a look. 'I was honest with Freya the other night—'

'No, you weren't. And you know it.'

'Anyway, she's still with Josh—'

They hear a noise coming from outside, commotion and shouting in the office. They stop and crane their necks out of the door.

'Everyone! Everyone, your attention. Please?'

Josh is standing in the middle of the room, his hands in the air. Everyone has paused – mid-conversation, phones slowly lowered to their receivers – looking at him. He smiles broadly. Not a trace of self-doubt on his stupid grinning face.

Mina and Robin move out of the kitchen to watch.

'What's going on?' Robin whispers to Mina. He looks over to Freya. She looks as confused as everyone else.

'I don't know,' Mina says slowly.

'I just want to… Wait a sec.' Josh pauses, then puts one foot on a desk and hauls himself up. He's now standing above everyone, wobbling slightly. 'That's better. So! As many of you know, I've been fortunate for a while now to be able to call the beautiful Freya West my girlfriend.'

Whooping and catcalls fill the air. Robin looks at Freya; her face has gone red.

'Oh, he's not…' Mina whispers next to Robin.

'He's not what?' Robin says, but Mina just shakes her head. Robin has a feeling that whatever this is, he's not going to like it.

'Well, I have to say, I've been a fool,' Josh continues. 'I've known what a wonderful detective she is, what an incredible person she is. How she's beautiful, and kind. But I've not realised how truly lucky I am. And I want to put an end to that today.'

With an athletic leap, he jumps off the desk, landing with both feet in front of Freya. She's staring at him, her hands covering her mouth, her eyes wide.

And Robin watches, horrified, as Josh gets down on one knee.

'Freya Elizabeth West,' Josh says. 'Will you do me the honour of being my wife?'

Josh pulls a small box out of his pocket and opens it. The room hushes. Robin feels his whole body drop; he barely breathes.

Freya slowly takes her hands away from her mouth. She blinks a few times, her eyes locked on Josh.

Then, 'Yes,' she says.

The room is a mass of energy. Cheers and applause fill the air. Josh leans forward and grabs Freya in a big hug, then takes the ring out of the box and puts it on her finger. She stands up, and Josh kisses her as she laughs.

Robin feels a gentle hand on his arm. He looks down and Mina is looking up at him, her eyes sympathetic, her mouth open in surprise.

He nods slowly with weary acceptance.

'Bugger,' he says.

68

'Robin…'

'Mina, it's fine. It's what she wants.'

'But…'

He pulls away from Mina's hand and goes back to his desk. Freya is over the other side of the room, surrounded by a gaggle of women, all cooing over the shiny new ring on her left hand. Josh is standing to their left, smiling broadly, talking to a matching group of men.

Robin stares resolutely at his computer screen. He clicks on a link and the recruitment pages for Devon and Cornwall load. *Express an interest…* the button says, and the next screen takes him through to *Apply.*

This is it. Decision time. If he clicks this, and they want him, he goes.

And why wouldn't he? Stay here, and what does he have? Months, years, of watching Josh and Freya plan a wedding, get married, have kids. How could they even work together? Not now it's all out in the open.

He said he had feelings for her, and she's made her decision blindingly clear. If he stays, he has to face that every day. That rejection. The humiliation.

But leave, go with Jo, and he has everything. She's pregnant with his baby – *his baby!* Why is he even hesitating? So they haven't been together for long, they're not in love. But those feelings will grow. In Devon, he has a future. A family. Here? Here, he has nothing.

He hears DCI Baker's voice. 'Come on, come on,' his boss is saying. 'Congrats to you both, but enough now. There's work to be done.'

Robin detects a frosty air to his tone and wonders whether Baker has an inkling about the feelings between him and Freya. But if so, it doesn't matter now. The crowd disperses; the chatter returns to normal levels.

He concentrates hard on his computer screen, switching tabs as he feels Freya come over and sit next to him.

'Robin,' she says quietly.

'Not now.'

'Robin, I'm sorry. I didn't...' Her voice tails off and he hears the creak of her chair. He assumes she's turned back to her computer, but when he chances a look at her she's still watching him.

'I didn't know he was going to do that,' she says. Her face is red, she looks like she's going to cry.

'You said yes, Freya.'

'Jo's pregnant!' Freya says it more loudly than she should have, and she looks around nervously. But no one's paying them any attention. 'You're having a baby with your girlfriend,' she repeats.

'You just agreed to marry him!' he hisses. Her gaze drops to her finger; she touches the ring awkwardly. But then Robin glances up, remembering where they are and what's going on around them. 'Listen, Freya. We can't talk about this now. If this is what you want, I'm happy for you—'

'Robin, I—'

'Congratulations, Freya!' the voice booms from behind them. It's DI Ratcliffe. 'Couldn't have happened to a nicer couple. Now, if I could just update you on what we need to do from here...'

Mouse tells them about his conversations with the CPS, the exhibit logging and evidence gathering they need to do to secure the prosecutions, and Robin tries to listen. But his mind feels numb, struggling to process what just happened. And the finality of the situation slowly dawns.

That's it now. Any hope he had that he might be with Freya – it's gone. Eighteen months of wondering, and pining, and thinking about her. That's it. She's getting married. To *him*.

DI Ratcliffe is still talking, trying to explain something to Freya. He gestures to the whiteboard, then the two of them get up and walk over.

Robin flips his screen back to the D&C recruitment page. His mouse hovers over the button.

'Butler,' his DI calls. 'Are you coming?'

And Robin clicks apply.

69

The ring feels tight on Freya's finger. Her thumb rotates it without thinking, the skin underneath already itchy and sore.

She's listening to Mouse talking, but all she can think about is Robin and how he must have felt to witness that. That wasn't her plan, not at all. She hadn't intended to say yes, but with all those faces watching and Josh gazing up, so handsome, so trusting, what else could she do? And it wasn't as if Robin had professed his undying love and was waiting, single and unattached, to sweep her off her feet. No – Jo is pregnant. Pregnant! Her brain can't even compute the thought.

There is too much on the line now. Her relationship – engagement, *fuck!* – with Josh. And Robin's future with the mother of his child. What if she got together with Robin and it didn't work out? What then? All they'd done was kiss. They'd never even slept together – although that thought alone makes her cheeks flush anew.

'West?' Ratcliffe says, finishing his download. 'Can I leave that with you and Butler?'

'Sure. Yes,' she replies, although she has no idea what he's just said.

Mouse leaves. Freya mumbles, 'Excuse me,' and heads off to the toilets. She needs space.

She walks quickly, pushing the toilet door open and going into a cubicle. She puts the seat down and sits with her head in her hands. Fuck. What now. What *now*?

She hears the toilet door, then a soft voice. 'Freya?'

'In here, Mina.'

Freya reaches forward and opens the cubicle door. Mina is standing there, hands on hips, eyes wide.

'What the...?'

'I know,' Freya replies solemnly.

'Did you know he was going to do that?'

'Of course not! It came out of nowhere. We've never even discussed getting married...'

Then she remembers her rant last night. Going on about marriage and kids and he must have thought... She groans and puts her head in her hands again.

'Let me see it then?' Mina says. Freya holds her left arm out, her head still bent. 'It's beautiful.'

For the first time, Freya looks up and properly studies the ring. It is gorgeous. It's platinum, she assumes – a diamond, emerald cut, surrounded by a ring of smaller stones. It's not what she would have chosen, but yes, it's nice. She pulls at it again, the ring feeling alien on her finger.

Mina puts a hand on her shoulder and sighs. 'Come on, you big slut, we've got work to do.' She's joking, and Freya smiles, appreciating that someone, at least, can find levity in the situation. 'You love Josh, don't you?'

'Yes,' Freya says.

'So much that if you were kidnapped and left in a dirty caravan you wouldn't tell them his secrets?'

Freya gives her a small smile. 'Maybe.'

'Well, then. Things could be worse.'

Mina takes her hand and pulls her out of the cubicle. They go to the sinks and Mina smiles at her in the mirror.

Then Freya frowns.

'That's the thing I don't get,' she says. Mina turns to her with a quizzical look. 'Chloe Somerset kept quiet the whole time she was in the caravan, yet the moment she gets out she hates Tiller's guts.'

They leave the bathroom and start walking back to the incident room.

'You can hardly blame her,' Mina counters.

'No. But then why not just tell them where it was?'

Freya stops dead in the corridor.

'That's it. That's fucking it!' She laughs, and for the first time that day all worries about Robin and Josh and her imploding love life are forgotten. 'All this time, it was right under our noses.'

And she heads towards the incident room at a run, Mina following, confused, behind her.

70

Tiller has spent a frustrating day at his desk.

He has written script after script, running them through the encryption, to no avail. One scrolled through every combination of numbers in less than two hours. Another scraped personal data out of Chloe's social media, looking for something she might have used as a keyword – but nothing.

He glances at the clock – it's eight p.m. Four hours before the system melts down and everything disappears. Why had he done this? Why? He curses himself for the hundredth time. Andrew often called him too clever for his own good – and, on bad days, a smug arrogant bastard – and now it seems he's right.

Years of work, training up the model. Inputting data, putting the lessons back into the brain of the machine. It'll all go. He hammers the keys with frustration.

The spaniel looks up from his feet at the noise. Tiller reaches down and fondles his soft ears.

'Why can't she just tell me?' he says to Max. 'Eh, wee dug?'

He debates heading back to the hospital to speak to Chloe, but he knows it won't be any use. Her face when he saw her – determination and pure abject hatred.

'If this makes you feel just a fraction of what I felt,' she spat. 'Helpless. Pathetic. Alone in that caravan. Because of you. Then it will have been worth it.'

He apologised, over and over. 'I didn't know this would happen,' he begged.

'You and Andrew messed with the wrong people. All this for money?'

'I didn't do it for that,' Tiller protested, and that was the truth. For him, the company had been about creating something new and revolutionary. Something his peers hadn't done before. Employing a whole load of equally brilliant brains who could challenge him.

He had never cared about the money.

So much has been lost. So much brilliance, locked up where even he can't get to it. He changes windows – stares at the blank command line trying to think of what he can try next. There must be a way through.

But before he has time to think, the dog jumps to his feet, so quickly it makes Tiller start. Max's whole body quivers on high alert, staring at the closed door.

Tiller listens, but he can't hear anything. Out here, there's rarely a sound, bar the hoot of an owl or the screech of a fox.

Tiller reaches out a hand to comfort Max but the dog's ears are raised, his head held high. Vigilant. Tiller pauses. And then he hears it too. A car engine, coming to a stop. Footsteps – slow and steady, approaching the door. Someone trying to be quiet.

Tiller's mind races. Is it them? The people that took Chloe? The police have Paul Freeman in custody, but maybe this is the bunch of armed squaddies they worried about all along. Evil, callous men, who wouldn't hesitate to kill Tiller. Cut his thumb off for the print recognition and leave him as a pile of bones by the roadside.

His breathing comes in short bursts, his heart races.

But then he hears it: two sharp raps. The dog rushes to the door of his study, and slowly he stands up. Mercenaries don't politely knock. They bash in, guns blazing. The tap comes again. The dog whines, then looks at him, waiting.

He edges out of the study, Max skidding on the floorboards in front of him, feet unable to keep up with his enthusiasm. Tiller slowly opens the front door, then wider when he sees who's there.

The blonde detective smiles broadly. Behind her, Butler's waiting. Seeing them both gives Tiller hope.

'You need to come with us,' West says. 'And we need to go, now.'

71

Freya is the last person Robin wants to be around right now, but when she and Mina had arrived in the incident room, talking ten to the dozen, he couldn't override his professional curiosity.

Eyes bright, she explained where she thought the encryption key was. And he knew she was right.

They'd gone straight to his car and driven at speed to the old manor house. The country roads were now familiar to Robin, and he put his foot down, the headlights illuminating recognisable hedges and fences as they cut through the darkness.

The large metal gates were open; he'd driven fast into the car park, stopping with a spray of gravel.

'Go,' he says to Freya now, the first words since they left the nick.

He feels the silence between them acutely. The unspoken words like thick fog, murky and threatening. But whatever needs to be said can wait – time is ticking.

'We need to go,' Freya says, once Tiller opens the old wooden door of the manor house. 'Now.'

Robin bends down and greets the excited spaniel, smiling despite himself as the dog leaps up enthusiastically, smearing a large amount of mud up his leg. Tiller doesn't reply, just grabs the dog's lead and follows them out to the car.

Robin drives, Freya reciting directions. Tiller sits in the back, the dog on his lap, panting happily as the scenery passes outside the window.

In the distance, a bright green light comes into view. 'Here,' Freya says. 'They said they'd be waiting for us.'

Tiller frowns, then looks at the dog. 'But what...' he begins.

Freya grins as they come to a stop. The sign overhead turns her skin a faint green colour. *Emergency Veterinary Clinic*, it says.

She turns round in her seat, facing Tiller. 'The dog. Max is the only thing Chloe cares about. The only thing she would have wanted to protect.'

Tiller opens his mouth in surprise. 'She would have worried that if she told them Max had the key, they might have hurt him. But where?' Robin watches as Tiller looks at the medal on the dog's collar. 'It can't be the phone number. I would have cracked it already.'

A figure has emerged at the door of the vet clinic, waiting. They all get out of the car.

'Thank you for meeting us,' Robin says, showing his ID.

'No problem,' the vet replies. 'But I don't understand how this is official police business. What do you want me to do?'

It's not officially police work. But that's a small detail Robin is hoping Baker will overlook. 'Scan the dog,' Robin replies. 'We need you to read his microchip.'

The vet nods. 'Come this way.'

It's done in seconds. The vet runs a small grey plastic handset over Max's neck and it beeps. Tiller has set his laptop up next to them and now waits, nervously glancing up at the clock.

The vet holds the handset out to Tiller. He goes pale.

'This is fifteen digits,' he says. 'And it's all numbers. We need a mixture of numbers and letters for the key. It can't be correct.'

'Try it anyway,' Freya says. 'Take off the first four. Or the last four.'

Tiller tries both to no avail.

The mood in the surgery sinks. 'I was sure I was right,' Freya mutters.

'Well... The dog is registered with the Kennel Club...' the vet says tentatively.

Tiller stares. 'Pardon?'

'Max. He's a pedigree cocker spaniel. We wouldn't normally hold this information, but I can see on our files that Ms Somerset recorded his Kennel Club membership.' The vet pauses, unsure, all eyes on him. 'That's a mixture of letters and numbers. What you're looking for? Right?'

'Yes, yes.' Tiller holds his hand out eagerly as the vet copies it down from the screen and passes the piece of paper across. Tiller blinks at it.

'This is ten digits,' he says, his voice rising to a desperate squeak.

'There's a space in the middle,' Robin replies. 'That makes it eleven.'

'But...'

'Type it in.'

Everyone waits; Robin barely dares to breathe. Then the screen jumps into life and Tiller lets out a whoop.

Robin turns to Freya with a grin. She meets his gaze and for a moment, everything is okay. Things are the way they were. Before.

Before they kissed. Before the proposal. His smile slips and his gaze shifts to her left hand. To the ring shining in the light.

72

With a contented sigh, Tiller disables the countdown, then packs up his laptop and tenderly puts it away. Max is given a treat by the vet.

They file out of the surgery, the vet locking up after them.

'That was an easy one,' the vet says. 'Normally I see much worse at this time of night.'

Freya thanks him and they head back to the Volvo.

'I'll drop you back,' Robin says, quietly. Now this is done, all he wants is to be home. By himself. Drink a beer – probably a few – and go to bed for a very long time.

But Freya's stopped at the back of the car, a few metres away from him.

'Get in,' he says. But she doesn't move. 'What?' he snaps, unable to keep the frustration out of his voice.

She glances at Tiller, then to the vet. They're talking, about the dog, and as yet unaware of what's going on between Freya and Robin. 'Can we talk?' she says quietly. 'When we get back to the station?'

'I don't think so, no.'

'Robin, I didn't know Josh was going to do that,' she hisses. 'You said yes!'

His shout echoes around the small car park; Tiller and the vet stop mid-conversation.

Freya goes red. Her eyes flare. 'You have no right to be angry with me,' she says, her voice low. 'No fucking right at all. I don't belong to you. I haven't promised you anything.'

'You turned up at my house in the dead of night and kissed me.'

'That was… that was…' Freya stutters.

'What? A bit of fun? Something to fuck with my head?'

'No! Because…'

'Because what?'

'Because I have feelings for you, Robin, and I wanted to know if you felt the same way.'

'Well, I bloody well do. You know that now. So what? You're marrying Josh.'

'And you've got another woman pregnant.'

'I told you – that wasn't planned.'

Robin's vaguely aware that both Tiller and the vet – the poor unwitting vet – are staring at them. Two police officers, shouting at each other, seemingly out of nowhere in a car park. But now he's started it seems he can't stop the outpouring of everything he's kept bottled up. For far too long.

'At least Josh is open about his feelings. At least he's not all scrunched up and repressed.'

'Scrunched up? Nice, Freya. Thank you. How wonderful to be you. Princess Freya and her Prince Charming. You and the perfect Josh deserve each other. How could I ever compete with him?'

'You were never supposed to be competing. For fuck's sake! Why couldn't you have just told me how you felt? Before Josh. Before Jo?'

'Because I'm your boss! How do you think that would have gone down?'

'I… I don't know. *Because you never said anything.*'

'And if I had – how would you have replied? You didn't like me. Not back then.'

'Not at first, no.'

Robin waves his hands, exasperated. 'So… What, Freya? What are you saying?'

'That I'm in love with you. And I love Josh. And I don't know what to do.'

That stops him then. Completely dumbstruck. He's known he's been in love with Freya for a while, but the idea that she might have felt the same way about him? It's unbelievable, and incredible, and heartbreaking – all at the same time.

He watches, mute, as Freya walks across the car park. Away from this, and him.

'Where are you going?' he shouts.

'Work. To get my car. Then home.'

'You're not walking all the way from here to Southampton nick.'

She turns and faces him. She's crying now, and all he wants to do is go to her. 'Why do you care?' she shouts back.

'Of course I fucking care. Jesus Christ, Freya!'

'I'm going that way,' the vet says awkwardly. 'If you want a lift.'

'Yes, thank you,' Freya replies and heads towards his car. Robin doesn't move, paralysed by indecision. What is he supposed to do? Rush over to her, sweep her up in his arms and declare his undying love? Right now, his legs are locked, his feet welded to the concrete. Even after everything that's happened, everything she's said, he can't tell her how he feels. The self-doubt, the fear, the insecurities haunt him.

The vet climbs into his car, and Freya opens the door to the passenger side. For one moment she looks back at him, tears in her eyes. Then she shakes her head and gets into the car.

Robin feels a bump – a fluffy black paw and a wet nose – nudging at his hand. He looks down to the dog as the vet's car pulls out of the car park. And she's gone.

'Are you… okay?' Tiller asks tentatively.

Robin clears his throat. 'Sorry you had to see that.'

Tiller shrugs. 'We're all human.' He looks in the direction of the road, where the car has just departed. 'So, you and DC West, then?'

'No,' Robin replies. 'I thought maybe it could be. But life's not like that, is it?'

Tiller smiles sympathetically, then gets into the car. Robin follows suit, putting the key in the ignition. The radio comes on, a Rolling Stones song, one he's heard a million times before. The choir sings, melancholy and wistful. It gets to the chorus, and Tiller hums along, under his breath. Then he stops and looks over at Robin.

'Perhaps we don't know what we want until we nearly lose it,' Tiller says thoughtfully. He clutches the laptop affectionately to his chest, the dog at his feet. 'Perhaps the song's right: we get what we need.'

'I bloody hope so,' Robin says quietly. 'I really do.'

73

The rest of the night passes in a blur. Once the bewildered vet had dropped her at the police station, she'd driven home on autopilot. Josh greets her at the door, glass of champagne in hand.

'Come on,' he says, giving her a big kiss on the cheek. 'We need to call my parents.'

Exclamation and squeaks over the Zoom call; laughter from Josh.

'When did you buy the ring, Josh?' his mum laughs. 'Let's see it.'

Freya holds it up to the camera. His mother sighs in admiration.

'This morning,' Josh laughs. 'I nipped into town on a break.'

'I can't believe you proposed in the office. Couldn't you have planned somewhere more romantic?'

'Sometimes you just don't want to wait,' Josh says, squeezing Freya tight. She feels like she can't breathe.

'Excuse me,' she mumbles.

She leaves the room and goes to the bedroom. She can hear Josh talking excitedly downstairs. She picks up her phone. Nothing from Robin. But what does she expect? She takes a long breath in and out, gathering herself together.

That's it now. She's put it all out there. Told him how she felt, and he'd said nothing. He doesn't love her. And soon he'll be moving to Devon. That argument was the hard dose of reality she's needed for some time. It's over.

She hears footsteps on the stairs, and Josh slowly pushes the door open. He pokes his head around.

'Are you okay?' he asks, quietly.

He comes over and lies on his front, resting his head next to hers.

She looks into his bright blue eyes, at the handsome face it's so easy to love. Her fiancé.

'Yes, I'm fine,' she says. 'I'm just tired. It was one hell of a day.'

He smiles. 'Yes, it was, wasn't it? And quite a week. Thank God that case is over. Did you find the key?'

She nods. 'Yes. It was in the dog.'

Josh frowns in confusion as Freya explains. 'Hamilton must have been pleased,' he concludes. 'They didn't charge Diane Freeman in the end. The CPS weren't convinced we had enough against her.'

'Even with the voicemails?'

'Yeah. They said there was no evidence she was behind the kidnap. Just that she didn't call the police. The fact they have both Paul Freeman and Stephen Dolan in custody is enough.'

'And Andrew?'

'He's buggered.' Josh laughs. 'The confession you and Robin got on tape? They'll charge him the moment he gets out of hospital. What a shit.' He leans over and wraps his arms around her; Freya rests her head on his chest. 'Aren't you glad you've got me, hey?' he says. Then he's quiet for a moment. 'Freya?'

'Yes?'

She cranes her neck up and meets his eyes.

'I know I put you on the spot, back there, at the nick. But do you want to marry me?'

Freya smiles. She feels the tension of the past week fade. The kiss with Robin, the argument, the baby – that doesn't matter now. She's marrying Josh.

'Yes,' she says as she reaches up to kiss him. 'I do.'

SATURDAY

74

A full night's sleep does Freya the world of good. She wakes late, bleary as the mid-morning sunshine seeps in through the curtains. Josh is lying on his back, his arms thrown above his head. A state of complete abandonment, his face tilted towards her, mouth slightly open.

She looks at him. Hair ruffled, features slack. And she resolves he will never know what happened that night with Robin. She will never betray his trust again. Her thumb goes to the now warm metal of the engagement ring. She holds it up in front of her face, enjoying the way the sunlight dissects the stone into an array of rainbows. She's getting married. To this incredible, amazing man. Who loves her, and isn't afraid to show it in front of the whole office.

She leans over and kisses him. He opens his eyes slowly.

'What time is it?' he mumbles, his voice husky.

'Nearly ten. Do you want coffee?'

'Yes. Please. How did it get so late?'

'I guess we both needed the sleep.'

A week of working all hours to solve the case, and both of them had passed out the moment their heads hit the pillow. Now she feels his arm creep round her middle as he pulls her close. He's warm, his skin soft, and she wraps her legs round his.

'How about we stay here for a moment,' he says with a slow smile. His lips meet hers; Freya gasps as his hands explore downwards.

And all thoughts of coffee and breakfast disappear.

–

After, they lie on crumpled sheets, Freya listening to the slow rise and fall of Josh's drowsy breathing.

'We could go out for lunch,' he suggests sleepily. 'Or just stay here all day.'

'I need to go to the nick,' Freya says. She meets his disbelieving gaze with a wince. 'I promised Baker I'd follow up on Ricky Hall. You know, the kid who made the false witness statement about Hamilton.'

'Can't someone else do that?'

'Yes, but.' She shrugs. 'I'm curious. Davis says they have some CCTV from outside the pub. There might be someone I recognise.'

'Fine, you go.' He grins. 'I might get another hour's kip.'

'Lazy shit,' she laughs. She climbs out of bed, heading for the shower, and for a moment she turns back. He's rolled onto his front, face down in the pillow, his bare back, soft skin, muscles, all on display. She savours the sight for a moment, and it's all she can do not to go back to join him.

–

The roads are clear, the car park empty as she makes her way up the stairs into the nick. She smiles as congratulations are fired her way; nothing spreads faster round the station than gossip.

When she gets to her desk, Davis has left a DVD and a Post-it attached. *CCTV from outside the Horse and Hounds. Scroll to 22.43.*

She boots up her computer and glances to Robin's desk. It looks neater than usual, obviously tidied by a cleaner overnight, and she wonders when he's going to be in. She needs to apologise. Clear the air; try to get them back onto an even keel. It wasn't fair of her to go over to his house that night. To kiss him and expect him to pour his heart out to her while she was still with Josh. And he with Jo. She feels a little pull in her stomach as she thinks about Jo being pregnant – Robin's baby – and wonders why. Envy, she decides. Because she wants a family, one day, with Josh.

She loads up the DVD and does as she's told; a blurry colour image from the outside of a pub comes into view. She scans the screen looking for the greasy blond hair of Ricky Hall. And there he is. He comes into shot, standing outside the front and lighting a cigarette. And as he does, another man appears.

She takes a quick gasp of air. That bastard.

Quickly she leans forward and picks up the phone. Then she pauses. Normally she would call Robin, but now? She makes a split-second decision and dials.

'Mina?' Freya says, when her friend answers. 'Can you come in? Yes. This afternoon. There's a few things I need to get sorted first.'

75

The uniforms bring him in, and Freya watches with satisfaction as he's booked into custody.

Haughty posture, supercilious air. Double-breasted tweed jacket. The man on the CCTV: Giles Kepner.

He has a lawyer with him this time and, formalities done, they're shown to the consultation room. Freya waits; she knows they won't be long, the lawyer grunting in annoyance when she refused to share anything in the initial discovery meeting.

'You're enjoying this a bit too much.'

Mina joins her in the corridor, file in hand. Freya smiles.

'Seeing that smug bastard in cuffs made my day,' Freya replies. 'We've arrested him for wasting police time. I'm hoping we can bump it up to perverting the course of justice.'

'You know he'll "no comment" the whole thing.'

'I don't care. I just want to see his face when we show him the video.'

'And the rest,' Mina grins.

The door opens and the lawyer emerges. He nods briefly.

'Come through,' Freya says, showing the way to the interview room.

The four of them sit down; Freya starts the recording and makes the introductions.

Kepner leans back, arms crossed, uttering the briefest of confirmations to the usual cautions.

'Mr Kepner,' Freya begins with a smile. 'Can you tell us where you were on the night of Monday the twenty-fifth of April? This Monday just gone.'

'No comment.'

Freya moves on to the next question. 'Have you ever been to the Horse and Hounds in Millbrook?'

'No comment.'

'Have you ever met a man called Ricky Hall?'

'No comment.'

'Get to the point, Detective,' the lawyer interjects. 'You know this line of questioning isn't going to get us anywhere.'

Mina passes her the laptop; Freya opens it, pulling up the CCTV footage she was viewing earlier. She presses play.

'This here,' she says, pointing to the screen, 'is Ricky Hall. And this here, is you. Isn't it, Mr Kepner?'

'Even if it is,' Kepner replies. 'And I'm not saying it is, there's no law against going to the pub.'

Freya feels a little jolt of satisfaction – the small victory of the deviation from 'no comment'.

'No,' she continues. 'But we interviewed Ricky Hall, and we gave him a selection of photos to look at. He picked you from the line-up. The person who paid him three hundred quid to put in a false witness statement saying he'd seen someone of Tiller Hamilton's description beat up Andrew Grace on Monday night.'

Kepner's lip curls. 'No comment.'

The solicitor sits forward in his seat. 'I want the full details of this line-up, DC West,' he says. 'And who's this witness? I bet he'll be easy to discredit, especially when he's already admitted to lying.'

He's right; Ricky Hall would be pulled apart in seconds under cross-examination. But Freya has a few tricks up her sleeve.

'What about this, Mr Kepner?' she adds. 'From the cashpoint across the road.' Mina puts the still on the table in front of them; Kepner is taking money out of the machine, Hall visible over his shoulder. 'And this, from the shop next door.'

Another photograph, taken from CCTV. The lawyer squints at it.

303

'Look at it closely,' Freya says. 'You can clearly see the exchange of cash between you. And you know we'll get a warrant for your bank records to confirm. All evidence that supports Hall's statement. Why did you do it, Mr Kepner?' she asks, and he meets her eyes, narrowing them slightly. She can tell he's annoyed; that in his arrogance he believed he could take advantage of a kid like Hall and get away with it. 'What was the point? You must have known we would get to the truth and Hamilton would be released.'

She pauses; he's still glaring at her.

'Or,' she continues with a smile, 'maybe you arranged the attack on Andrew Grace. Maybe we should be adding GBH to the list.'

'I had nothing to do with that,' he snaps, as his lawyer interrupts.

'Where's the evidence, DC West?' the solicitor says. 'You have nothing to implicate my client in that attack.'

'But he knew it was happening. Didn't you, Giles?'

Freya's been busy working, following fresh lines of enquiry. Based on no more than a suspicion, but one that paid off.

She takes a piece of paper out of the file and pushes it across to Kepner. He ignores it, his arms still crossed; the lawyer picks it up.

'Registration plates?' he says scornfully.

'Car registration numbers recorded by ANPR at Leisure World on the night Andrew Grace was beaten up. And this one,' Freya leans across and points to the highlighted line, 'is registered to you, Mr Kepner. Isn't it?'

The lawyer shows him the piece of paper.

'It's a company car,' he says, scornfully. 'Could have been anyone in it.'

'Anyone that works for Parapet Holdings,' Freya adds. 'Yes. I agree.'

'That's not what my client said.'

'But you admit that that's a company car?'

304

Kepner looks chastised. 'No comment,' he says.

Freya sighs in mock sympathy. 'I can understand your annoyance,' she says. 'Hamilton Grace are looking for a buyer. You offer them millions. And then they say no. How did that feel?'

'No comment.'

'Did they say why?'

'No comment.'

'Maybe it was because they thought you didn't really understand what you were buying, is that it? Tiller said he was needed as part of the deal. Was the technology too complicated for you?'

She meets Kepner's gaze. Something has hit home: his face is turning red, he's shaking. His arms are still crossed but his hands are pushed into fists so hard his knuckles have blanched white.

'I get that Hamilton's a computer genius. But Grace? Even he thought he was too good for you—'

'That fucking moron,' Kepner explodes. 'He was desperate for us to buy. Even knocked a few mil off to keep us interested. And then he comes back and says they've changed their mind—'

'Mr Kepner...' the solicitor warns.

'How fucking dare they? That weirdo Hamilton. Could barely string a sentence together. We had buyers lined up at our end. People you don't mess around. And he *changes his mind*? He deserved a night in the cells. I know people like him. I knew he wouldn't be able to cope. We didn't have to lay a hand on Grace, someone else did that for us. But when we saw—'

'Giles!' The lawyer's shouting now, and at last Kepner listens. He clamps his lips shut and sits back in his seat, scowling.

'So you got Ricky Hall to issue a false statement just to put Hamilton through hell?' Freya asks, disbelieving.

Kepner glares. The lawyer answers: 'No comment.'

'Don't speak on behalf of your client,' Freya says. 'Giles?'

'No comment,' Kepner replies.

76

Out of the interview room, Freya and Mina do a quiet high five in the corridor.

'Nice work in there,' Mina says as they walk back to the office. 'That's as good as a confession.'

'I'm sure his lawyer will disagree, but it's a start. You head off, Mina.'

Mina pauses, uncertain. 'Are you sure?'

'Absolutely. I'll pull it all together for the CPS. Get authorisation to charge. See you on Monday.'

Freya watches her go, then slumps back in her seat. She had an ulterior motive for sending Mina home – she wasn't sure she could face the questioning about Robin she was guaranteed to receive.

The one person she wants to phone is him. She knows how pleased he will be that they've got Kepner; she can imagine the grin on his face, the quiet nod of approval.

'Do you live here now? I'd have thought you'd be spending the weekend with your new fiancé. Especially after that good work.'

Freya turns with a smile at the booming tones; DCI Baker stands behind her, off duty in an England rugby shirt and jeans.

'You heard?'

'Nothing gets past me,' he smiles.

'Just tying up a few loose ends,' Freya replies. 'And then I'll go.'

He nods. 'Doing some paperwork of my own.' He leans down and runs a finger along the edge of Robin's desk.

'Do you know when Butler's going to be in today?' she asks, in what she hopes is a casual tone.

Baker stares at her for a moment. 'I thought he would have spoken to you?'

'No?' Freya feels her body turn cold.

'He's been and gone,' Baker replies. 'It seemed the right thing to do. The investigatory side of the case is pretty much over, and Devon and Cornwall want him as soon as possible. We agreed he'd finish yesterday. He had some holiday to take, and you know Robin. He's not one for tearful goodbyes.'

Freya swallows. She nods quickly.

'I tried to get him to have some sort of leaving do. Drinks down the pub, dinner, but he wasn't having any of it. He said he'd rather just creep away.' Baker pauses, and Freya feels him studying her face. 'I assumed he'd speak to you though. You two. You had something special.'

Freya blinks again. Do not cry, she tells herself. *Do not cry*.

'I'm sure he'll call me,' she croaks. 'Anyway, guv,' she continues, turning away from Baker and back to her screen. 'I'd better get on. Get home before Josh finds someone else to propose to.'

'Yes, you do that.' For a moment, she feels a light pressure as Baker puts a hand gently on her shoulder. Then she hears his soft footsteps echo away.

Freya stares at her screen for a moment longer, tears threatening. He's left. Without a word? Without even a goodbye? She hears chattering in the corridor, and not wanting any of her colleagues to see her she gets up quickly, walking into the tiny kitchen.

She picks up the kettle with an unsteady hand and fills it under the tap. A pile of dirty mugs and crockery lie in the sink and for a moment, she pauses. In the mess is Robin's Little Miss Sunshine mug. Originally a sarcastic Secret Santa present, she's come to associate it so closely with Robin that seeing it left here is almost a physical shock.

He's gone. He's just gone. Their partnership, that she valued so much, has dissolved. And with it, their friendship. Without so much as a conversation or a hug goodbye. She picks up his mug and turns it round, looking at it. She has fetched him coffee in this more times than she can count. Him, holding it tightly in both hands, as if gaining strength from the caffeine by osmosis, as they rally back and forth about a case. The omnipresent frown – Robin thinking, and that constant, *annoying*, tap tap of his middle finger on the wood of the desk.

But it's not just that. His massive feet in pink woolly socks on the sofa as they watch TV. The smell of his Reading Festival sweatshirt when she puts it on because she's cold. The worn-out holes in the sleeve he tells her off for putting her fingers through and making worse, but he never hides it, never puts it away. The way he buys her favourite tea, even though it's his house and he says it stinks of cat piss.

All of that, one awful argument in the car park, and he is gone.

That's how much she means to him.

She turns the mug around in her hand and, without another thought, she drops it decisively in the bin.

TWO WEEKS LATER

SATURDAY

77

Tiller misses the dog. Ever since Chloe came by to pick him up, with a rev of her engine and a furious scowl, the old house has seemed strangely quiet. He finds himself putting his hand down to the side of his desk, looking for soft warm fur. He still wakes at seven on the dot, thinking he needs to take him outside.

The habit of the daily walk has stayed. Every morning he strides out across the fields, rain or shine. Wellies on his feet, fresh air in his lungs. Sometimes he even watches the sun come up, a blaze of optimism as the heat scorches away the low-hanging fog.

He has learned that things can change – for the better.

It's the weekend, so he works from his office in the manor house. Even so, he looks out of the window and sees cars arriving down the tarmacked driveway. He smiles with recognition: engineers with nothing better to do than come in and twiddle with the latest bit of code that has caught their eye. He feels like an indulgent parent; he knows that disposition well.

He looks at his own little bit of code on his screen now. He's still playing, changing a line here, an instruction there. But the overall algorithm remains the same.

Last week he'd gathered everyone together – all forty-two of them, crammed into the tiny space they use as a canteen. Tiller had rigged up a screen and projector and slowly taken the team through the algorithm. He swelled with pride as they realised the potential of what he'd created, gasps and eager excitement filling the room. It would only get better with more brilliant minds.

It was theirs now. And it would stay that way.

Tiller hears a gentle knock on the door, and frowns. Even though they know he's there, nobody ever bothers him.

He gets up and makes his way down, opening the door. Laura stands on the front step. She smiles.

The bruises have faded to smudges of yellow and light brown, although Tiller knows the emotional scars remain. He's spoken to her a few times since – mainly affectionate messages late at night when Laura can't sleep and Tiller is working. He wasn't expecting her here today.

'Can I come in?' she asks.

'Of course, of course.' He moves out of the way and she walks into the hallway, looking with interest at the peeled wallpaper, the stripped floorboards.

'You've made some progress,' she says.

'Slowly.' He grins. 'It's going to get worse before it gets better. I have finished one room though.'

He shows her through to the main living room at the front of the house. It's a big space, and one Tiller has always loved. Bright sunshine reflects through the huge bay windows. One of the panes has been pushed open, and a late spring breeze blows through, moving the light white curtains.

Tiller has no sense of interior design or fashion, but he knows what he likes. The floorboards are plain wood, varnished. The walls are white and bare, bar the aged iron fireplace and original tiles in the hearth. There is no furniture yet, no television. But he's proud of what he's achieved.

He looks over at Laura. She's smiling.

'It's lovely, Tiller. You were right to keep the house.'

He nods, speechless at her approval. Then he remembers his manners. 'Do you want a cup of tea? Coffee?'

'No, I just... I just came over to say thank you. For what you did for Andrew.'

With permission from the detectives, Tiller had been in to see Andrew, under guard in the hospital. He'd presented him with a legal document.

'This is my first and final offer,' he'd said. 'To buy your stake of the company.'

Andrew paused, then picked up the stack of pages. He flicked though, looking for the vital information. Then he'd looked back to Tiller.

'How do you have this sort of money?'

'I buy next to nothing. I don't go abroad. I don't own property. I've had the same car for ten years. And I've been earning the same as you. I've invested well. Played the market. Do the maths.' He paused. 'Do you want it or not?'

'This is a fraction of what we were offered before.'

'We don't have any buyers now. Nobody's interested – not after the mess you caused. And besides, I'm going to keep it. Make the employees shareholders. We'll run it our way.'

'What you always wanted. You must be pleased.' The words seemed bitter but his tone was sad. He looked through the pages again. 'It says here that only half goes to me.'

'More than enough for you to pay off your debts. And get some help.'

Andrew signed. The deal was done. Andrew would be okay, assuming he survives whatever punishment comes his way for his role in the attack on his family.

And now Laura is here.

'I did it for you,' Tiller says. The other half of the money had gone to Laura and the kids.

'I don't know how to thank you,' she says. 'But I need to ask another favour.'

'Anything.'

'There's no way we can go back to the house. Tim's having nightmares. I twitch at every sound. So we've been staying with

311

Mum and Dad. And it's…' She laughs. 'They're driving me nuts, Tiller. We're selling the house, but until we do…' She looks round the bare living room again. 'Can we stay here? With you?'

He thinks for a second. In the past, any suggestion of an intrusion into his space would have caused him to baulk in horror, but after everything that's happened, he's changed. He finds himself smiling.

'It's a mess,' he says. 'The rest of the house is a mess.'

'But you have heating? And Wi-Fi?'

'I have the best Wi-Fi money can buy,' he laughs. 'The heating I'll get to next.'

'It's a big house. I promise we'll keep out of your way. And I can cook. Help with the renovations.' She takes a step forward and gently touches his arm. 'And I'd like to spend a bit more time with you,' she says softly. 'If that's okay?'

Tiller remembers meeting her for the first time. Catching sight of the book in her hand. The feeling of promise, and the potential of something good. Andrew had taken that from him, but now, maybe now, he can have it back.

'Just one question,' he asks. She tilts her head to one side, waiting. 'How would you have split the prize money? If you found Halliday's Easter egg?'

It's a *Ready Player One* reference, and he hopes she'll get the joke.

Sure enough, she grins. 'With you, Wade,' she replies. 'We're going to make the world a better place, right?'

He laughs, then nods in agreement.

'So we can stay?'

'You can.' He leans forward; for the first time in years, he gives someone a hug. Her body folds into his, her arms go round his waist. The comfort of contact from another person, one he really likes.

It feels good.

78

Robin lifts up the box and carries it through to the hallway. It joins the stack; a wall of cardboard encompassing his whole life. He has surprisingly few belongings. Clothes, books. Ancient CDs and outdated DVDs. His sofas, the beds, the dining table – they'll remain. The house is being rented out as furnished and the first tenants move in next weekend.

He hears Liam in the kitchen, the bashing of plates and saucepans confirming he's packing. Liam offered to come and help – help that he didn't really need, but the company has been appreciated.

His phone rings, and he pulls it out of his pocket. Jo starts talking the moment he answers.

'I did it!' she says, her voice excited. 'It's ours!'

'That's great.' He tries to muster the same level of enthusiasm, but he knows it's tempered. Luckily, she doesn't notice.

'I can't wait for you to see it. Three-bed. Detached. Driveway. And a gorgeous nursery for bump.'

She calls it bump, but it's barely that. Seven weeks now, the first scan booked in a month. And that, he can't wait to see. The white blob of their baby on the screen. The *thump thump* of the heartbeat – the thought of it fills him with unmitigated joy. This is good. Good things happen.

He tells himself that.

Jo chatters for a moment longer, then they say goodbye, knowing he's going to be driving down tomorrow to join her. He lowers his phone, and as he does so the doorbell rings.

He looks towards it.

Every morning he expects her to message. Every knock on the door he imagines to be her. And tonight is no exception.

But once again, he's disappointed.

His DCI stands there, almost filling the doorway.

Robin smiles. 'Guv. Good to see you.'

Baker moves forward and gives him a hug. Then he surveys the wall of packing boxes.

'You're almost done?'

'Leave tomorrow,' Robin confirms.

Baker nods. 'I came to bring you this,' he says, and he holds out Robin's ridiculous mug. 'Someone tried to get rid of it,' he smiles. 'But I couldn't let Little Miss Sunshine leave without a fight.'

Robin takes it. 'You came all the way over here for this?' He wipes a dirty line of coffee off her bright yellow face. 'Couldn't you have washed it first?'

'They don't pay me to wash up,' Baker scoffs. 'And while I'm here, Giles Kepner pleaded guilty to perverting the course of justice.'

'He did?' Robin's pleased. Anything to wipe the smug grin off that man's face.

'For what good it'll do us. His expensive lawyer will probably get him off with a suspended sentence. But he wouldn't have confessed without Freya. She put together a solid case. She didn't tell you?'

'Mmm-hmm.' Robin knows Baker's waiting for a reaction to Freya's name; he stays quiet. 'Did he say why he did it?' Robin asks instead.

'Not in any great detail. But West reckons—' her name again, as subtle as a freight train '—that he was trying to mess with Hamilton. Revenge for refusing to sell.' Baker shrugs. 'Not that it matters.'

'And the loan sharks. The ones that beat up Andrew Grace?'

'Disappeared like farts in the night.' Robin laughs as Baker continues. 'We have our suspicions, but that one will remain open for now. Until they beat up the next punter and fuck up somehow. Which they always do. Anyway, I better go. Tina will give me hell if I'm too late back, even if I am seeing you.

'Good luck, Butler.' He holds out his hand, and Robin shakes it warmly. 'You look after yourself, you hear me?'

'You don't need to worry about me, guv.'

'I always worry about you, Robin.'

With a final nod, he opens the front door and leaves Robin standing in the doorway.

He listens to Baker's Range Rover drive off, then closes the door behind him. He swallows, hard. It's going to be difficult to work for someone new. No one has helped him, supported him as much as Neal Baker. No one except Freya, that is.

He pushes that thought out of his head, then picks up an empty cardboard box. He can't put this room off forever.

He can still hear Liam in the kitchen. He glances back for a moment before he pushes the handle down and opens it. His spare room. Abandoned, ignored. For years.

He switches the light on and stands in the doorway. The curtains are drawn; the bed untouched. Cartoon dinosaurs in the paintings on the wall. The bumpers and plug protectors pushed into the sockets remain, and now he bends down and pulls one out.

This is the room he decorated in preparation for his nephews to come and stay. Georgia was pregnant again, and she trusted him enough to increase his uncle duties. He remembers the feeling – apprehension mixed with excitement at the things they could get up to, Alex and James's personalities coming to the fore as they hit their second birthday. Alex – always the brave one, the first to walk, the first to graze his knee. James – waiting for his brother, quieter, more introspective. Happier curling up on Robin's lap with a book. Both surprising him in ways he had never thought possible, least of all with the all-consuming love that accompanied them.

But then they were killed, and something in Robin died along with them. He closed up all optimism; the joy, the part of his life that let him hope and dream.

He drops the plug protector into the empty box, then drops to his knees and pulls the large flat container out from under the bed. These are his most valued possessions. Photos of him and Georgia as children. Shots of the boys laughing, playing. A few items of their clothing – matching T-shirts with robots on the front. And the two battered purple elephants. Their constant companions, given by Robin when they were born. Sucked, washed and loved into near oblivion.

He takes them out and pushes them against his nose. The biscuity baby smell has faded over the years, barely a trace of it remains, but enough. He remembers their soft pudgy cheeks, their fine baby hair as he kissed the top of their heads at bedtime. Their laughter, hysterical screams of joy as he'd boot a football across the park, chubby legs charging after it.

He feels the emptiness again now, the aching pang of loss, and he worries about the baby that's going to be his. Already he wants to lock Jo away, stop her from going to work where some shitbag might hurt her – and the child hasn't even been born yet. How is he going to feel when it's a living breathing person? When they can walk, talk? When Jo goes out in the car?

'They loved those elephants.'

Robin turns; Liam is standing behind him, bending his lanky frame to lean in the doorway.

'I hoped you still had them.'

'Of course.' He holds them out to Liam and he takes them, lying them down his forearms, the heads cupped in each hand the way he might have once held his twins. He looks at them in silence, then gently raises them to his mouth and kisses them. He blinks a few times, then hands them back to Robin, who places them tenderly in the box.

'It won't happen to you,' Liam says. He comes in and sits on the bed in front of Robin.

Robin nods, looking at the elephants, his throat tight.

'How do you know?' he asks quietly.

Liam shrugs. 'I don't.' He manages a half-smile; his eyes are wet, on the edge of tears. 'But you have to tell yourself that. Otherwise how will you ever allow yourself to be happy again?'

Liam reaches down and takes a photo out of the box. It's one of the five of them, one Christmas. Liam and Georgia, one of the twins on each of their laps. Robin to the side, his head bent to Alex, laughing at something he must have done.

'Times like this, they were the happiest I'd ever been.' Liam's looking at the photo, running his finger across the image of his dead wife and sons. 'I wish every day that it hadn't happened – the crash.' His voice cracks and Robin feels his own vision blur. 'But I have never wished I hadn't met Georgia. That we hadn't had the boys. Even with what I know now. Even with the grief and everything that I – we,' he adds with a crooked smile to Robin, 'went through. I am always thankful for the time we had together.'

'Are you okay? With Lizzie?'

Liam nods. He takes his glasses off and wipes his eyes before putting them on again. 'Lizzie will never replace Georgia and the boys, but she makes me happy.' He pauses. 'We're going to move in together. I'm going to sell my place. Buy somewhere with her.' He glances to Robin to see how Robin's taken the news.

But Robin smiles. 'That's great. I'm pleased.'

'So am I. And I couldn't be happier at your news. The move down to Devon. Baby on the way. Fresh start.'

Robin nods slowly, taking it all in.

'Rob?'

He looks up at Liam, waiting.

'Are you happy? Is this… is this what you want? I don't mean the baby. I can see how happy you are about that…'

'You can?'

'Yeah. When you told me, and every time you've talked about it since. Your whole face lights up.'

'But?'

'But the move? And Jo? You seem hesitant.'

Robin pauses. Ever since Jo told him about the baby it's just felt… right. Like he's ready to be a father and take that next step in his life. But he hasn't got his head around the fact he's leaving.

'It's just sudden,' he tells Liam. 'It's a lot to get used to. A new nick, new boss.'

'New partner?'

Robin's told Liam the bare bones of their argument but Liam's well aware of the subtext and the extent of Robin's feelings for Freya.

'Have you spoken to her?' Liam asks softly.

Robin shakes his head slowly.

'Will you?'

Robin laughs sharply. 'I think I've missed that boat,' he says. 'It's nearly eleven. And I leave first thing tomorrow.'

Liam puts a large hand on Robin's shoulder, then stands up, placing the photograph back in the box.

'You should,' Liam says as he walks through the doorway. He turns back for a moment. 'One thing I've learned,' he continues quietly. 'Is you should never leave the important things unsaid.'

He leaves Robin alone. He listens to Liam walk back to the kitchen, his footsteps echoing in the empty rooms.

Robin puts the photographs back in the box, then tenderly replaces the lid. He sits back against the wall and looks up at the ceiling, trying to make sense of the surge of emotions he's experiencing.

Freya's words from the argument in the car park bounce around in his head. The reality is she had only been articulating what he knows to be true – the emotions he pushes so far inside, the words he swallows day after day out of fears of inadequacy and self-doubt.

But she said that she loves him. A declaration only tempered by the knowledge that she's marrying another man.

He can't even start to imagine what's been going on in Freya's head – what brought her to his house that Wednesday night. How she felt when she kissed him. And he doesn't know how things are going to work out between him and Jo.

But one thing he does know: he can't leave it like that with Freya.

He just can't.

79

Freya can't sleep. She lies in the dark, shifting, restless. Next to her, Josh snores. She glares at him in the darkness for a moment, blaming her insomnia on him.

But she knows it's not his fault; she knows where the cause of her sleeplessness lies. For the past few weeks it's been the same.

She sighs and sits up, pushing the heels of her hands into her eyes. The room is chilly, her feet cold, and she reaches to the chair by her bed to put a jumper and socks on over her pyjamas.

The silence haunts her.

The two weeks since her argument with Robin have passed in a haze. Josh has been talking excitedly about the wedding, and work is busy, as they tie up loose ends at the same time as managing a flood of new cases. She's missed him; felt his absence acutely. She looks for him first thing in the morning; smiles when she sees or hears something he'd find amusing.

But he's gone.

She feels sadness threaten. She's so loved working with Robin. Their partnership, their friendship. It's been everything to Freya over the last few years, and she's never told him.

Instead, she said all those awful things. Things she didn't mean, even for a second. She'd seen the wounded look in his eyes. She hates herself for that. For hurting him in that way.

She's almost called him a thousand times, but always stopped herself before she dialled. Nothing she says now will be enough.

She lies back on the bed and wipes a stray tear away from her cheek. Everything has to change, she tells herself sternly.

And good things will happen as a result. She'll apply for that promotion, become a DS and get to make the decisions herself. Yes, she thinks. It will be okay. She can manage without Robin Butler.

She closes her eyes again, but as she does so she hears a car drive slowly down the road. The shine of headlights, the slow stop outside her house. She opens her eyes and listens. The engine is switched off but there is no other sound.

She climbs out of bed and goes to the window, opening the curtain a fraction. Parked in the road is a car very familiar to her. A battered old black Volvo V60.

She feels a jolt. She quietly gets to her feet and hurries out of the bedroom. Socked feet patter on the stairs as she goes down. She stands by the door for a second, hesitating. Why is he here? What could he possibly have to say to her at this time of night?

She turns the latch, carefully, and pulls open the door. She can just see Robin, sat in the driver's seat. His face is tilted down, illuminated by the phone in his hand. Then, as if sensing her, he looks up.

Their eyes meet. She waits as he gets out of the car and walks across to her. The night air is cold, and she wraps her arms around herself, realising how crazy she must look, in striped blue pyjamas and fluffy white socks. But he doesn't seem to notice.

He stops in front of her.

'Hi,' he begins. He smiles hesitantly. He's wearing jeans, trainers and a hoodie, his hair a mess, and he looks so much like the Robin she's come to know and love that her breath catches.

'Do you want to come in?' she whispers.

'No. I...' He glances up to her bedroom window, clearly imagining Josh behind the closed curtains.

'He's asleep,' Freya says. 'An earthquake wouldn't wake him.'

He frowns. 'I shouldn't be here, I should go.' He turns to leave but she catches him by the arm.

'Robin, please. I'm sorry.'

He pauses.

'I shouldn't have said all those things. I didn't mean them.'

'You were right—'

'No. No, I wasn't. I know you find it hard to talk about how you're feeling. I know what you've been through. And I shouldn't have just turned up on your doorstep that night.'

'You should have, Freya. I should have told you, sooner. How I felt.'

He pauses, his brow lowered. Then his gaze shifts to her hand, to the engagement ring on her finger she hasn't got used to.

'Are you happy, Freya?'

He says it softly, and his eyes meet hers. She feels their connection physically – an ache and a desire long held, demanding to be acknowledged. The air stills, the moment charged. She knows that whatever she says now could change the course of their lives completely.

She thinks of Josh. Of the promise of their life together. But she also thinks of Robin, and this baby. This is his chance – to have a family with Jo. The thing he's been missing for so long. Freya wants that for Robin – to be happy. To fill the gap left when his sister died.

She swallows hard. 'Yes,' she says.

He nods slowly, his lips pressed together in an apologetic smile.

'Then I'm happy for you.'

He goes to leave, but suddenly she can't bear it. That he'll go and that will be the end.

She steps forward and grabs him round the middle, hugging him to her. She rests her cheek against the soft cotton of his sweatshirt, and his arms go around her, holding her close. He feels his head lower as he rests his face against her hair.

They've hugged before, but not like this. Her whole body is pressed against his; her face resting almost to his neck. He smells of washing powder, of the shampoo she's come to associate with long car journeys and late nights in the office. It's comfort, and warmth, and safety. It's exactly where she's supposed to be.

They stay that way, neither daring to move, then she feels him bend his head towards her, his hug releasing. She looks up, and tentatively, she lifts her lips to his. A deliberate kiss, a gentle kiss. Lasting no more than a few seconds, until he pulls away.

He gives her a lopsided smile.

'You'll call me?' he says. 'It won't be the same as seeing you every day but promise you will?'

'I promise. And maybe even a text message every now and again.'

'Once a month?'

'Maybe more.'

He laughs softly.

'You're going to make an amazing father.'

He nods slowly, like he doesn't quite believe her.

'I hope so,' he replies. And with that, he turns. 'See you soon, West,' he says, and walks to his car. He opens the door, then turns and lifts a hand.

She returns the wave, and he gets in.

She watches him start the car and drive off down the deserted street, his Volvo fading into the darkness.

'See you, Butler,' she says, quietly.

She turns and goes back into the house, closing the front door with a quiet click. She stops, swallowing hard, then sags, leaning against the wall. She gently touches her fingers against her lips, remembering the kiss.

And she knows, deep down, that this is not the end.

She will see Robin Butler again.

Acknowledgements

Over fifteen years ago, I worked for a software engineering firm in the middle of the Hampshire countryside. It was a magical place and it left an indelible mark, evolving into a fictional company called Hamilton Grace that I always wanted to write about.

At last, the story worked, and I thank Louise Cullen at Canelo for liking the book I presented out of nowhere, and not demanding the manuscript originally promised. Thank you to the rest of the incredible team at Canelo Crime – to Francesca Riccardi, Siân Heap, Claudine Sagoe, Elinor Fewster, Alicia Pountney, Iain Millar and Nicola Piggott. Thank you to Miranda Ward for the copy editing, and Jenny Page for the proofreading – dream team!

As always, I owe an everlasting debt of gratitude to Ed Wilson and the team at Johnson and Alcock for making it all happen.

This book wouldn't have been possible without the expertise of Rob Noble, Rob Coles and Joe Allnutt. A huge thank you to them for their advice on the technical aspects of encryption, software engineering and VR.

Thank you to Dr Matt Evans for his help on the medical side of things, even though in this one nobody died. (I know, standards are slipping.)

Thank you to PC Dan Roberts for ever-entertaining school run chat and answering the same questions about police procedure over and over again. (MG11! It's an MG11!)

Thank you to Divinia Hayes for the French translation for Durant's interview.

Thank you to Meenal Gandhi, AR, Laura Stephenson, Charlie Roberts and Steph Fox.

As always, all mistakes, deliberate or otherwise, are down to me and me alone.

Thank you to the Criminal Minds group for their daily entertainment, badgers, crabs, jellyfish, llamas and support. Especially to Heather Critchlow and Dominic Nolan for feedback and encouragement after an early read (and for Heather's Kennel Club resources!), and to Rachael Blok and Jo Furniss for their help with the Prologue.

Thank you to my family, to Chris, Ben and the real-life Max, and to Mum and Dad – I couldn't do it without you.

Last but not least, this book is dedicated to Susan and Jon Scarr. Susan has been a huge cheerleader of my books from the beginning, reading them all with enthusiasm, as well as being on hand to help with everything pharmaceutical – and with Tiller and his Scottishness in this instance. Jon has had to endure being the namesake of Freya's ill-fated lover – a dedication is deserved for that alone.

CANELOCRIME

Do you love crime fiction and are always on the lookout for
brilliant authors?

Canelo Crime is home to some of the most exciting novels
around. Thousands of readers are already enjoying our
compulsive stories. Are you ready to find your new favourite
writer?

Find out more and sign up to our newsletter at
canelocrime.com